Praise for Gerri Russell's

A Knight to Desire

"*A Knight to Desire*—The sweeping story of a powerful love born in the crucible of war and duty. I couldn't put it down!" ~*Alexis Morgan, author of My Lady Mage, book 1 of the Warriors of the Mist.*

"Nobody writes Templar Knights like Gerri Russell! With pages full of sword-swinging adventure, sizzling romance, exciting treasure-hunting, and blood-thirsty villains, there's no putting this book down once you start reading." ~*Ann Charles, Award-Winning Author of the Deadwood Mystery Series*

"If you love fast-paced adventure and red-hot romance A Knight to Desire is the book for you!" ~*Joleen James, Award-Winning Author*

For more reviews, check out Gerri's website, as well as the reader reviews for her books on Amazon, Barnes & Noble, and Smashwords.

Book One in the
Brotherhood of the Scottish Templars Series

To Tempt a Knight

"Russell begins a new series with a wonderfully thought-provoking, emotionally insightful glimpse into what it meant to be a Templar knight after the order was outlawed by the French church. This highly charged romance portrays the emotional agony of a stalwart hero and the woman who comes to love him. Medieval enthusiasts will thrill to this adventurous love story and its explosive conclusion." ~*RT Book Reviews*

"[*To Tempt a Knight*] has all the elements: a powerful and handsome hero, a vulnerable but determined heroine and a long journey that forces them together intimately. Romance and treasure make a combination that's hard to beat and Russell fans will not be disappointed." ~*Fresh Fiction*

"*To Tempt a Knight* is a thrilling, fast-paced romance jam-packed with adventure after adventure after adventure. It's only natural movies like "The Indiana Jones Trilogy" would come to mind during the read – and just like the movies, *To Tempt a Knight* is a well-researched history lesson made into entertainment. Intense action sequences ensure the action plays out like a film in the mind's eye of the reader, while complicated, dramatic emotions tug at the reader's heart strings." ~*Romance Junkies*

Book Two in the
Brotherhood of the Scottish Templars Series

Seducing the Knight

"Action and wildly exhilarating adventure propel the second book of the Brotherhood of the Scottish Templars series forward. Russell packs the pages of the Indiana-Jones-meets-Lara-Croft tale with nonstop action." ~*RT Book Reviews*

"This is the second in the Brotherhood of the Scottish Templars series and [includes a] change of scene to the lands around the Mediterranean and the introduction of the paranormal. This creates a whole new aspect and brings out the power of the biblical elements. The love story between Jessamine and Sir Alan is almost secondary to the power of the Ark. A good story for Russell fans." ~*Fresh Fiction*

"Russell transports our hero and heroine across vivid locales spanning Spain, the Holy Land, and Scotland – as only an adventure of these epic proportions deserves. The combination of such vibrant descriptions of the environs, a fast-paced storyline, and the quintessential quest for the Ark of the Covenant makes for a very quick and pleasant read." ~*Romance Junkies*

A Novella in the
Brotherhood of the Scottish Templars Series

The Border Lord's Bride

"Set around both a holiday and engagement theme, [this] novella is the perfect way to escape a hectic schedule. Even in a short format [Russell's] style shines through and charms readers." ~*RT Book Reviews* ear Reader:

As an author I am often asked about where I get my inspiration for certain books and characters. The answer is simple. Anywhere and everywhere. My inspiration for writing the Brotherhood of the Scottish Templars series came from a quick annotation in a history reference book that described a band of knights united under Robert the Bruce who were sent on a mission after the king's death to return his heart to the Holy Land.

That brief little reference got me thinking, and I had to know more. Why would a king of Scotland want to send his heart on to the Holy Land? Who were the men he entrusted to see his wish fulfilled? It was these questions, and their answers that piqued my imagination and sparked the creation of the Brotherhood of the Scottish Templars series.

I hope you enjoy reading about the knights of the Brotherhood of the Scottish Templars and the women who guide them through their journeys. I'll take you to exotic locations in the Holy Land as well as the heathered hills of Scotland. There will be danger and lots of adventure as the characters find their way to true love.

My very best to you,

Gerri

A Knight to Desire

Gerri Russell

A Knight to Desire
Copyright © 2012 by Gerri Russell

All rights reserved. Except as permitted under the U.S. Copyright Act of 1976, no part of this publication may be reproduced, distributed, or transmitted in any form or by any means now known or hereafter invented, or stored in a database or retrieval system, without the prior written permission of the publisher, Gerri Russell.

This book is a work of fiction. Names, characters, places, and incidents are the product of the author's imagination or are used fictitiously. Any resemblance to actual persons, living or dead, business establishments, events, or locales is coincidental.

Cover Art by Visual Quill

Printed in the United States of America

First Edition
First Printing, 2012

ISBN: 978-0-9838997-8-5

Dedication

Some people come into our lives only briefly, others come in and stay forever. April Rickard, you are a joy, a friend, and the sister I never knew I had. You are so very appreciated and loved.

Also by Gerri Russell:

To Tempt a Knight
(Brotherhood of the Scottish Templars Series: Book 1)

Seducing the Knight
(Brotherhood of the Scottish Templars Series: Book 2)

The Border Lord's Bride
(Brotherhood of the Scottish Templars Series: Book 4)

The Warrior Trainer
(Stones of Destiny Series: Book 1)

Warrior's Bride
(Stones of Destiny Series: Book 2)

Warrior's Lady
(Stones of Destiny Series: Book 3)

History is filled with treasures from cultures all over the world. Some of the treasures are real. Some of the treasures are legend. Sometimes the treasures are both, and the artifact and the legend blur together to become something more...

So it might be said of two such historical artifacts: The cup of Christ and the sword of Charlemagne. One gives eternal life, the other ultimate power.

What happens when two such artifacts fall into the wrong hands?

Perhaps that is when fact and legend become fiction...

A Knight to Desire

Chapter One

Scotland, 1329

The abbess leaned back in her hard chair and folded her hands serenely across her stomach. She asked the same question she always asked, "Are you prepared to admit to the sins of stubbornness and pride?" The older woman didn't smile, but there was nothing harsh in the lines of her face when Brianna Sinclair took a quick glance.

"No, Reverend Mother," Brianna answered, just as she did every morning.

The abbess didn't sigh. She leaned forward once more, and perhaps now her face appeared a bit softer. "Brianna, tell me why you should remain here among us?"

Brianna startled at that. She was used to lectures about willingness, and the patience to accept what God had sent her way, and surrendering to His will. But this, however kindly couched, was a threat. "Reverend Mother, I must remain here. My father will not take me back into his house until I learn to act more like a lady should."

The abbess waved her claim away. "We do not teach young women to become ladies here. We teach them to honor God."

"I do honor God."

"Dear child, I have watched and waited, and I must tell you I see no change in your heart. No ability to bear what must be borne. No trust that God has set your feet on a new path."

Brianna did not let her anger show on her face except for the uncontrollable flush of red that flooded her cheeks. She struggled for a long moment, then managed to state calmly, "I cannot admit to stubbornness and pride because I have been forbidden to lie."

This time Mother Superior did sigh. She shook her head, but her features did not fill with repudiation as much as weariness. "You still believe it is God who gifted you with the skill of a warrior? And with the ... visions?"

Brianna did not glance up again, did not show the abbess that her face had set with determination. "I do."

The abbess tapped the simple table between where she sat and Brianna knelt, the latter's hands pressed together in the aspect of petition. The abbess sighed again. She sat silent a long time, long enough for Brianna to have to ignore the ache of her knees against the hard stone of the floor.

"Would that I could declare this is not God's touch. Would that I could call it the Devil's work," Mother Superior muttered. She tapped the table again, harder, before abruptly ceasing in order to lean back in her chair once more. "Yet even if I did not wish to honor your father's wishes — which I uphold as an example of that good man's mercy and patience — I must declare for myself that I have never found you to be a liar or a braggart."

In her surprise, Brianna forgot to keep her gaze down. "You believe me, Reverend Mother?"

"I believe God gives us wit and will," the abbess snapped. This was more like her usual manner and Brianna's gaze retreated to the floor. "I believe the words I have heard from your lips, not least because I have seen those words come true. I have asked myself why I, like St. Thomas, was made to see proof? Can I say these visions come from God? No. But neither can I claim ill has come of them, not discontent, nor discord." She considered for several beats, not looking terribly happy about her claims.

Brianna wanted to blurt out that Sister Agnes's life had been saved because she'd dreamed of her weighted down by her heavy skirts, drowning in the mill pond. Or that the sisters had come to Agnes's aid just in time because Brianna had confessed her dream to the abbess. She wanted to call out a dozen other examples of how her visions had aided the convent. But she knew better. She did not want unhappiness or uncertainty to cloud Mother Superior's face further, so she kept silent.

At last the abbess spoke again. "Regardless, I have been charged with your care. To see to your well-being, in your person and your faith. As I say, despite your willfulness and your inability to be meek, I believe your heart is good." The abbess paused, perhaps embarrassed, but she went on. "Your heart is strong, and it could be loyal if given the right motivation."

For the first time since her father had sent her to the convent, tears formed in Brianna's eyes. "Could be? Have I not proved loyal to the order?"

Mother Superior stood and came around the table. She put a hand on Brianna's shoulder, giving silent permission for the younger woman to meet her gaze. "No," she said gently, and went on speaking over Brianna's protest. "Not in your heart of hearts. You have tried, but I am forced to acknowledge it is not your nature to lead a quiet life."

Brianna lowered her head, penitent. "I will try harder. I will pray. And reflect. I will ask for guidance—"

"No, child," the abbess said, her hand squeezing Brianna's shoulder. "Yours is a worldly nature. Do not argue with me. We both know there is something you have yet to confess to me, beyond your prowess with a sword or these visions of yours." She patted Brianna's now stiffened shoulder, and turned to go back to her chair. "I have seen that faraway look in your eyes when you should be concentrating on the Mass." Her gaze met Brianna's fully. "What is it, child? Tell me."

She straightened. Now was the time to tell the abbess the truth. Things could not get any worse than they already were, nor could the abbess think her any more sinful. "God made me the equal to any man with a blade. He gave me eyes to see the feints, the strategies. I move with speed, quickly, silently, more deadly—"

"Do not boast to me of dealing death," Mother Superior said softly, instantly shaming Brianna who fell silent. "While it falls to man, sadly, to raise a sword in His name, to keep the barbarians from the door, it is false to speak of war as glory. Glory belongs only to Him."

"Aye, Mother."

"But I do admit, from what I have seen of you practicing in the narthex when you think no one is looking, you appear very skilled."

"I most humbly admit that I am."

"And such skills do not lend themselves to the abbey."

"Mother, I beg you not to cast me out."

"Your future does not lie here at the convent, Brianna," the abbess said, her voice brusque. "I give you two choices, my child."

Brianna's chin dipped to her chest. The abbess would be rid of her and her visions and warrior ways, just like her father.

"Your old nurse. She visits you now and then, am I not correct?"

Brianna slowly looked up at the unexpected words.

The abbess nodded. "She brings lavender when she comes and kindly donates it to us for our wash days. She seeks my blessings — but I confess mostly she desires my company to learn more of how her old charge prospers here. She oversees an inn, as I recall. I think ... yes. There may be a place for you with her."

Brianna swallowed back disappointment. "I have nothing to offer her. I would be nothing less than a burden. At least here I can help with the washing we take in—"

"Your other option is to become what you do not confess. You desire knighthood."

Brianna's mouth worked for a moment before she managed to say the longing that truly was in her heart of hearts as the abbess had called it earlier. "More than anything, aye, I want to be a knight."

"Why? It is not natural for a woman to desire such."

"There is nothing natural about me," Brianna whispered. "Not since I was very little. I have always battled, using sticks as weapons, with my brothers, much to my nurse's dismay. Abigail tried to break me of my unwomanly ways."

"At least Abigail has some sense." Mother Superior didn't quite harrumph; it was more of a sniff, but it spoke volumes.

"What are you offering, Mother?" Brianna asked, almost afraid to hope.

Mother Superior stood and reached for something she had confiscated months ago. She came back around the table and pressed the sword into Brianna's hands. "I know the abbot at Crosswick Abbey. He is looking for men of skill to initiate into the Templar Order."

Brianna gasped at the unbelievable offer. "But I am no man."

"No," the abbess agreed. "But you do have gifts, gifts I can no longer dismiss, gifts that might very well be divinely sent. You must choose with your heart, Brianna, either a life with Abigail or a life of deception and deceit, for only you will bear that stain of sin upon your soul."

Brianna stared down at the metal, too long unpolished. She felt its weight, and could not suppress a shiver of deep longing. Still, she looked up with trepidation. "You would offer me another chance to take up the sword against my father's wishes, fully aware that I must sin against my true nature to secret myself into this Order?"

"I have prayed. This is what God has revealed to me." She signaled Brianna to rise. "I do not understand the ways of the Lord in all things. We do not glory in violence. As women we work to build God's paradise on earth. But we also do not close our eyes to what God has given us. You were given your visions and your skill with a sword for a reason. Now is the time for you to follow where that leads."

Brianna looked down at the sword carefully balanced on her palms then back to the abbess. "You know what my choice must be."

The abbess turned back to the cupboard where she'd only moments ago retrieved the sword and handed Brianna a pile of clothing: breeches, boots, a shirt, and a homespun tunic. "These will aid you in your disguise."

Brianna accepted the garments. "Thank you, Mother," she said past the thickness in her throat. "Thank you for believing in me."

"I send you forth to pray for what is good and right, but also to stand against what is foul and wrong in this world. My wish is that the sword seldom be used," the abbess said with the tiniest hint of a smile, "but if it is, that perhaps it may be used to remind some man who has forgotten God's commandments and is in need of a pointed reminder."

Brianna smiled at the abbess's words, but also at the unexpected turn her life had taken this morning. She had come to do penance. She left following a life-long dream. She would become a knight. "How soon do I leave for Crosswick Abbey?"

"As soon as we can change Sister Brianna into Brother Brendan."

It couldn't be soon enough.

Chapter Two

Teba, Spain 1331

"Leave this battlefield immediately." Sir Simon
Lockhart, a knight in the Brotherhood of the Scottish
Templars, brought his warhorse alongside Brianna's Arabian.
'Twas a horse she'd taken from the Moors as a spoil of war
when her own horse had been killed.

Brianna tried to maneuver around Simon, but he
blocked her way. The Templar army had advanced on the
Moors, yet Simon held her back at the edge of the battlefield.
She was one of them — a Knight Templar. She had been for
over a year now, despite the fact that the man before her had
discovered her true identity in only a few months of her
entering the Order. "I'll not abandon my fellow knights,"
Brianna cried. She turned her mount to the left, only to be
met with a wall of horse. They hadn't sent her back to
Scotland after they'd discovered her deception; despite the
fact that she'd tricked them all, she could fight as well as any
man there.

Simon knew that. So why didn't he get out of her way
and allow her to help?

"Get … out … of … here," Simon repeated, his tone
sharp.

"You know I can hold my own with a sword. You
trained me in the Templar ways yourself."

"I was a fool to allow you to continue your journey with
us. Had I known the dangers… Nay, Brianna, you must go."

The thunder of hoofbeats crashed against the dry
ground, filling the very air. A battle cry rose from forty
thousand Moors, its challenge answered by only a hundred

men. Brianna's palm tightened around her sword. Her muscles tensed as she leaned forward in her saddle, seeing an opening in the Moor's advance. "Simon, please?"

Was this the battle she'd had visions of since the age of seven — the battle in which she would turn the tide? A shiver of anticipation rippled along her spine. Her gift of sight had shown her the path. She had prepared, and she was ready. She would save the Brotherhood.

Wasn't that what her visions had revealed time and time again? She and her sword would save her own brothers, as well as the man before her. Her visions had revealed it all. And she trusted her visions even if Simon did not. "You deny me my destiny?"

"Your destiny was never to be a Templar. 'Tis unnatural for a woman to fight as you do," he growled. "Hasn't enough been stripped from you in the past weeks? Must you now lose your life as well?"

They had taken everything from her once they'd discovered her deception. They'd punished her all right. They'd removed any record of her from the Order. They'd taken her Templar tunic; thankfully, they'd allowed her to keep her sword, but that and her pride were all she had left. They'd taken away the only purpose she had left in this life: to be a knight.

The hiss of blades being drawn from their scabbards brought her back to the moment. She felt the weight of her own drawn weapon in her hand and prepared to charge into the fray. "Let me fight. I'm not afraid."

"You should be."

Brianna's gaze moved beyond Simon to a surging tide of black that rippled toward them. The Templars were outnumbered. A desperate yearning built inside her chest. They might be few, but they were mighty. She twisted back to Simon. "You might not believe it, but it is my destiny to be in this battle, to fight alongside the Brotherhood."

"You will not die today. Please, Brianna, do as I say."

She caught her breath. He'd pleaded with her. Simon never pleaded with anyone. Her gaze moved beyond Simon to the wave of black that swallowed the flecks of white and red. Brianna could not hold back a gasp at the sheer violence of the confrontation. Hooked swords came down, leaving death in their wake. She gripped her sword, desperate to help. The smell of blood and death reached out to her. "Let me pass," she cried, feeling as though she were strangling, suffocating.

The tide of black surged ever closer. The cries of the wounded, the screech of the horses added to the cacophony of sound. The Moors pushed the Templars back, devouring them like a dark and foreign beast.

"Simon, they are dying. We must help the Brotherhood. My own two brothers are in that chaos." A great cry of despair welled up in her chest, filled her lungs, her throat. How could she make him understand? This battle was what she'd been born for? Why else would she have terrifying visions unless she was meant to do something about them?

Simon brought his horse close to hers, making the newly acquired animal quiver. "I'm your superior officer. You will leave the field of battle." His gaze had been dark before, but now it turned to liquid steel. "That is an order." His horse pressed her back, farther from the fighting. Her horse quaked in response.

The enemy drew closer. Dust lay heavy in the air and fine grit filled her mouth. Brianna steeled herself. "You cannot mean for me to run." Her voice cracked. Sweet heavens! Brianna clenched her jaw. She was not a silly female to be ordered about. She was a fighter, a warrior.

"Do as I say, or I'll kill you myself." Simon drew his sword.

"You wouldn't," she gasped, leaning back in her saddle. At her actions, her horse skittered nervously backward.

"Try me."

"Simon—"

A sick wave of agony passed across his features and then was gone. "If they capture you, what you'll suffer will be so much worse than death. I cannot allow that."

Her grip tightened on her reins, causing her horse to dance closer to Simon.

His blade snapped out and came to rest beneath her chin. "We are losing this battle, can you not see that? I'll not lose you as well."

She startled at the intensity and meaning of his words. "We've not lost this battle yet. You cannot know that we will." Again, a hint of desperation entered her voice. "Please, Simon, allow me to fight. I must protect my brothers."

"Protect them with prayer." His blade vanished from the underside of her chin. In the next instant, he brought the flat of his sword down against her horse's flank. Hard.

Her Arabian shrieked, then bolted, propelling her away from the battlefield as a wave of black-turbaned Moors slammed into the space she'd just occupied.

Brianna tried to pull back on the terrified horse's reins, to turn the fleeing animal around. But the high-spirited horse panicked and gave her no heed as it darted up the hill separating the Templars from the tiny town of Teba.

"Nay!" Brianna cried. She twisted to look back. Templar blood spilled into the dry earth. Shouts resonated against the hills in the distance, turning her blood cold. Her gaze moved to Simon. He reeled around as six men engaged him at once. Simon struck one to the ground. The others sliced his torso, his legs, his horse. The horse went down. Simon followed. Brianna's breath caught in her throat as she watched him pull his dirk free, twist then thrust up, taking another Moor to the ground with him.

He blocked the swords of the others, blocked and blocked again. Brianna clutched the hilt of her sword in her palm. If only she could help Simon; if only she could help them all.

As her horse raced up the hillside still terrified by the sights and sound behind it, she could see far below. Her heart stopped at the sight of the massacre. Her body went numb. Her mind refused to follow. A single sob escaped her.

Her brethren were crushed, destroyed. She hadn't had the chance to help them or to die beside them. Her visions had been for naught. She turned away from the sight of blood and death that would forever be imprinted on her mind.

Simon had saved her life by forcing her away. She would never forgive him for it.

Chapter Three

Scotland, Spring 1332

Heat prickled the back of Sir Simon Lockhart's neck as he climbed on foot up the Scottish hillside before him. His body tensed and sweat itched along his hairline. He turned his face into the hot breeze that rippled over the land as a familiar sensation came over him. Why did he sense danger here? He and his men were in the middle of nowhere. They'd been climbing this hillside for two days now. No one followed them. They'd been careful to make certain of that.

There was no danger here. He was home. He was safe.

Simon took a deep breath and forced his curled fists to relax. He sloughed off the odd sensation of danger and concentrated on the beautiful scenery around him. He paused, forcing the other nine men behind him to do the same. He looked down over the path they'd just traveled up the Cairngorm Mountains. Rowan trees dotted the hillside, and far below fields of green grass and purple heather stretched as far as the eye could see.

And still the sensation of danger persisted. Simon squeezed his eyes shut, forcing back the memories of his time in Teba when he and the Brotherhood of the Scottish Templars had attempted to return Robert the Bruce's heart to the holiest of places, and failed.

God had abandoned them then.

"Why do we stop?"

Simon's eyes snapped open at the sound of Kaden Buchanan's voice. He drew a sharp breath and banished his thoughts to the darkest recesses of his mind. "The Mother's Cave is within sight." He turned toward the mountain and pointed off in the distance. They were near the secret cave that had harbored the Templar treasure for years. He and his men were to relieve the ten knights who had guarded the treasure for the last fortnight.

Since its rediscovery less than a month ago, the treasure had been under constant guard while Simon and others determined the best way to move it to a new secret location.

"We are almost there, men," Simon said, forcing a tone of excitement into his voice. It wouldn't do for his men to see his uncertainty. Besides, it was his memories that had brought forth the sensation of danger. Nothing more.

The weariness on his men's faces vanished as excited conversation rippled among the knights who would replace the guards already in the cave. A soft smile came to Simon's lips as his men's good humor lifted his own spirits.

"Come, men." Simon continued hiking toward the small opening in the mountainside. "I am certain the others are eager for their replacements to arrive."

They journeyed up the hillside in no time, and stood at the opening of the cave. Suddenly the air thickened and silence fell around them. Scattered knights lay face-down upon the ground.

Dead.

Simon's heart refused to believe. He heard his men shuffle to a stop behind him. He ran forward, dropping to his knees beside his fellow Templar, John McCrae. Rolling him onto his back, Simon stared down into the vacant gaze. 'Twas a look he had come to know well. Bitter regret swept through Simon. With his hand, he closed John's eyes and stood, proceeding to the next man who lay reposed in death, his sword still clutched in his hand.

"Are they..." Kaden asked from beside him.

Simon stood, drew his sword and nodded, unable to answer just yet as he swallowed thickly. Quietly, he moved farther into the dark, winding passageway — into the bowels of the earth itself. The soft hiss of steel leaving other scabbards filled the silence as his men followed close behind. They proceeded deeper into the cave, then down a long passageway where two more knights lay dead.

"Someone outside of the Templars has discovered the treasure," Simon said, his voice rough as shock rippled through him. More men were dead. They'd lost so many already at Teba, then to the maniacal madman, Pierre de la Roche.

Simon's heart twisted at the thought. Nay, it couldn't be. The man was dead. He stood. "Come, men, be prepared for anything."

At the end of the tunnel a wooden ramp angled down into another cavern. The soft sounds of a waterfall came to Simon's ears, and he knew they were close to the treasure. He'd been told before he'd left the monastery that the treasure could be found in a cave behind the waterfall.

Two flickering urns lit the cavern and revealed a waterfall on the opposite side. But despite the light and the air that flowed freely through the cavern, Simon's chest tightened, his breath stuttered in and out of his lungs as though he'd been buried alive. An odd sensation raced down his spine. Was the villain who'd killed these men still here?

Simon tightened his grip on his sword and moved silently forward. The flame from the urn created a kaleidoscope of distorted, twisting light around the cavern. Golden-hued spirits seemed to dance on the walls, spirits of those who had died here, of those who had originally brought the treasure to this sacred place, of those who had come before any of them. Their presence comforted Simon as he edged toward the falls.

"I'm right behind you," Kaden said. Simon nodded and proceeded toward the underground lake that separated the cave's entrance from the treasure itself. His heart sped up as he strode into the water at the base of the waterfall. They'd have to go through the falls to enter the cave beyond.

In the chest-high water, his mail dragged him down. He clenched his jaw and tapped new strength and determination to put one booted foot in front of the other, dragging himself forward, desperate to find the men behind that waterfall still alive.

He held his breath and plunged under the falls. He emerged, sword at the ready, on the opposite side. Light splashed across the chamber. His heart missed a beat as he blinked, then blinked again, until his vision cleared. The treasure remained. Gold, riches, jewels, artifacts from every culture crowded the large room.

"Oh, heaven above," Kaden breathed beside him.

The air in the chamber was warm, dry and scented not with earth, but with the smell of something as sweet as honey on a warm summer's day. Simon shook his head, dispelling the magic of the moment and forced his gaze from the treasure to the five bodies that lay face-down on the ground.

"Check them," Simon commanded his men as he hurried across the chamber to the familiar body of Brother Bernard. Simon fell to his knees beside the fallen Templar and carefully turned him over.

"Bernard."

The man's dark eyes fluttered open.

Simon drew a sharp breath and crossed himself. "You're alive." Carefully he separated the leather tunic that covered Bernard's chest to reveal a long but not deep gash low on his belly. The wound had already stopped bleeding. But the purplish red color that surrounded his injury spoke of putrefaction. They'd have to take him back to Crosswick Priory if there was to be any hope of keeping the knight alive.

"He left … me alive … to warn you."

Simon pulled the bladder of water from his belt and held it up to Bernard's lips. The young Templar tensed as he drank thirstily, then relaxed back into Simon's arms, his relief palpable. "Who did this?" Simon asked.

Bernard's eyes widened with fear. "De la Roche."

Simon flinched at the unexpected words. "That madman is dead."

Bernard shook his head. "Nay. He somehow infiltrated our ranks." On a deep shuddering breath Bernard continued, "He came here as one of the ten knights. He worked as we all did at first, then artifacts started to disappear. A crown here. Jewels there. Then the Holy Grail vanished and he struck. Using a sword from the treasure — Joyeuse, Charlemagne's sword — one by one he took us down. He took from the treasure only what he could carry ... but he took the Grail. The healing cup." Bernard's head fell back against the earth beneath him, as though suddenly drained of energy.

"How long ago?" Simon asked.

"It feels like forever."

"Is there anything else you remember?"

"His looks, his voice, were so different from before. But I should have recognized those eyes — those light unearthly eyes." Bernard took a deep, shuddering breath. "He pretended to be one of us ... the man who killed our brothers."

Pierre de la Roche, the fanatical Frenchman who had terrorized the Templars in Scotland for months, torturing and burning the knights without remorse — a man who they all had thought was dead. "Why the Grail?" Simon asked with a mixture of anger and curiosity.

Bernard closed his eyes. "I can assume only that he needed to heal from his fall over the castle wall the last time we confronted him. He walked with a limp we all assumed he'd acquired at the battle of Teba. But now I know better. He has used the powers of the Grail, for when he battled us at the end, the man was as strong as any warrior."

The temperature in the chamber suddenly seemed cooler than it had been as Simon's breath jammed in his throat. De la Roche was still alive and determined to kill them all.

His premonition of danger had been real.

Simon straightened and looked about the chamber at his men. He had to keep them safe. He'd lost too many men already. He would not lose any more. Treasure or no treasure, he had to keep them safe because de la Roche could return at any time with more men.

Simon's gaze moved from his men to the artifacts in the chamber. Instead of splendor, this time he saw only the enormous amount of work involved in moving the treasure. It would take days to move it all with only ten men — time they didn't have, even if they knew where to take it.

Simon turned to Bernard. "Can you walk?"

"I'll try."

With Simon's help, Bernard stood and leaned heavily on the arm Simon offered.

"Are there any other survivors?" Simon asked his men.

"Nay," Kaden said as he gripped Bernard's unsupported arm. The others gathered around, awaiting orders.

Simon nodded. "We must leave. De le Roche is responsible for these men's deaths. But Bernard reports he was alone at the time. That was perhaps two days ago, judging by the state of Bernard's wounds and the rigor of the dead men. De la Roche could return with support at any moment."

"What about the treasure?" Kendall, the youngest knight among them, asked. "We can't just leave it for that blackguard."

"We won't." Simon tightened his grip on Bernard's arm and led him back to the waterfall. The others followed. Moments later, they plunged through to the opposite side of the water and made their way up the ramp on the far side of the chamber. Once all the men had completed the passage through the water, Simon looked back at the falls. He knew what he had to do. He just prayed his fellow Templars would understand the decision he'd been forced to make.

"Kaden, lead Bernard and the men to the cave's opening and hold them there. I'll join you soon."

"Why?" The knight frowned. "What are you going to do?"

Simon gripped the hilt of his sword, drawing the weapon from its scabbard. "I must protect the treasure the only way I can, by bringing this cave down upon it."

Silence crashed down upon the small group until only the sound of the falls rumbled behind them. Jacob stepped forward, his eyes wide in his weathered face. "We've only just found the treasure."

"Nay!" Thomas exclaimed. "If you destroy the treasure then de la Roche wins."

Simon straightened. "'Tis our legacy to keep the treasure safe. This is the only way to do so with de la Roche at our heels. Do you not agree?"

The men exchanged looks, each judging the other's response. "Aye," they said in unison, then turned and headed for the cave's opening, leaving him alone at the opening of the long, narrow passageway that led to the outside. Simon turned back toward the water. He had to think. How could he bring the cavern down? He stared blindly into the silver gray pool.

He'd hoped beyond hope that, once he returned to Scotland after the slaughter at Teba, he would find only peace and contentment. And he had for a short time. He and William had been happy returning to their old lives for a few weeks. Simon had gone home to Lee Castle and left the precious Charm Stone he'd acquired in Spain in his mother's care.

Then de la Roche had crossed onto their shores. Nothing would bring peace to any Templar ever again. Not while de la Roche roamed their country torturing and slaying all who had connections to the Templars.

Instantly Simon's thoughts moved to Brianna. Would she be safe? Could de la Roche know her association with their unfortunate band of brothers? Simon clenched his fist around the pommel of his sword until the metal bit into his palm. Nay, he had to believe she was safe. Thinking of anything else would make him feel only more defeated and alone than ever before.

Her survival had kept him going during the dreadful aftermath in Teba. He'd managed, with great cost to himself, to keep his feelings hidden from her after he'd discovered her deception. He'd treated her as a brother, but his feelings had always gone deeper than that, despite his vows. The memory of Brianna plunged into his gut. The last few years had been such a torment. He was a man whose two loves couldn't possibly coexist, and between which he could never choose. A monk in love with a woman; a man dedicated to God.

Never had he allowed his feelings to compromise his vows — or at least those were the lies he told himself at night as he lay in his lonely bed thinking of her, praying she was well and whole and away from the evilness de la Roche had brought to this land.

Looking around him now, at the men who'd lost their lives to de la Roche, and at the treasure that was now vulnerable to attack, he wasn't so certain of her survival any longer. She was but one woman against that man…

Simon shivered involuntarily. It wasn't up to him to protect her. It was his duty to keep his Templar brothers and the Templar treasure safe. He forced thoughts of Brianna aside and stared at the challenge before him.

The Templar treasure was as vulnerable as it had ever been. Without thinking about the magnitude of what he did, Simon raced up the passageway to the four pillars that the previous treasure guardians had carved into the rock. Between each pillar stood a statue of a Templar. The guardians had spent years creating this underground temple. All of it would be destroyed if his plan succeeded.

Simon moved to the pillar closest to the cave's opening. But even the guardians had prepared themselves for a day such as this. If the scroll Siobhan Fraser, the daughter of one of the guardians, had shown Simon was correct, then he'd find what he searched for here on this first pillar. Carefully he examined the stone, searching in the golden light of the torches for a flaw in the carving. It took several moments before he found it. A deeply grooved cut in the lower half of the stone pillar. A carefully designed flaw in case such an emergency as this should arise.

Simon stepped back and lifted his sword. For a moment he thought about praying, but banished the idea. Why pray to a God that abandoned those who needed him most? Or perhaps it was Simon's own faith that hadn't been strong enough. Perhaps if he'd believed more?

He clenched his fingers on the pommel of his sword. Nay, 'twas God who had left them in their time of need. Now when they had need of divine assistance once more, it would be Simon's own might and the guardians' careful design that would bring the pillars down and collapse the rest of the cave.

On a sharp breath, Simon tightened his grip on his sword and let the weapon fly with all the intensity his muscles could provide. An explosion of sound echoed through the hallway as steel met stone. Pain ricocheted up his forearms and lodged razor-sharp in his shoulders. He clenched his jaw against the agony as the pillar snapped, wobbled, then fell toward the statue and the pillar beside it.

Simon took several steps back, as the second pillar crashed into the third, then the fourth tumbled down to crash upon the rocky ground. The stone beneath him rocked, making it difficult to stand as he struggled toward the exit.

All around him, the rock shuddered. The air filled with a terrible grating sound. The shriek deepened, grew louder. The world began to shake and sway around him as the ceiling above cracked at the lack of support and tumbled to the ground in huge, raining chunks. In surreal slowness, Simon ran for the opening of the cave. Over his shoulder he watched the cavern fall. One rock tumbled, then another until an avalanche of noise boomed all around him, rattling the walls — the sound both earthly and unearthly.

The walls were collapsing in upon themselves. Simon surveyed the destruction that intensified with each beat of his heart. If he didn't hurry, he'd be buried along with the treasure. With the earth twisting and rutting upward in his path, he raced down the dark corridor. Ahead he could just make out a splash of light. He fixed on it. Power surged through his body, made his heart beat faster as dirt showered all around him, spattered on the rock beneath his feet. The light ahead became his single hope for salvation. Large chunks of rock rained down from above. He leapt around them. His breath ripped from his chest at his exertion. He pumped his arms, moving faster. The sound of his ragged breathing pounded in his ears, mingled with the thrumming of his heart, drowning out the noise.

He broke through into the light on a cloud of dust and rock to find his men waiting with alarmed faces. The shaking stopped as suddenly as it had begun.

A slight breeze stirred and whistled through the treetops below. A bird chirped. The warm rays of the sun kissed the back of his neck, drying the sweat that had gathered there. The world around him went on as though nothing had happened. Yet a vast, impenetrable emptiness invaded his soul.

What had he just done to the Templar treasure? A treasure his Order had painstakingly gathered and protected over the centuries, a treasure he had re-buried with a single stroke of his sword. Simon drew a sharp breath, forcing the emptiness aside. He'd done what he'd had to do to keep the treasure safe from de la Roche and others until the Brotherhood could dig it out of the rubble.

Kaden immediately came to Simon's side. "I was afraid you wouldn't make it out."

For a moment, so was I," Simon said, straightening and searching his men's faces. "Our mission has changed."

"Where do we go from here?" Kaden asked.

"Kaden, you'll join me; the rest of you will escort Bernard back to Crosswick Priory. He needs to heal, and the healing baths there will serve him well. The important thing is that we leave here before de la Roche's army arrives."

Kaden frowned at his friend. "Where are we headed?"

"To the north." God have mercy on him. He couldn't leave her vulnerable to attack. It might be a dreadful sin to bring her back into temptation's reach, but he didn't have a choice. Brianna Sinclair had a skill that could help them. "We are heading to the one person I know with the gift of sight."

"Brianna Sinclair."

Simon forced away the ripple of awareness that hearing her name brought to his flesh. "Aye, Brianna. Her visions may help us identify any disguise de la Roche has assumed. She will help us find the man who means to destroy us all."

Chapter Four

Pierre de la Roche shivered as the morning mist gathered around his feet. His hip ached and his ankle burned as he stood at the edge of the loch. His healing was progressing, but he still had a ways to go before he would be whole once more. He held the cup of Christ in his left hand and the sword of Charlemagne in his right. His days of pain were at an end. It was time to restore himself fully. With these two artifacts he would be invincible.

The sword and the grail.

Ultimate power and eternal life.

The weapons of a true champion.

He bent to the water's edge and filled the unremarkable tin cup with clear, almost sweet-smelling water. He bit back another jolt of pain as his hip and ankle protested the movement. Instead of focusing on the pain, his thoughts turned to all that had happened. He'd damaged both his hip and ankle when he'd fallen from the tower of Stonehyve Castle. The twisted disfigurement of his leg seemed a small price to pay for escaping with his life. But the days and weeks and months since the accident had worn him down. He'd managed to overcome the pain with thoughts of revenge. Revenge that had driven him to do things he'd never imagined. The idea had come to him one cold, rainy, miserable night when he'd happened upon a group of Templar scouts.

Three of the men had stayed with the horses. A fourth man had wandered to the edge of a loch to fill their water skins. That man had never returned, at least not the man the others knew as the Templar Knight, Roinald Brown.

Roinald Brown had taken on a new persona that day along with a slight limp. He'd captured the three other knights one by one and tortured information enough to start his masquerade as one of them. He'd become the thing he hated that day, all for the purpose of bringing them down.

De la Roche's gaze shifted to the cup filled to the brim with liquid. Anticipation flared inside him as he brought the cup to his lips and took a small sip.

Disguised as one of them, he'd stolen the holiest cup on earth, along with the most powerful sword ever forged. A warm and heady power flowed through him, giving him the strength he craved.

The Holy Grail.

A healing cup, and a cup that gave those who drank from it eternal life.

He took another swallow of the liquid, allowing the water to spill past his lips in his haste to consume it. The water rolled down his chin, along his neck, to his chest. Again strength flowed through him, through his body and into his damaged leg. He stared down at his damaged limb. The slight twist of his ankle remained unchanged, yet the appendage felt as though it had never been shattered.

He gulped the remains of the cup, feeling the pain in his hip subside. He drew a breath deep into his lungs, then another. An energized life force that he'd never experienced filled him.

He took a step away from the water's edge. No pain seared his side and his foot and ankle seemed straighter and steady beneath him. He took another step, then another until he was running free from pain and filled with joy.

The Grail had healed him, saved him, and would continue to do so. His steps slowed, then stopped. It was all happening just as he'd hoped it would.

He'd wormed his way into the Templar nest, stolen the Templar's treasures, and now he would use those things to destroy the unholy tyrants once and for all. He would have his revenge against the man who had caused him torment every moment of every day since he'd fallen from the tower and injured his body.

William Keith. De la Roche would see the bastard fall. But first, he had to contend with another Templar. A smile came to de la Roche's lips as he looked off into the distance, imagining his newest target. Simon Lockhart. As the self-appointed leader of the Brotherhood of the Scottish Templars, once Lockhart fell, the others would flounder. Their weakness would be his triumph. With a renewed sense of power, de la Roche gripped the sword of Charlemagne more firmly in his hand. Hunger for revenge raked his soul. With this weapon and the Holy Grail in his arsenal, he would be unstoppable.

"Brianna," Abigail MacInnes called from the back door of the small inn she ran with Brianna's help. "We have visitors and I need you to help serve them their supper."

Silence met her call.

"Brianna?" Abigail stepped out onto the stone path. "Where are you?"

"Up here," Brianna replied from the branches of a stout oak tree that grew to the left of the path. Her private retreat. She quickly replaced the silver spurs she held in her hands into a wooden box, then wedged it between the two branches where she kept it hidden. The pieces of silver were all she had left of her life as a knight. Even that small remnant would upset her old nurse if she found out Brianna still possessed them. Abigail had taken her in when no one else would. Brianna would never intentionally do something to harm her one and only friend.

Abigail came to stand beneath the tree and looked up. "My child, get down from there! You'll hurt yourself."

Brianna gathered her skirts in her hand, then made her way back down to the ground.

"Ladies don't climb trees, Brianna."

"My apologies. Old habits die hard," she said softly, studying her toes with great intent. She'd tried to let that part of her life go. Lord knew her father had made her suffer enough for wanting something different than what she'd been allotted by life. Brianna swallowed back pain and schooled her features into a look of calm acceptance before she met Abigail's searching gaze.

There was a slight frown on Abigail's face. "My child, I know this is hard for you, but you must try."

Brianna nodded. She did try. She tried every day, but some deep-seated need in her heart always brought her back to the tree, to those bedamned silver spurs and the memories she should let die.

Her thoughts moved to the one man she blamed for her current situation. He'd taught her everything she needed to know about fighting and warring, yet he'd also been the one person who had crushed her dreams. In her mind's eye she saw not a vision, but a memory of Simon Lockhart the day he'd discovered her ruse…

They'd been training all day, sparring with each other. She'd taken him to the ground twice and his pride had been injured. That's when he'd pushed his attack harder than he'd ever pushed it before.

He'd brought his sword down, inside her defenses. Then, with an upward stroke, he'd sliced through her tunic and the bindings that held her breasts into place. He'd seen for himself that she was no boy as she'd pretended.

Had they been closer to Scotland, Brianna would have been sent home. Instead, Simon had offered to serve as her guardian when her own brothers would have nothing to do with her.

Simon had made her his squire and allowed her to keep her sword, more for her own protection than anything else. The other Templars were angry with her for her falsehood. And everyone except Simon went on ignoring her even after Teba.

Brianna shivered as she swept the memory from her mind.

"Come inside. I need your help. We have guests," Abigail's tone grew light. "Knights. I thought perhaps you'd be interested," she teased with a quirk of her brows.

Brianna offered her old nurse a tight smile before she followed her inside the cottage. Torture and punishment. That's what the next few hours would be. She'd be confronted with a life that was denied her by one cruel man — Simon Lockhart.

In the small kitchen, Abigail handed Brianna a thick cloth and waved her toward the steaming iron pot near the hearth that contained mutton stew. "Take that in and serve it to the men while I gather bread and cheese."

She would serve the men because she had no choice. Yet she had wanted to serve her country in another way ... by following the visions that haunted her dreams. But so far, her visions had only led her to a life with no purpose.

She'd had a vision last night, one she did not understand. It seemed so real — more real than any vision she'd ever had before. A man she did not recognize appeared in her chamber dressed in a white tunic that bore a Templar's cross. He'd leaned over her and taken a lock of her hair.

Her fingers strayed up to her unbound tresses. A shiver of foreboding rippled through her. The odd thing was, a hunk of her red hair was gone. But such a thing was impossible. Dream apparitions did not steal locks of hair. Unless it was no dream?

Brianna forced the thought away. 'Twas only a dream. She wrapped a cloth around the warm iron handle of the pot Abigail had indicated. She took a deep breath and moved toward the dining area with exaggerated care. Knights? Here? Why? The click of her leather boots on the wood floor broke the silence as she moved through the doorway, prepared for the battle with her own spoiled hopes and dreams.

She stepped up to the table where two men sat with their backs to her. Focusing on her task, she dipped the ladle into the kettle and scooped out a hearty serving for the man on her right. She glanced at the stranger and her throat went dry. She stared, gape-mouthed at the man she'd hoped never in her life to see again.

Handsome, elegant, yet rugged. Sir Simon Lockhart.

"Brianna?"

Brianna swallowed roughly. His voice sounded as she'd remembered, like the darkest ale — rich and smooth. Her heart thundered in her ears. "Get out!"

His expression darkened.

Good. That frown dulled some of his perfection.

"You can't mean that," he said slowly, fixing her with a steady, searching gaze. He looked at her, through her.

Brianna set her shoulders back. He'd see no weakness in her. "But I do." Her teeth came together with a snap as the urge to say more swelled inside. Nay, she wouldn't give him the satisfaction of knowing just how deeply he'd hurt her.

His expression grew more intense. "I've spent the last fortnight looking for you. I went to Rosslyn Castle, but your father would not meet with me. He sent a message through his steward saying his daughter was lost to him. What did he mean by that?"

She tensed, but remained silent.

He leaned toward her. "'Twas the stable boy who told me where I might find you. He said when you left Rosslyn that you left with only a horse and a sword. Why?"

Memories flickered through her mind. A horse and a sword were all her father would give her. He'd tossed her out as if she were last week's pottage. She squeezed her eyes shut and forced the memories back into the deep recesses of her mind. "Get out." She repeated and snapped her eyes open.

"Brianna, you don't mean—"

With a slight twist of her wrist, the stew slipped off the ladle and into his lap.

A curse left his lips as he shot to his feet, sending his chair flying backward. The wooden chair hit the floor with a crash. He brushed frantically at his lap.

"Merciful heavens," Abigail cried as she rushed into the room, a wooden tray with bread and a wedge of cheese balanced in one hand while she scooped the chair from the floor with the other. "Whatever is going on out here?"

Brianna dipped the ladle back into the kettle and took a quick step back. "Nothing of importance," she said at the same moment Simon replied. "Fool girl."

The memory of her father saying the same words to her upon her return from Teba darted through her mind. "Your brothers are dead because of you. You'll never be a knight, you foolish girl. You'll never be anything to me again." The memory of his disapproving voice sent a new wave of old guilt and loss through her.

"You have no reason to be here. Please leave," she repeated with more politeness than he deserved.

"Brianna," Abigail gasped. "Of course he has a right. Whatever could you be thinking?" the older woman turned to Simon. "Pray forgive her, Sir Simon."

He straightened and something close to understanding flickered in the depth of his gaze. "I came to talk with you. To be civil. You owe me at least that for the fact that you are still, after all, alive."

He was right. His actions that day in Teba had saved her life. Brianna clenched her fists. He had dashed her dreams, but she hadn't given up. She would be a knight someday and prove to him and anyone else in her life who had ever doubted her visions that she wasn't mad, that she was as good as any man with a sword, that her life had a purpose.

Abigail remained silent, but her gaze spoke volumes. Once again feeling a sense of obligation to her benefactor, Brianna forced a smile. "Yes, your-knightliness, milord," she amended at Abigail's harsh glance. "Please be seated." She waved her hand toward the righted chair. "I promise not to accost you with more stew." As if to prove her point, she ladled the stew into both bowls, then stepped back. "There, see, it's quite safe, I assure you. Abigail cooked the meal, and the belladonna has yet to bloom."

Abigail gasped.

Simon smiled. The effect was devastating. His features brightened, his eyes warmed, and against her will, her heart stuttered.

Brianna cleared her throat and looked away. "Sit down. You're safe with me."

Simon sat back down and accepted the length of linen Abigail handed him. He wiped himself off while keeping his gaze focused on Brianna. "Sit with us," he said when he was finished cleaning the stew from his leather tunic and breeches.

She thought about refusing until she turned to Abigail — a warning lingered in her eyes that dared her to refuse. Brianna dropped into the chair the farthest from him. His gaze held hers. An unexpected understanding, deep and penetrating, shone from the bottom of his dark eyes.

Brianna shifted in her seat. She didn't like the way he looked at her — like he searched her soul for secrets. God knew she had enough of them. She twisted slightly away, shielding herself.

Once Brianna had complied with Simon's wishes, Abigail placed the platter of bread and cheese on the table before the men. "Sir Kaden, would you be so kind as to help me in the kitchen for a moment?"

Kaden rolled his eyes and scooted his seat back. He followed Abigail, looking almost pleased to escape the non-verbal sparring that filled the small room with tension.

When they were alone, Brianna turned to Simon. "What do you want?"

"I need your help." At her startled look he added, "It's important."

Intrigue dulled the edge of her anger. She sat forward and fixed him with a stern gaze. "What could be so important that you would belittle yourself by coming to me?"

"The survival of the Templars."

She sat back. Again, he'd surprised her. "What?"

"I don't know how much, if anything, you've heard about the notorious Frenchman Pierre de la Roche."

She frowned. "I live in isolation. What could I possibly hear about the state of things?"

"I'm somewhat relieved to hear that," he said, his expression so serious that a lump of unease formed in Brianna's chest. "De la Roche came to Scotland with the sole purpose of annihilating what remains of the Scottish Templars and taking back to France whatever he can of the Templar treasure. He tried first to take the Spear of Destiny, but now that he has failed with that, he appears to be after the entire treasure."

Brianna eased back in her chair, stunned. "I'm sorry for the Templars he's deceived, but how can I possibly help you with any of that?"

He scooted his chair close to hers. Too close. "Disguising himself," Simon continued, his voice low so only she could hear, "De la Roche infiltrated what remained of our organization. He went on patrol with the men who were to guard the treasure until Lucius Carr could organize the men to move the artifacts."

"I still don't see how I can possibly help you."

Simon leaned closer. Brianna felt his soft breath against her cheek. She closed her eyes. Why did his nearness have to feel so reassuring and upsetting at the same time? When she opened her eyes she found herself staring into his dark-eyed gaze.

"Your visions, Brianna," he said slowly. "They seem to focus on things that are important to you."

"Aye," she agreed, still not understanding how she could help.

"We can use your visions to tell us not only what de la Roche looks like now, but where he is. Your visions can help us stop him from harming anyone else and aid us in locating the treasure he stole."

She opened her mouth to tell him no, when his finger touched her parted lips. The clean scent of lye soap filled her nostrils, and the words that formed on her tongue slid back down her throat. She stared at him in silence.

"Before you say anything, I want to make you an offer."

Brianna swept his finger away from her lips. "I want nothing from you." Her words lacked her earlier anger.

"You might want this." He grinned. "I can give you a chance to be what you've always wanted."

Brianna's heart lurched. Could he mean...

"You can ride with me as a knight if you help me figure out what de la Roche will do next to destroy the Templars."

Despite her attempt to appear unimpressed by his offer, excitement flared. The images from her earliest vision came back to her.

She was dressed as a Knight Templar.

Her sword was held at the ready.

Her brothers were in danger.

Only she could save them from certain death. Only she.

The vision had haunted her for years.

It was that vision and so many others that had forced her from the convent and onto her path with the Templars. It was in Edinburgh, among the other Templars, that she had seen her two brothers once more. Pain swelled in Brianna's chest as her thoughts turned to William and John Sinclair.

Suddenly her fingers trembled. She shoved her hands into the folds of her heavy skirt. Her brothers were dead, but not by anything she had done to distract them during the battle of Teba as her father had accused her. But now Simon offered her a chance to save other Templars from a similar fate at the hands of a new enemy. Could she grasp what Simon offered and let go of her anger? Stop blaming him for destroying her dreams and preventing her from saving her brothers?

Slowly she relaxed the death-grip she had on her skirt and brought her hands atop the table. "Give me your word you'll not send me away again at the first sign of battle."

His gaze narrowed, scrutinizing her. "You don't trust me."

"Should I? If you want my help, give me your word."

"I promise not to send you away."

She reached out and grasped his forearm, waiting for his grasp in return. It was how they'd once greeted each other in the Brotherhood. "I will hold you to your word, Simon."

He hesitated only a moment before responding in kind. "I shall not fail you, milady."

At his words, warmth flared where his fingers touched. She pulled her hand away to rest it in her lap. Words of gratitude flooded her throat, but she held them back, unwilling to give him that much power over her. They had reached an agreement. He still had yet to prove his word. "I shall go with you."

"Brianna, no. You mustn't leave here," Abigail gasped.

Brianna twisted toward Abigail, who stood framed by the kitchen doorway. A sick feeling crept into Brianna's stomach. "I must."

Abigail brought her aging fingers to her cheeks. "Your father would not approve of you warring again."

Brianna straightened, relieved that feelings of betrayal slammed into her now instead of her own guilt. "My father's opinion matters not." He had given up that right a year ago when he'd disowned her.

"Abigail, I very much appreciate all you have done for me. You saved my life. You gave me hope when I had none." She stepped up to her friend, taking her fingers from her cheeks to wrap them in her own hands. "I don't understand any more than you do why I behave so unlike my own sex. But I know, deep in my heart, I wasn't born to wield a needle and thread, but to wield a sword, to protect others, and to fight for my people in any way I can. You must understand that about me by now?"

Long absent color filled Abigail's cheeks. "Aye, my child. Even at your birth, you entered this world backwards, fighting convention even then." She gave a little laugh. "Nothing has changed, has it?"

Brianna responded with a soft smile. "So you see why I must go with Sir Simon, Sir Kaden? I am needed." She bit back her own admission of "finally." Admitting such a thing would make her too vulnerable to Simon. Nay, she would keep her insecurities to herself.

Abigail nodded and gave Brianna's hands a squeeze before pulling away. She untied her apron, folding it in two, then set it across the back of the wooden chair nearest her. "I understand." She turned to face Simon. "I hope you also understand that this child has suffered enough ill treatment in her young life. I'll not allow you, or anyone else, to add to her burdens. If she must go with you, then I must go with her."

Brianna gasped. "Abigail, I could never endanger you so."

The older woman ignored Brianna as her gaze fixed on Simon. "Do we have an accord, Sir Simon? I shall serve as a chaperone while you two do whatever must be done."

"Abigail," Brianna took two steps forward, then stopped when she realized how close she'd come to Simon. She needn't move any closer to smell the hint of fresh, clean soap lingering on his skin, or feel the warmth radiating from his nearness. Nay, she needed to keep her distance. She could think better that way. "It will be dangerous."

"Sounds intriguing," Abigail said with a lift of her brow.

Brianna frowned. That was not the response she wanted. She tried again. "The man we must find has ruthlessly tortured and murdered our countrymen."

Abigail nodded. "Then let's hope you young people find him before he has a chance to do that anymore."

"What about the inn? Who will run it while we are both gone?"

She shrugged. "I can close it for a time. You know how few people stop here at present. Perhaps they are afraid to travel with this de la Roche on the loose. Finding him might help create more business." She set her jaw firmly. A sign Brianna had learned long ago meant the discussion was through.

"You are not making this easy." Brianna said, trying to reason with her friend once more.

Abigail fixed Brianna with an all-too-familiar glance. "You are not the only Scottish female with a will of iron, my child. I am going with you, and that is that."

Brianna sighed. "When do we start?" she asked with a note of concession in her voice.

"At first light if you can be ready by then," Simon replied, his tone lighter.

"We'll be ready," Brianna said. Nothing in heaven or on earth would stop her from seeing her visions through this time.

Nothing.

Chapter Five

Simon studied the woman beside him. He hadn't seen Brianna for more than a year. Time had changed her, but not in the way time usually changed people. Nay, if anything time had been her friend. Her features had lost their last vestiges of youth, revealing a goddess. Dark red wisps of hair curled against her pale, perfect skin.

How could he have ever thought she was a man, even for a heartbeat? Looking at her now, it would be impossible to see anything but her feminine loveliness. Her classically beautiful face was expressionless as she stood at his side, yet Simon could tell deep emotion simmered beneath that façade.

She made no pretense as to why she was angry or at whom that anger was directed. Him. He clenched his jaw. He'd sent her away from the battle at Teba.

To save her life.

Why did she not see that? He could feel the beat of his pulse pound against his jaw. Women. Why were they such a mystery to him? They shouldn't be ... his family should have prepared him for anything.

Simon watched as Brianna and Abigail headed from the room to make plans for their departure. The tension that had filled the small space moments before dissipated, and the chamber seemed larger for it.

"We accomplished our first goal," Kaden said from the kitchen doorway where he'd remained while Brianna and Abigail had negotiated their terms.

"Aye," Simon agreed. "It appears the women have as well."

Kaden laughed. "You always were overprotective of the gentler sex."

Simon frowned. "I was doomed at birth, having been raised with seven sisters."

"Seven? 'Tis no wonder then why your family sent you away to the monastery to study amongst other men, or why you took vows to remain in that world of men."

Simon relaxed at Kaden's banter. "Let's not discuss women any longer, for I fear we are sadly inadequate to the matter."

Kaden nodded, his expression suddenly quite serious. "Being that we are Templars."

"Being that we are men." Simon had a feeling he would never truly understand why women thought the way they did. Why Brianna wanted more than her gender allowed. She had risked everything to train as a knight. She'd disguised herself as a distant cousin to the Sinclairs.

No one had questioned her as she gained entrance into the sacred circle of the Templars to become one of them. It was only once they were on Crusade, living in close quarters, that Simon had uncovered her guise. He hadn't seen her femininity in the way she battled, walked, or talked. He'd seen it in the simpler moments like when they ate; she always waited for everyone to be served before she took her first bite. Or when they slept at night; she'd tuck one hand beneath her head, cushioning her cheek.

Looking back now, he also realized she bathed by herself, never changed her clothing with the rest of them, and refrained from their rough and tumble games. Yet she'd thrown herself into many battles alongside the other men over and over again. Simon frowned. Why would she risk death or discovery to follow her visions? Did what she saw in her mind empower her or frighten her into seeing things through?

Simon stared at the doorway through which Brianna and Abigail had left. Fear or strength, it did not matter to Simon what her visions did to her; he would see that she had them, many and often, in order to learn what they could about de la Roche.

"What do we do now?" Kaden asked, interrupting Simon's thoughts.

"For a start, you and I are going to the stable to see what kind of horseflesh these women own, then make our plans from there."

Kaden frowned. "It's going to be a long night, isn't it?"

"You never had any sisters, did you?"

The young knight shook his head.

Simon clapped his friend on the shoulder. "Prepare yourself, Kaden. It could be quite some time before we know a moment's peace again."

At dawn the next morning, Brianna crept silently into the stable where Simon and Kaden had bedded down for the night despite the fact they had every room available at the inn. The men had preferred to sleep with their horses. On tiptoe she moved to the two horses Abigail kept for travelers' needs.

Brianna grasped her favorite harness and saddle from the rest of the tack. She made her way to Magic's side. At her approach the horse lifted her nose and eagerly rubbed it against Brianna's outstretched hand. "My beauty," Brianna whispered against the horse's ear. "Good morning. Are you ready for this?"

The horse tossed its head, and a responding wave of nervous anticipation flared in Brianna's chest. She couldn't sleep last night, not one wink, as her mind had raced through the possibilities that lay ahead of her.

Her gaze crept to the reclining figure of the man who had, in part, given her back a small glimmer of hope that her life might amount to something — that the dreams she had each and every night had meaning. Yet caution held her back. Would he be true to his word? Would he allow her to see this journey through, to fulfill her destiny? Would she be able to prove to herself and the rest of the world that she was as good as any man — that her visions were a gift as the Mother Superior had once called them and not the ravings of a madwoman as Brianna had begun to suspect? Brianna pressed her lips together at the thought. It wasn't the rest of the world she wanted to convince she was worthy — for her, the world amounted to only her father and Simon.

A familiar hurt centered in her chest. Damn them both for not believing in her, for rejecting her. Brianna straightened. One thing she had learned over the last year was that no one could take away her sense of worth unless she let them. And she wasn't about to let that happen to her again.

"What are you doing?" a male voice came at her from behind.

Brianna lifted the edges of her dress and turned to face Simon. He stood with his sword drawn. She frowned down the length of the blade. "You have no need of that weapon here."

"Answer my question." Slowly he lowered his sword, no doubt reacting more from habit than from any threat by her. "What are you doing?"

"Haven't you ever seen anyone saddle a horse before?"

"With what intent, Brianna?" he asked, his tone brittle.

Her frown deepened at the distrust in his voice. "I'm excited to get going. I didn't want to waste time waiting for you to prepare the horses. I thought I'd take care of it myself."

"Because as well as fight, you can saddle a horse better than I can. Is that it?"

"You taught me how to saddle a horse, you fool. Why would I think I could do it better than you?"

"Because to you, everything is a challenge you must excel at. Saddling the horses is no different than winning a sword fight."

She turned away from him to slip the bit between Magic's teeth then fit the bridle comfortably around the horse's ears before securing it. "Believe whatever motive you like. I've told you the truth." She moved to the tack and snatched up two more bridles. She faced Simon and thrust them into his joined hands, avoiding the sword he still held.

"Make yourself useful and saddle the horses you brought with you."

The spark of challenge lit his dark eyes. He sheathed his sword as he strode to Diago's side. "I see the last year has not dulled your tongue."

""Twas the only weapon I was allowed." Brianna grabbed the horse blanket and settled it over her horse's back, followed by the saddle. A heartbeat later she moved on to Abigail's old gray mare. He moved on to Kaden's horse at the same moment.

She wasn't racing him, Brianna reminded herself as she finished setting the bridle in the mare's mouth faster than she ever had before. The old horse's gaze followed Brianna as she tossed the saddle onto its back. It was a look that said, "Go easy on these old bones."

Simon darted a glance at her and picked up his pace.

Brianna's fingers flew over the lashings. When she'd finished she patted the horse on the neck and turned to see Simon had finished at the same moment.

"Well done," she acknowledged begrudgingly.

He gave her an arch look. "You had a head start."

His words rang in her head and ignited her temper. She had lived for the past year in isolation from her family, sacrificing everything she held dear, and he had the audacity to insinuate she'd cheated. "I'm done here."

"Where are you going?"

"Away from you." She stopped at the door and turned to face him. "We might be partners in this search for de la Roche, but that doesn't mean I have to like you, Simon Lockhart. You are still as arrogant and pigheaded as ever." On those words, she disappeared.

Pigheaded. Him?

"She's right, you know." Kaden sat up in the pile of straw that had been his bed for the night. He yawned, then stretched. "Have you always been like this around her?"

"What do you mean? I'm no different with her than with anyone else."

Kaden's laughter filled the morning air. He stood, dusting the remnants of the straw from his leather jerkin and breeches. "Watching the two of you is like watching two deer with their horns locked, battling over territory. You're both all muscle and no brains."

"I resent that."

Kaden shrugged. "Resent it all you like. It's the truth."

Simon was surprised by Kaden's words, though he shouldn't have been. Brianna's presence had always set him on edge. Why would today be any different? "What do you suggest?"

"Let the woman win occasionally. She and her visions are helping us, after all."

Let her win. She would win most of the time even if he didn't let her, but a part of him still couldn't accept her skill. She was first and foremost a woman. "Come on," Simon said, heading for the door that Brianna had vanished through. The sudden silence was heavenly, but that's not why they were here. They'd come to find Brianna and make use of her dreams. He frowned at her retreating back. Before they began this adventure, however, he had one more stop to make.

He had to return to Rosslyn Castle. And this time he would speak with her father no matter his excuses. During their journey to Teba, William and John Sinclair had mentioned secret underground catacombs that existed beneath the old chapel at their home. The catacombs would be the perfect place to relocate the treasure. The chapel was close enough to Edinburgh and the Templar brothers who lived there, that they might help protect the artifacts without major disruption to their lives.

Simon clenched his jaw. Moving the Templar treasure was almost as urgent a task as finding and stopping de la Roche. He had to convince Brianna's father to allow him to use the already excavated tunnels. If not, it might take years to prepare another hiding place as secure as the Sinclair brothers had claimed the catacombs to be.

And perhaps while he was there he could also help bridge whatever divide had come between Brianna and her father.

It seemed like the perfect solution.

He only prayed Brianna would see it that way.

Of course, he didn't have to tell her.

Chapter Six

Brianna tasted fear as the scenery where they headed became familiar. They'd passed many rolling green fields dotted with acacia trees, but at the sound of the River North Esk, the scene resonated in her memory. They came to the top of a rise and she looked down to see the familiar sight of Roslin Glen bathed in late afternoon light. "Simon, where are we heading? I thought you said it was to Crosswick Abbey?"

"We needed to make one stop first," he replied, bringing his horse alongside hers. "I wish to speak with your father."

"He won't see you." He won't see anyone. "He went into deep mourning after the loss of his sons."

"It's been more than a year since they—"

"Grief resolves in its own time," she snapped. She hadn't meant to snap, but then she hadn't ever meant to come back here either. She glowered at Simon. "You should have told me."

"Would you have come?" he asked with a lift of his brow.

"Nay." She'd suffered enough hurt and rejection at her father's hand. She needed no more.

He smiled faintly. "That's why I didn't tell you. I need you with me. What I ask of your father is great. I thought perhaps…"

She laughed. "My presence will only turn my father against your cause." She reined to a stop at the edge of the bridge approaching the castle. "He is more likely to do as you wish without me nearby. I shall wait here."

His smile faded. "Are you frightened of the man?"

A heaviness came to her throat and she cursed herself for it. The man deserved no more of her tears. "Let's just say my father and I see the world differently."

He studied her as Kaden and Abigail brought their horses alongside Brianna and Simon.

"Is there a problem?" Kaden asked.

"Of course not," Brianna replied, catching the look of concern on Abigail's face. Abigail understood.

Simon's gaze continued to probe Brianna's.

She straightened and looked away, hiding her pain.

"Trust in me, Brianna."

She glanced back at him. She could almost believe him. Sweet heavens, she needed someone with whom she could talk who understood her need to pick up a sword. She was so alone.

Brianna shook herself. What was she thinking? After the turmoil she'd been through, had she learned nothing? She could trust no one. She smiled with an effort. "I need nothing from you, Simon."

A flicker of disappointment crossed his face. "Then if we have nothing to discuss, let us proceed."

Brianna shook her head. "You and Kaden will go alone. Abigail and I shall remain here and set up camp for the night. By the time you get back, darkness will be upon us."

Anger darkened Simon's features. "Have it your way then. Set up camp and, by the heavens, you had better prepare our evening meal before we return."

She looked directly into his eyes. "Good fortune with my father; and by the way, beware the dead wolfhound that haunts these grounds. Mauthe Doog has terrified many a man away from Rosslyn Castle with his eerie baying and sudden ghostly appearances."

His gaze narrowed. "I am not scared of ghosts, your father, or you, Brianna. Be forewarned yourself."

Brianna felt a gust of cold wind as he and Kaden sent their horses cantering over the bridge toward her one-time home. Her gaze followed Simon's broad, mailed back. Trust him? The last time she had trusted him, he had exposed her secret identity to the Templars, and broken her heart. She closed her eyes, blocking out the sight of the man's strength and power. A part of her realized he'd had no choice but to betray her. That perhaps things might be different between them now. What would it feel like to have an ally? She was terribly weary of battling her dreams and desires alone...

"He would be kinder to you than your father."

Brianna opened her eyes and glanced at Abigail. "Or he will tear me apart." She shook her head. "I don't want to think about my father or anything else right now except making camp." Brianna dismounted and drew her horse to a thicket of grass. She tied the reins loosely to a nearby branch so the animal could feed. "I will see to the shelter if you prepare a meal."

Abigail slid from her horse. "Or, you could allow me to teach you how to cook over a fire. There will be a day that you might need to know how to cook, Brianna."

She ignored, once again, Abigail's attempt to domesticate her. "I'll go find us a hare."

Abigail sighed, and handed Brianna her horse's reins. "All right, child. But someday..."

Brianna felt her lips pull up in a smile. Not if she could help it.

The sound of baying filled the night air.

Brianna stared up at the twisting shadows cast by the moonlight through the woven ferns and sticks overhead. The shelter she had built for herself and Abigail, and another further away for Simon and Kaden, protected them from the rain and mist, but not from the sounds of the night keeping her awake.

She wasn't scared of Mauthe Doog. She'd seen his apparition twice before in her life: Both times had been on nights before her father had sent her away, first to the abbey, then to the woods.

Darkness closed in on Brianna, wrapping around her like a shroud of black cloth. Thick, lifeless, and deceptively soft, it covered her nose and mouth, pressed against her lungs, suffocating her with memory. She drew a gasping breath and glanced around wildly, trying to see something, anything that would not feed her fear of being sent away again.

Her heart thudded in her chest, pounded against her rib cage as she lay against the ferns. She could only be hurt by rejection if she allowed herself to care. The problem was that she did care about Simon and about helping the Templars rid themselves of their enemy. Would he make her a knight as he'd promised? Or would he reject her in the end as her father always had?

Her mind raced with unanswered questions. Silently, she slipped out of the shelter. She grasped her sword, and securing it about her waist, made her way to the grassy field a hundred paces to the left. She needed to do something to clear her mind and bring the exhaustion her body needed if she were to dream as Simon had asked.

If only she could find sleep.

She drew her sword from her scabbard and balanced it in her hand. She gripped the hilt, feeling the grooves of the metal beneath her palm. It felt right having a sword in her hand. Natural.

Despite the darkness, her gaze drifted to where she knew Rosslyn Castle sat. She was a woman warrior. Why could her father not accept that? Simon had accepted her ... eventually. He had accepted her quite readily when he'd thought she was a boy. He'd sparred with her and taught her many things. Until he'd discovered her secret.

That's when everything had changed between them.

Brianna concentrated on the blade in her hand. She drew a deep breath and felt the sword as though it were an extension of her arm. She brought the blade up in a slow, controlled movement, then down, releasing her breath as she did.

Breathing helped to center her as her blade came up, then down, over and over again in a punishing routine she'd developed for herself. She had to keep herself strong and keep her skills sharp, even if she hadn't had any use for them since her return from Teba.

From the shadows at the edge of the field, Simon watched the woman before him as she put her lean muscular body through the primal steps of a dance. Her battle dance. Despite the fact she wore heavy skirts now instead of breeches, he'd seen such movements before. Her lithe movements had captivated him as much then as they did now. Brianna, the woman, the warrior, and if he were honest with himself, his equal on the battlefield.

Simon narrowed his gaze upon her as she danced in and out of the moonlight, bringing her blade up with a swift, sure stroke, then down with the same proficiency. The simple cut of her dress did nothing to hide the curves hidden beneath. The fabric fluttered with each step, only to hug her body with each turn. He stared at her, transfixed. How could he have ever thought she was a boy?

Simon closed his eyes, bracing against the onslaught of emotion flooding him. Deep within himself he must have known the he was a she, for he had been attracted to her from the beginning. And yet he had not realized her deception on some level as well. The first time he'd touched her and a strange spark had passed between them, he'd thought he was going mad. Perhaps he'd taken too many blows to the head.

He had tried explaining his need to be near the new knight "Brendan" as his own desire to train the lad in the ways of the Templars. And when he'd discovered her deception, he had to admit his first thought had been that of gratitude a moment before the rage set in.

He'd been as angry at her as many of the other knights had been. They had wanted to abandon her in Spain, but he couldn't do that. He'd seen a raw vulnerability in her eyes that he'd connected with even then.

That vulnerability was back in her eyes now. Her concentration focused on her movements and on her technique. With all her efforts elsewhere, her guard had dropped, leaving her exposed. And along with the vulnerability he also saw hurt and betrayal. By her father?

"Simon?"

The sound of her voice brought him out of his reverie. "I did not mean to disturb you. I saw you slip from the camp and wanted to make certain you were well." What was it about her father that disturbed her so?

She lowered her sword and he could see her chest rise and fall from the effort of her movements. She batted at the sides of her face with the back of her hand. "I am done here." She stiffened and turned away, as though afraid to look at him.

Simon studied her downcast face. She was hanging on to her self-control by a thread, trying so hard to be invincible. But he could see past her facade. And the scared, lonely woman standing before him tore at his heart. He recalled his own moments of doubt as a young man who'd been sent away from home to learn how to become a warrior. He remembered the cold, lonely nights in the monastery, staring into the darkness, praying for something more.

The fear and painful loneliness was something he understood. An almost aching tenderness unfolded within him. He needed to reach out to her, to weave his fingers around hers. He wanted to take her into his arms and, without words, let her know she wasn't as alone as she thought.

"Brianna?" Her name, spoken so gently, hung between them.

Slowly, she lifted her gaze to his. In her eyes he saw a faint, hesitant stirring of hope. "Couldn't sleep?"

She shook her head as she sheathed her weapon. "I thought exhaustion might help."

He curled his fingers at his side, fighting the urge to draw her near. "Did it?"

She released a tired sigh and leaned back against a human-sized boulder at the edge of the field. "Not in the way I needed."

He strode toward her and positioned himself next to her with his back against the rock. Her nearness sent a jolt of warmth down his spine. He looked up at the night sky, seeking a distraction. Above him stretched an inky cloak speckled with thousands upon thousands of stars. "It seems we both failed to attain our goals this eve." He brought his gaze back to her.

She turned her face to him. Even in the meager moonlight he could see the paleness of her skin, the slight lines of worry that bracketed her mouth. "I am sorry my father refused to see you. What did you come to ask him?"

"Are there truly catacombs beneath Rosslyn Chapel?"

She nodded and her lips lifted in a partial smile. "They are deep and many. It's where I used to practice with my old iron sword as a young lady when my father and brothers stopped allowing me to train with them." Her smile faded. "That was until my father caught me and sent me away."

It was his turn to frown. "He sent you away?"

She nodded. "To a convent. He was determined to make me a lady, one way or another. When Abigail's teachings failed, he thought the sisters might have better luck." A lost, almost tortured expression passed through her eyes.

"I didn't know."

She shrugged and pushed away from the rock. "There are many things you don't know about me."

He stared into her huge, pain-darkened eyes and felt as if he were drowning in the need to hold her. She stood right beside him, so close and yet distinctly separate, alone as always, untouchable. And now he understood the pain that was ever-present in her eyes. She waited for the world to attack her, to blindside her, to betray her yet again.

He moved awkwardly toward her as pain snagged his heart. She expected him to betray her as well. "I didn't understand before, but I do now."

Even in the darkness he could see the shimmer of tears in her eyes. "I don't want to talk about this anymore."

Neither did he. He needed distance if he were to keep his thoughts focused on their mission. Simon drew a sharp breath of the cool night air into his lungs, the coolness reminding him with crystal clarity what his true purpose was: to locate de la Roche and stop him from harming anyone else. Both he and Brianna had a task to do. That duty allowed for no interference from their past. He straightened and pushed away from the rock. "Do you think you are tired enough to dream now?"

She turned away. "The only way to find out is to try to sleep."

"Then let's return to camp," he said, his words sharper than he'd meant them to be. Her dreams were the key to their success.

And nothing else besides finding de la Roche mattered. Nothing at all.

By dawn, Brianna had yet to fall asleep, let alone to dream. Simon forced back his disappointment as he, Brianna, Kaden, and Abigail prepared to ride out. They had only just mounted their horses when Simon noticed a haze of coiling gray smoke in the east that rose against the pink hues of dawn.

"What is that?" Kaden asked beside him.

Simon could only stare into the distance as he felt the color drain from his face. A knot of fear tightened his stomach. It couldn't be...

Brianna brought her horse alongside his, gazing at the black smoke rising in the distance. "The morning air carries the scent of—"

"Death," he filled in, as pain engulfed him. He knew what that smoke meant. He knew who was responsible. "We must hurry." He kicked his horse into a gallop.

Brianna kept pace beside him. Kaden and Abigail followed.

"What is it?" Brianna asked.

"De la Roche." Pain throbbed at the base of Simon's neck.

"How can you know that from the sight of smoke?"

His fingers tightened around the reins in his hand until his knuckles turned white from the force. "It's the scent of burning flesh that tells me it's him."

Her eyes went wide. "He's burning the countryside?"

"Nay, Templars."

Brianna fell silent as their four horses flew over the open terrain. Desperation constricted Simon's chest, yet he couldn't help but glance at the woman beside him. She rode with remarkable skill. And despite the horror he knew his words must have evoked in her mind, a look of determination settled across her delicate features.

They had reached the crest of a hill when the punishing flames came into sight against the backdrop of the small village of Roslin at the bottom of the hill. One figure stood erect, tied to a stake. Flames lapped cruelly at the human form engulfed within.

"Abigail and Brianna, stay back. Kaden and I shall—"

A cry of distress sounded beside him. Brianna bolted forward.

"Brianna, nay!" Simon's heart pounded wildly as he saw Brianna's slim form outlined against the red-orange flames. At her approach, seven men leapt from the bushes.

An ambush.

Simon spurred his horse toward those who would kill them.

Brianna must have sensed the danger. She drew her sword and expertly dispatched two men before they realized she'd drawn her weapon.

Simon joined the battle, his heart hammering as he watched Brianna engage the men with skill that was deadly and precise. He fought one attacker after another, yet despite the danger, his focus remained on her, on the way she and her horse moved as one, as though in the steps of a macabre dance. Five new opponents rushed forward on foot. Simon watched her back between a trio of trees. She'd cornered herself. His heart sank — until it buoyed again when he saw she'd made it impossible for more than two men to come at her at once. She deflected their blows with grace and ease. He'd never seen anything like it, like her, wild red hair catching the wind, the silver streak of her weapon as it slashed through the empty space to catch their foes. One by one the men fell. The echo of steel died away until the only sound remaining was their own harsh breathing as it mixed with that of the horses.

A heartbeat later, Brianna slid from her horse. She sheathed her weapon as she ran toward the flaming timbers.

"Where are you going?" Simon slid from his horse and in two steps he gained on her. He gripped her arm and pulled her back against his chest.

"We must help that poor man."

"Brianna," Simon whispered against her ear, holding her close. His gaze strayed to the blackened figure bound to the stake. His throat tightened and he couldn't swallow. "We are too late." Smoke stung his eyes, seared his lungs.

She stopped fighting as his words sank home. "De la Roche?" she asked, her voice raw with emotion.

"Aye. He tortures then burns the Templars he captures," Simon said as he studied the woman beside him. Her eyes glittered brightly in the glare of the fire.

Behind them, hoofbeats sounded. Simon's hand tightened on his weapon only to relax once again as he saw it was Kaden and Abigail who approached. "I'll retrieve the body," Kaden said.

"Do you have any idea who this poor man was?" Brianna asked over the pop and hiss of the flames.

Simon prepared to answer that he did not know when his gaze caught on the ground near the burning stake. Scratched into the earth were four words: You are next, Lockhart.

Chapter Seven

Brianna stared at the ground and the words etched there. "Simon?" The word was barely a whisper. "He is after you?"

"Aye. He's been after me and all the Templars for some time now. And he has two holy relics that may help him accomplish that task. He'll continue until he gets what he wants. That's why I need your help so desperately. Your visions are the only advantage we have."

"I want to help." Simon studied her with a gentleness that brought a catch to her breath. She pushed out of his arms. She stepped away as guilt and anger consumed her over the senselessness of the deaths of all the men this day.

The pain of loss was nothing new to either one of them. They'd lost many warriors in the days they'd fought together. They would lose many more before this was over, if the ambush today were any indication. Her gaze swept the ground and the eleven men who lay dead. "De la Roche's men?"

Simon came to stand behind her. She could feel him, sense him standing there. As always, he was close enough to lend her comfort, yet kept a distance between them as well. "We must leave here, Brianna. Until we have reinforcements and know more about de la Roche's identity, we cannot risk anything happening to you."

"To me?"

He nodded. "You are everything. The edge we need to destroy de la Roche for good."

Before she could reply, Simon gripped her waist, then lifted her up onto the back of her horse. "This is no time for us to delay. De la Roche could be anywhere."

Simon assisted Abigail onto her horse before he mounted his own. Kaden bundled the charred remains of the Templar into his cloak then lashed the body to the back of his horse before mounting. "We must ride as far as we can this day. Only once we reach the priory and the other Templars there will we be safe." Simon turned his horse to the southeast. They all fell silent as they picked their way through the dense forest.

"How could de la Roche know you were on your way to find me, or that you'd head to Rosslyn Castle?"

Simon frowned. "I don't know, but from this moment forward we must proceed with absolute caution. It was probably best that Abigail came with us. I'd hate to have left her for de la Roche to use as bait to get to you."

Brianna twisted back toward Abigail. She was too far back to hear their conversation. Pain squeezed Brianna's chest. She loved Abigail and had never intended to put her in harm's way because of her own choices. "Will Abigail be safe at the priory?"

"As safe as any of us."

Brianna frowned. "You mentioned that de la Roche possesses two holy relics. Why does his possessing them concern you so?"

Simon twisted toward her. "He stole both the sword of Charlemagne and the Holy Grail. With those two items, he holds the power to slay and to heal in the palm of his hands."

A shiver rippled down Brianna's spine. "He will be a formidable foe."

Simon nodded, but said nothing further.

As they rode, Brianna glanced at the man beside her. She had not seen Simon for a year. He sat his horse with more confidence than he had when they were in Teba together. His bearing was proud, his gaze thoughtful, yet she didn't miss the lines of worry that were etched beneath his watchful eyes. And in those eyes there was a sadness that had not been there before. No doubt Simon had seen many horrific things in the time they'd been apart, but was that the reason for the sadness or something more?

Her gaze shifted to his hands. They were large and well-shaped, strong, masculine, and lightly scarred. They were the hands of a capable warrior who was used to fighting. She shifted her gaze to her own hands. A light scar laced the back of her right hand that she'd received in one of the many battles leading up to Teba. Her left hand bore two smaller scars from early days of sparing with her brothers. The hint of a smile tugged at her lips. They both wore the evidence of their chosen life. The thought warmed her.

Brianna allowed silence to fall between them as they traveled for what felt like forever. At nightfall, her muscles screamed at the lack of movement and exhaustion settled over her. A glance at Simon told her he was as tired as she, yet he wasn't about to give in.

Brianna straightened. If he could take the relentless motion and stiffness in his muscles, so could she. But a quick glance at Abigail confirmed that not everyone in their party was so stubborn.

Abigail came forward. "My horse is tired. As are yours," she said. "Will we be stopping soon?"

"There is a village ahead."

A wave of relief swept across Abigail's weary face. "Where we will stay the night?" she asked hopefully.

"Nay," Simon responded. "We will stay only long enough to trade the horses and eat something warm; then we shall continue onward."

"With so little rest?" Abigail asked.

He shrugged. "I have no desire to give de la Roche time to catch up to us. Do you?"

"Nay, but how can you fight him if you are exhausted?"

"You'd be amazed at how hard you can fight with no sleep whatsoever when the need arises."

"Simon's right," Brianna agreed. They'd both fought against their foe when exhaustion had been heavy upon them. "We had best keep moving until we know we are safe."

Though a look of disappointment shadowed Abigail's features, she nodded and let her horse fall back into step beside Kaden and his horse.

As they continued on, Brianna tried to focus her thoughts on the trees, the slight wind that picked up as dusk fell over the land. No matter what she tried, her thoughts turned back to the quiet man beside her. What had happened to him since his return to Scotland? They'd parted suddenly after the battle of Teba. She'd been escorted by four of the surviving foot soldiers back to Rosslyn Castle along with the bodies of her brothers.

She shuddered at the memory. Suddenly she had to know more of what had become of Simon after that day. "You mentioned going back to Lee Castle after Teba?"

"For less than a day. That's when I received word from Sir William that it was urgent I meet him at Crosswick Priory. That's when we learned about the threat de la Roche had brought to Scotland's shores."

"You've battled de la Roche before?"

"It did not go well. The man escaped." As if saying the words released him from some spell, he finally met her eyes.

Every question she asked raised only more questions. Brianna met his gaze as suddenly she needed to know all of what he did not say. Was he protecting her or himself? Without thinking, she brought her horse next to his and reached out and touched his hands as they clutched his horse's reins. "I'm sorry for the pain he's added to your life."

Her nerves flickered as the scent of soap teased her senses and warmth curled down her spine.

He didn't pull away, but his breathing quickened. "He'll not get the chance to do so again."

Through her fingers she could feel the tension thrumming through him. "Does anyone else know about de la Roche infiltrating the Templars?"

"I sent the others who were with me at the treasury ahead of us to the priory. By now, I have hope they've been able to spread the word as far and as wide as possible." He sighed and some of the tension left him. "But that is why it is imperative we get to the priory because none of us knows what the man looks like — how he's disguised himself." His gaze warmed. "That's why we need you. Your dreams can tell us what we do not know."

If only I could dream. Brianna looked down at where their hands were joined. It had been a year since they'd been this close. She could feel the heat of Simon's body pass into her own, sensed the raw desire that lay just below his surface — the energy that was always there. She'd not forgotten how it felt to touch him. How she felt charged with tension and yet renewed each time.

She drew a shuddering breath, trying to keep her thoughts centered on the challenges ahead. "What do you expect de la Roche will do with the artifacts he has?"

A flash of pain darkened his eyes the instant before he pulled his hand from her slackened grasp. "He's obviously injured which explains the Grail. And the sword, no doubt, is to help him overtake the Templars. He almost accomplished that feat last time when he stole the Spear of Destiny, but thanks to Sir William and Lady Siobhan Fraser, that attempt was thwarted."

"I know this might be unpleasant for you, but what can you tell me about him physically? Does he have any notable features? Things he could not disguise? It might help me."

"His eyes." Simon's voice became hard. "He has unusually light blue eyes."

"Merciful heavens," Brianna whispered. "Blue eyes…"

Simon's gaze snapped to hers. "What is it?"

"I've seen him before in my dreams." She reached up and toyed with the place where the lock of hair that had gone missing the night before Simon had arrived. "Or perhaps in person."

Simon's expression darkened. "Explain yourself."

She lifted the hair that had been left blunted after that night. "I had a dream one night that there was a man in my chamber. He stood over me and clipped a lock of my hair. Why would he do that?"

Simon stopped his horse then reached out for her bridle, forcing her to do the same. Fear and anger mixed in the depths of his dark eyes. He reached for her hair, running his finger and thumb along the severed ends. "He did not hurt you, did he?"

"I could have taken care of myself if he had tried anything."

Simon released her hair. "Nothing good can come of this."

"What could he possibly do with my hair?"

"I don't know for certain, but since I've come to you, it has seemed as though the man has known our every move."

Abigail and Kaden stopped their horses. "It's the old magic," Abigail said with a frown. "I've heard tales from my mother and her mother before her that a lock of hair from one who has visions can allow others to partake in those dreams."

"Is there any way to sever the bond?" Kaden asked, bringing his horse up next to Brianna.

"Brother Kenneth might know." Simon glowered, quietly smoldering, but there was worry behind his eyes. "I know you are all tired, but with this new development, we absolutely must continue to the priory."

All the color drained from Abigail's countenance. "It's that serious?"

Simon nodded.

Abigail stiffened. "Then let's go."

"There is a small village ahead." Kaden paused, then added, "We can refresh the horses and perhaps ourselves there."

Simon inclined his head. "When we reach the village, you and Abigail will gather food while Kaden and I see to the horses. Agreed?"

Abigail gripped her horse's reins. "I'll do whatever it takes to get this man away from us," she said as they started forward once more.

None of them spoke again until they entered the village. "How long do we have?"

"Not long. I'll come back for you as soon as Kaden and I refresh the horses."

Brianna turned toward the small inn to find a large, buxom woman opening the door to welcome them inside. About the same age as Abigail, the woman had graying black hair and kind brown eyes.

"Good eve," the woman said, smiling brightly. Her smile faltered for a moment as her gaze fixed on Brianna's sword. "Will you be needing a room for the night?"

"Nay, just a bit of food before my companions and I are on our way again."

The woman looked past her as Simon and Kaden headed for the stable. "Judging by the tall one's steps, he appears to be in a hurry."

Brianna nodded.

"Then we'd best get you taken care of before he returns." The woman stepped aside to allow Brianna and Abigail to enter. "Go on into the common room. We have mincemeat pies and roasted lamb."

They needed food that would be easy to carry. "We'll take four pies, two skins of ale, and apples if you have them, please?"

The woman nodded and left the two of them alone in the empty common room. An odd sensation fluttered across the back of Brianna's neck. She scanned the empty chamber.

Even for a small town, it was unusual for the inn to be vacant at suppertime.

Brianna sat in a chair near the hearth to wait. With her gaze on the door, she gripped the hilt of her sword.

"There's no need for that." A frown pulled down the corners of Abigail's lips as she sat down next to Brianna.

Brianna opened her mouth to speak, then paused as she heard something odd from outside. If she didn't know better…

A dagger whizzed past the right side of her head, narrowly missing her.

Abigail shrieked and dropped to the floor.

Before Brianna could unsheathe her sword, the door slammed open and a body dressed in a green tunic and black breeches rolled to the floor.

Four long steps took her across the room where she rested her blade at the man's exposed neck, only to find him already dead.

A heartbeat later, Simon stepped through the door with his dagger in his hand. "We must leave now."

"De la Roche's man?" Brianna asked.

"It has to be. We must keep moving. That is our best defense until we know more."

Abigail joined them. Her face paled as she gazed at the man slumped in the doorway. "What about the food?"

Simon bent down and hoisted the dead man over his shoulder. "Our hunger won't matter much if we are dead." He vanished into the darkness of the inn yard to return a moment later without the man.

Brianna shut the door to the inn, then she and Abigail strode toward the horses Kaden held for them at the center of the yard. Silently, they mounted and under the cover of darkness, left town.

As they made their way through the dark forest, Brianna couldn't stop the frantic beating of her heart. Who was this de la Roche? He'd sent men to attack them twice now. Would more follow? How did the Frenchman know where the four of them were? Did the man follow them as well?

Suddenly the burden of what Simon had asked of her settled around her shoulders. How many more men or women would die before she could identify who or what de la Roche had become? Her visions would tell her. "Please," she whispered into the night. "Let me sleep."

De la Roche frowned as a torch, illuminating the buxom woman he'd paid to set his trap, came toward him, revealing his hiding place on the far side of the inn yard.

A few more days of drinking from the Grail and his shattered leg would be fully healed. Then he could challenge Lockhart and all the Templars himself. Each day he grew stronger, the damage to his body improved and the pain was less crippling.

"They left in a hurry," the woman cried. Her face was pale and her expression void of the friendliness with which she'd first greeted him. "I tried to make them stay. I did everything you asked."

De la Roche pulled his brown robes around him and stepped out of the shadows.

The woman stopped an arm's length from him, quivering. "They killed your man."

At her fear, his anger faded and a smile tugged at the corner of his mouth. She was only an innkeeper's wife, yet the effect his presence had over her was everything he'd ever hoped for. It was about time someone saw him the way he saw himself — powerful and indestructible. The woman's fear was palpable. To him it was as heady and as intoxicating as the finest wine in France. "Did you poison their pies and their apples?" he asked, his voice hard, filled with the power that ran through his veins.

Her face became ashen. "They left without the food."

Joyeuse swung free of his scabbard, and displacing a mere whisper of air, cut her down.

She dropped to her knees as her face contorted with pain. "Milord…" The words faded into the night as she fell to the ground at his feet.

The air still vibrating with the song of death, de la Roche sheathed the mighty weapon. Armies throughout history had fallen before Charlemagne's sword. The Templars would be easy prey once he was fully healed.

De la Roche lifted the pouch filled with the lock of Brianna Sinclair's hair that he wore suspended by a silken cord about his neck. Just as the old woman who'd helped to harbor him after his fall from the tower of Stonehyve Castle had said, the lock of hair he'd taken from Brianna Sinclair gave him an odd connection to the girl. Through her hair, he had known where to go next to find Lockhart and his band of warriors.

De la Roche stretched his broken and battered limb, feeling no pain. The Grail would continue to heal him. But the time was past for sending assassins to do what must be done. He must face his enemy himself. Before he met Lockhart face-to-face, he would strike the man in a more subtle way — a way that would hurt him far more than a sword to the chest.

And de la Roche knew just where to start. Lee Castle was not too far from here. The Lockhart estate would most likely hold many treasures worth destroying. With a satisfied smile, he headed for the innkeeper's kitchen.

The unprotected sisters of that bastard Lockhart would welcome a basket of beautiful apples. They would accept a gift from one of Lockhart's many associates. He would make certain of it.

Chapter Eight

They rode through the night and all the next day, until once again night fell. The sky was bloodred as the last rays of sunlight pierced the horizon. The rays turned the glimpses of the sea peeking out between the trees on their left a blazing red. Instead of taking in the breathtaking beauty, Brianna frowned at the sight. She hated the color red. Since Teba, she'd not been able to separate the color from the sticky red liquid that had covered the battlefield that day.

Pulling her gaze from the sky, she slowed her pace to bring her horse next to Abigail. They'd been riding for hours. The older woman was as dusty as she from their travels, yet Abigail's oval face and sparkling gray eyes showed no sign of weariness. In fact, with each mile they rode, it seemed as though Brianna's exhaustion increased in proportion to Abigail's excitement.

"Are you truly that excited to be away from your home?" Brianna asked when Abigail laughed after turning her face into the slight breeze.

"I've been in that inn for so long. I had forgotten what the world around us looks like — the hills, the trees, the sky. They are all so beautiful!"

Brianna wished she were enjoying the scenery as much. It had been so long since she'd been free of the confinement of the inn as well. But instead of joy, she felt the incredible pressure of forcing a vision to come to her. What if nothing came? She'd been given a chance to change her future and now what if her gift of sight refused to cooperate?

"That's a very dark look on your face for such a beautiful sunset," Simon drew his horse up to ride beside her.

Brianna frowned. Was she the only one who thought the sky appeared wrathful? "How much farther until we reach the priory?"

"Another day's travel at least. We will have to beg shelter from the lord in the castle just beyond the trees at the shoreline."

"Is the lord someone we can trust?" Out of habit, Brianna's hand moved to the hilt of the sword at her hip. She fingered the Celtic design carved into the haft, ready to draw if needed.

Simon smiled. "With our lives." Simon gave his horse a command. His steed leaped to a gallop through the woods.

Brianna, Abigail, and Kaden followed his lead as they crossed a wide, fast-flowing stream. Moments later, they emerged from the trees to see a shimmering four-square tower made entirely of red stone, rising from the edge of a bluff with the sea stretching endlessly behind it.

"Red Castle," Simon said, slowing his horse beside her. "The home of Sir Alan Cathcart and his wife Jessamine."

"Sir Alan is no longer a Templar?"

Simon nodded. "He helps the cause in other ways now."

Silence fell as the four of them progressed up the lane to the drawbridge. Before they reached the gate, the portcullis went up and a tall man with dark hair stepped forward to greet them. Brianna held back. Abigail did the same, allowing the men to talk privately.

The dark-haired Sir Alan clapped Simon on the shoulder and laughed. Simon's staid demeanor brightened and pleasure lingered for a moment as he smiled, before all emotion vanished once more. Simon turned to Brianna and signaled for her and Abigail to come forward.

Brianna paused, uncertain of how Sir Alan would greet her. He had been upset when he'd learned of her deception. She worried her bottom lip between her teeth. Most of the other Templars had been angered by her ruse, but none of them had been mean to her after the fact. They'd mostly just ignored her.

Sir Alan offered her a welcoming smile. "Brianna, 'tis good to see you again. Come." He waved her forward. "I want you to meet my wife."

She and Abigail joined the men and headed through the gate, across the bailey, up a flight of steps, and into the castle's great hall. Just past the doorway stood an exotic woman with long black hair and honey-colored skin.

Her dark eyes were kind as she met Brianna's. "Welcome to Red Castle. Alan has told me so much about you. I feel as if I already know you."

Brianna's eyes moved to the woman's rounded belly and back to her face. "You are with child?"

"I sure hope that's what this is!" She laughed as she cradled her belly with her hands. "Very soon there will be a little warrior in the castle and in our lives."

Sir Alan strode to stand behind his wife and placed his hands on her shoulders. A tender smile pulled up the corners of his mouth. "We are blessed."

Brianna could only stare. Never once, in all the time she had spent with the Templars had she ever seen Sir Alan smile. And yet he smiled easily now, standing beside his exotic bride and his soon-to-be baby. He appeared content. "Sir Alan, I am pleased to see you so happy. But what about de la Roche? Doesn't his presence in this country worry you? How will you keep your family safe?"

Sir Alan's smile slipped. "De la Roche's presence here concerns us very much. But is it not infinitely better to hope for the best than to fear for the worst? Jessamine and I have every confidence that you, Simon, Kaden, and the others will find a way to do what must be done. And if you have need of me, all you need do is ask."

"If you will excuse us," Jessamine said to the others. "I would like to speak with Brianna alone."

Simon nodded as he and the others walked past them into the high-roofed hall. They'd arrived at suppertime. Men sat at long tables clustered near a raised dais at the opposite end of the chamber. A cheery fire crackled in the hearth along the far wall. Busy serving maids carried platters of savory-smelling meats to each of the tables already laden with bread, fruit, cheese, and tankards of malty-smelling ale. Roasted mutton and onions were scents that reminded Brianna of home and should have brought her comfort. Tonight, they only made her stomach churn at the impossible task that had been placed on her shoulders. She needed to sleep, not eat, if she were to help them continue their journey.

"Alan tells me you have the gift of sight?" Jessamine said with a gentle smile as though reading her thoughts. "He truly believes your visions will help the Templars find and destroy de la Roche once and for all."

"I have dreams of things that have come to pass." Brianna could not keep from smiling back. There was something about the pregnant woman that reminded her very much of the abbess where her father had sent her to be cured of what he felt was a disease.

Brianna shook off the memory and studied her hostess. Did an iron will lie beneath the woman's genuine kindness as it had the abbess?

"Come, let us get you something to ease your weariness." Jessamine placed her hand on Brianna's arm and guided her toward the raised dais at the front of the hall. "I am familiar with dreams of prophecy."

Brianna startled at her words. "Do you have visions as well?"

She shook her head as they approached the table. "I was the keeper of a prophecy that brought Alan and I together. The prophecy changed both of our lives for the better. Perhaps it will do that for you and Simon as well."

As if he'd heard the statement, Simon turned, his gaze locking with hers. Brianna tore her gaze from his and frowned at Jessamine. "It's not like that between Simon and me."

Jessamine nodded thoughtfully. "I had thought ... oh, never mind." She led Brianna to the table on the dais and signaled for her to take the chair next to her own. "It is my most ardent hope then that your dreams will help the Templars overcome their greatest foe."

"Mine as well," Brianna glanced uneasily about the chamber. All these people and so many others needed her dreams to guide them. She swallowed back a moment's fear. What if she let them down?

"You have strength, Brianna. More than I've ever seen in a woman before," Jessamine said as though reading Brianna's thoughts, her doubts.

"Sometimes I fear it is just my stubborn pride that guides me."

Jessamine laughed. "It is more than that, my new friend. Even I, who am no seer, can tell you are different — special." Jessamine's gaze met Brianna's. "You are a blessing."

Brianna felt her throat thicken. "Thank you, Jessamine."

"Now, we must set you to rights so that you may dream these dreams of yours." Jessamine poured a tankard of ale from the pitcher on the table and handed it to Brianna. "Try this. It is made with honey and has a reviving quality to it."

Brianna took a deep drink, letting the warming liquid slip down her throat. The ale was sweeter than other ales she'd tasted. And her hostess was right. She did feel less fatigued even after only one swallow. "Thank you for giving us shelter tonight. Sleep, and I hope, the necessary dreams, will find me now without having to worry about our safety outside."

"Let's get you fed so you may retire, and with luck, you'll dream the dreams you need to free this country from de la Roche's terror."

Brianna found herself staring at the ceiling of the bedchamber she shared with Abigail. Her friend had fallen asleep immediately. Hours later, Brianna still had not. She'd tried relaxing into the soft heather ticking beneath her. When that hadn't worked, she strolled about the chamber, praying for weariness to overtake her. When that had failed, she had moved to the small shuttered window and had opened the latch to allow the night air to brush her heated cheeks.

From the tower in which she was housed, she could see the lists below. Four torches had been set at the corners of the field, illuminating the now empty area that would be used by the castle's knights to practice their warring skills.

As Brianna gazed down at the open space, an idea came to her. Silently, so as not to wake Abigail, she dressed then slipped her sword soundlessly into her scabbard. Practicing her warrior's skills would serve as a way to help her find the sleep she so desperately sought.

Smiling, she hurried through the silent corridor and down the stairs. Brianna hesitated at the open doorway that led into the great hall where Simon and Kaden supposedly slept with the castle's other knights. Only soft snores greeted her as she slipped past the doorway, heading outside.

The moon hovered full and round above the mountains to the east and the cool night air brought a shiver from her. But Brianna knew she would warm herself in a moment with her efforts in the lists. She could go through the motions of a mock battle against an invisible enemy as she had during so many other practice sessions in her early days, before the Templars.

Sorrow streaked through her for a heartbeat and her steps faltered at the reminder of her folly. She was here in the lists tonight to force herself past the point of exhaustion so she might dream about a man who had disguised himself. She knew how she had disguised herself and infiltrated the ranks of the Templars. Would she be able to figure out how de la Roche had achieved the same end?

She had to.

Brianna entered the lists and drew her sword. She held her weapon out before her and bowed to her invisible enemy. "To the death or first blood?" she asked.

"First blood."

Brianna gripped her sword and spun toward the voice. Simon stood not two paces away. By the light of the torches she could see him fully. "What are you doing here?"

"I could ask you the same thing. Aren't you supposed to be sleeping, or dreaming, or having a vision or whatever it is you do to give us the information we need?"

She lowered her weapon. "I still cannot sleep. I thought a bit of practice might help tire me." At the sight of Simon, her tension eased. Why? Did she truly find his presence comforting? Or was it that he understood the kind of pressure she was under to start them on their way.

"Would you like a true opponent, not just the air?" he asked.

She smiled. He knew her so well. A challenge would ease her mind. "If you dare," she replied.

"I dare that and much more."

Brianna raised her sword, waiting for Simon to draw his weapon.

Instead of drawing his sword, he walked away toward several benches along the side of the list. He strode back toward her after reaching for two long poles. He offered her what she now recognized as a quarterstaff. "I have no wish to kill you with my sword. Quarterstaffs will be safer. Put your weapon away."

Brianna sheathed her sword before she accepted the staff. "That's very kind of you, but you need not spare me. I can hold my own against you no matter the weapon."

He laughed. "We shall see about that."

Brianna glowered at the man. "I promise not to hurt you either." She turned the staff in her hands. Finding the balance off, she strode toward a rock not too far from her and laid her staff along the edge. She drew her sword. With both hands, she brought the weapon down against the wood, taking a handbreadth from the end. She sheathed her weapon and picked up the quarterstaff once more. Another twist of the staff confirmed the weapon was the proper length and balance for her height. "Now, we battle," she said, joining Simon in the center of the lists.

He laughed as he circled her.

Brianna kept her staff at an angle across her body just as Simon swung his quarterstaff. She misjudged the distance he could reach, knowing her mistake too late as he swept her off her feet. With a groan, she hit the ground. Her head rang from the blow resonating through her, and her eyes refused to focus. She heard a sound coming toward her. She rolled. A heartbeat later, Simon's staff tapped the hard-packed earth where she had been seconds before.

She scrambled to her feet, grabbing her staff by one end and swung it. He held up his staff, blocking the hit, but her blow sent him stumbling back several paces. Surprise widened his eyes. "You've improved since we last sparred with quarterstaffs." His mouth tightened and he came at her again.

Brianna met each swing of his quarterstaff. He was taller than she was, and his staff longer than hers, but she was quicker. That was her advantage, and she used it.

Round and round they went, striking and feinting. She watched Simon's hands closely, gauging his next move. But he moved to strike high, then went low, knocking her off her feet when he scooped the staff around and hit the back of her knees. She hit the ground hard.

As he leapt forward to press the staff to her throat, she raised her staff and caught him in the belly. She pushed hard, forcing him to her left. Using one end, she swung, striking him in the chest this time. He fell. From the ground, she shifted her hands and mimicked his move, slashing the quarterstaff against the back of his legs when he struggled to stand. She rolled away from him as he hit the ground with a thud.

Jumping up, she readied herself for the next attack, but Simon remained on the ground with his eyes closed. She inched toward him. Wary of being tricked, she reached out with her staff and poked him. He did not move. She batted his quarterstaff away from his right hand and lifted the appendage. It fell back to the ground lifeless.

"Simon?" She drifted closer. "Simon, did I hurt you?" She leaned down. His hands shot up and grasped her arms.

He pulled her down hard against his chest. Her staff fell and came to rest just out of arm's reach. His gaze narrowed on her face. "It is unique to find a woman who can wield a sword and a staff as well as any man."

"I practice as often as you do," she replied coolly.

"You are a decent warrior ... for a woman." His grip lessened enough for her to roll away from him. She gained her feet.

Brianna snapped up her staff and curled her fingers around the solid wood. "Does it give you solace to believe my skills are inferior to yours when both of us know—"

Simon was on his feet in a heartbeat. He grasped the staff on either side of her hands. He raised it with one quick motion to rest beneath her chin. He brought his face forward until he was only a handbreadth from her.

She tried to shove the staff down, but he was too strong. She took a step back. He matched it. She edged to the left. He followed. He kept the distance between them the same no matter what she did to try to avoid him. Finally, he pushed her back until the stone of the castle stopped their progression.

She lifted her chin and met his suddenly fiery gaze. "Remember it was you who challenged me."

He brought his face closer. "Because I want you to understand you are a good warrior, but even good warriors have a weakness. De la Roche will find what yours is and use it against you. So be forewarned and be prepared."

"I have no weakness."

He lowered the staff to her chest and stepped even closer. She hardly dared to breathe as she became aware of every hard angle of him against her. His muscular legs pressed against her skirt and she felt the force of his breathing move the rigid bulk of his chest against the softness of her own.

His gaze dropped from her eyes to her lips a moment before his mouth clamped over hers. At first there was anger in his kiss. She tried to turn her head away, but found she physically could not. He jerked the staff out of her hands and tossed it aside while his lips continued their punishing exploration.

She brought her hands up to press against his chest and tried to stamp on his foot. But he shifted his threatened appendage to the left and pulled her closer. A soft groan escaped his lips. She used his momentary distraction and tried again. She stomped down hard.

He broke the kiss and muttered a curse. His hold lessened and she twisted out of his grasp. She dove for her staff. He followed and grabbed her arm. He spun her to face him. "That wasn't very ladylike."

"There's no need to insult me." She brought her elbow up against his thumb, breaking his hold. She grabbed his shoulders before he could recover and gave a half turn. Simon flipped easily over her hip and hit the ground for a second time that night. He groaned, closed his eyes, and did not move.

This time she kept her distance. She would not fall for that trick twice. "Get up and dust yourself off like a man."

His eyes snapped open. "How did you do that?"

"I attacked your thumb. It is weaker than any other finger. Putting the right amount of pressure on it will easily break a stronger hold, allowing me to escape."

He rose to his elbows and glared at her. "Why did you attack me?"

"I did not want you to kiss me."

He sat up. "You could have just said no."

"You didn't give me a chance."

She put her hand out to help him up. "Are you all right? I didn't hurt you, did I?"

He brushed her hand away and stood. "I'm unharmed," he said and winced as though in pain.

She knew he probably did hurt. She'd taken such falls herself while training with the Templars. Had he damaged his head in the fall? She reached up and ran her fingers along the side of his face and along the back of his skull.

He grasped her hand and held it. "What are you doing?"

"I am only trying to examine the damage I might have caused you." She matched his fearsome scowl.

"You should be less concerned with the damage you do your enemy and more concerned about your survival."

"I can take care of myself."

He pulled her close against his chest once more. "Are you so sure about that?" He turned her wrist over and bent toward it. His breath rushed warm and swift against her tender flesh, sending shivers up her arm. "Can you defend yourself against this?"

He pressed his mouth to the inside of her wrist. The sensitive skin heated beneath his lips. She clutched her skirt with her other hand, fighting the warm sensations that nearly weakened her knees.

He raised his head slightly. "Can you defend yourself if de la Roche attacks without a sword?"

"I can, and I will." Her voice shook.

"What if he does this?" He nuzzled her neck and ran his tongue along the edge of her jaw to the base of her ear.

She could not contain the moan that escaped her as tingles sizzled along her spine. She released the hold she had on the fabric of her dress and found she clamped the fabric of his tunic instead as sensation after sensation battered her defenses.

His breath burned against her ear. She shut her eyes, savoring the exotic sensation.

In the next heartbeat he captured her lips once more, this time more gently. His fingers splayed across her shoulders as his tongue brushed against her lips. She could not deny him the deepest secrets of her mouth or anything else he wanted in that moment. His tongue slipped into her mouth and she responded by curling her fingers around his nape, drawing him even closer until she realized what she was doing.

She dropped her hand, broke the kiss, and stepped back. Her breathing came in ragged gasps as though she'd been battling for hours instead of the fleeting few moments that had passed in his arms.

Simon stepped away, his eyes still burning with the same desire she'd seen there earlier.

"You're a Templar," she whispered. She should not be kissing a Templar for so many reasons she could not begin to count them all!

"Thank you for the reminder," he said, his voice low and cool and suddenly remote.

She reached for her staff, held it tightly in her hands, fighting the urge to pull him close and lose herself in this Templar's kiss once more. "Simon, I—"

"That is enough practice for one night. Perhaps now you will find you are able to sleep. We need you to have a vision, Brianna. That is the only hope we have of identifying de la Roche in his new disguise."

Brianna's lips burned with the memory of Simon's kiss. She knew what was expected of her. "I'll try," she said even though she knew finding sleep now would be nearly impossible. Every nerve in her body leapt to life just thinking of Simon, his kiss, and the thrilling warmth as his body pressed against her own. That wasn't supposed to happen. Not with Simon.

"Do not try, Brianna. Just like battle, there is only one victor and one loser. Do not lose this battle for us all."

Chapter Nine

He should have left at sunrise. Simon frowned at the others seated at the long wooden table with him in Sir Alan's great hall. Four of the knight's men had agreed to go with them as they journeyed the rest of the way to the priory. Four men Simon knew well from his early days as a Knight Templar. They would each be an asset to their small band of warriors.

"Where are the women?" Kaden asked impatiently beside him.

"The extra hours will be time well-spent if Brianna had a dream," Simon replied, trying to conceal his own impatience. "I'm sure it won't be much longer."

Kaden frowned. "Are you certain Brianna's dreams are divinely sent?"

"Of course they are sent from God." Simon startled at Kaden's unexpected words. "Her dreams have saved many. Why would you believe otherwise?"

Kaden's gaze shifted to the tabletop. "I'm trying to be cautious where de la Roche is concerned."

"That is wise, Kaden. But we do not have to suspect Brianna of falsehoods."

Kaden lifted his gaze to Simon's once more. "She played us false once before."

"That was in the past." Simon stood and strode about the chamber, coming to a stop near the smaller hearth at the back of the room. He stared into the red-gold flames. They already had plenty to worry about with de la Roche on the loose. He didn't need his men questioning Brianna's dreams or her intentions. They needed to trust her as he did.

What they needed was action. Brianna's actions would demonstrate to the men that she was trustworthy. He glanced back at the door. It remained empty. He released a sigh of frustration. Why was he delaying their departure? He could march up into the tower room and demand Brianna and Abigail join them. Yet he did not. Was he ready to see her again after last night?

He should never have kissed her, even if it was out of spite. He was angry she'd beaten him. He'd been bested by others before. But never by a woman ... and not by a woman who stirred him in ways that she should not. She reminded him of all he'd set aside when he'd taken his Templar vows.

That had been many wars and a long time ago. Yet her one kiss had unleashed an urgent desire for more. The image of Brianna's face suddenly alight with desire formed in his mind. He'd forgotten what it felt like to have a woman in his arms. He clenched his fists.

The woman was desirable. She was definitely skilled in the art of battle. But she was not for him. He had to put the memories of last night out of his mind. Such a distraction could get him and every one of the men in his care killed if he wasn't focused and ready for whatever de la Roche had in store for them next.

Simon straightened and turned away from the fire just as Abigail and Brianna entered the room, Alan and Jessamine following in their wake. Just the sight of Brianna's wild, untamed hair brought warmth to his chest. He forced his response deep inside himself and hastened to greet the foursome.

Brianna stopped her progress and her gaze dropped to the rush-covered floor. Why would she not meet his eyes? Was it because of last night or—

"I did not dream," she said solemnly. "I still could not find sleep even after..." Her words faded away as she finally brought her gaze to his. He saw unbanked fires in her eyes and knew he was not the only one affected by their kiss last night. But it was a kiss that could never be repeated.

Jessamine placed her hand on Brianna's arm, breaking the moment. "You need to stop chasing the dreams. Relax and let the dreams find you instead."

Simon swallowed his disappointment. It would not help Brianna to see how desperate he was for her to dream. He realized the kind of pressure he'd placed on her to perform. "Dreams or not, we can delay no longer." Simon motioned for all the men to join them. "We'd best be on our way. We thank you for your hospitality, Lady Jessamine, Sir Alan, and for the additional men."

Sir Alan clapped Simon on the shoulder. "Until we meet again, Brother."

"Until we meet again." Simon clasped his friend's arm in the Templar salute.

"Your horses are saddled and ready in the bailey and loaded with food and skins to see you through the rest of your journey," Sir Alan said as he gathered his pregnant wife against his chest, facing their guests.

Simon nodded and headed from the hall with Brianna at his side. In the bailey, they mounted their horses and silently proceeded through the gate and over the drawbridge, heading for Crosswick Priory.

Perhaps at the monastery Brianna would dream and reveal the direction of their quest.

Brianna watched Simon as he led them through the open countryside. They were vulnerable here in the open lands. All of them had to be alert to the dangers. Even so, Brianna couldn't help but steal a glance at Simon. He kept his face at an angle to her so that she could not read his emotions, but his commanding presence and power were undeniable. This was a man who had led a hard, harsh life. And yet, there was a gentle side to him as well. He'd shown her that last night when he'd kissed her. Not at first. At first his kiss had been rough, punishing, but then his lips had gentled and he had allowed that part of himself to be seen.

It was that gentler Simon whom she'd missed over the past year. She craved his warmth instead of the remoteness he showed her now. "How far is the priory?" Brianna asked, knowing it mattered not how far away their destination was. They would travel hard until they reached it.

"If we move quickly, Crosswick Priory is but a day's journey to the southeast. We should make it shortly before nightfall."

As though not wanting to converse any longer, Simon took the lead, while Brianna and Abigail rode side by side, with Kaden and the other warriors at the rear in case de la Roche should find them.

Just as Simon had predicted, it was a hard day of riding, with them stopping only to rest the horses. Night was fully upon them when the walls of the priory came into view. The light of the full moon shone brightly against the stark gray stone. They dismounted and while she and Simon settled the horses, Abigail and Kaden untied the charred remains of the Templar they'd brought with them.

"He deserves a proper burial among his kin," Kaden said as he gripped the cloak-covered body in his arms. Together, they headed to the small alms door at the back of the priory.

Simon rapped on the door. Two knocks then a pause. Then three more knocks. After a brief moment, the door was flung open to reveal a tall man with a hood obscuring his face. The man took a step closer and drew back his hood, settling it around his shoulders. His lips turned up in a smile. "Stinger?" a gruff voice asked. "Is that you, Brother?"

"It is I," Simon replied. "As well as Viper and—"

"Mistress Brianna, or, as you are known to the Templars, Shadow Walker." The tall man she remembered as Reaper dropped his gaze to her, appraising her from head to foot, then bowed his head. When he straightened, curiosity blossomed in his dark eyes. "Good to see you in Templar company again."

"It's glad I am to be here," Brianna greeted the abbot with a smile. Once her identity as a female had been discovered among her Templar brothers, Brother Kenneth had been the first to forgive her. He had taken her under his wing, like a protective older brother.

Simon stepped forward. "Brother Kenneth, may I introduce Mistress Abigail MacInnes."

The man's smile increased. "A pleasure, milady."

A heartbeat later the abbot's smile slipped when his gaze settled on the body in Kaden's arms. "Who?" Brother Kenneth asked.

"We don't know, but we wanted to bring him back here where he belongs," Kaden said, moving past the abbot and into the hallway. "I will join you all in the refectory after I see our brother settled in the chapel."

The abbot nodded. He motioned for the others to follow him to the refectory where the evening meal was still being served, seating them at one of the long wooden tables. Many of the other monks in the chamber stared at Brianna. She kept her head high, refusing to let them see they had any sort of effect on her. It wasn't because she was a woman in a place where very few tread. It was because they remembered her and her deception.

Her thoughts were interrupted when moments later bowls of steaming mutton stew and a platter filled with chunks of dark bread and golden cheese were placed before them. Brother Kenneth said a prayer before he and the other men started eating. Sitting across from Simon at the table, Brianna could only stare into her wooden bowl as she allowed the familiarity of being back among the Templars to settle over her.

"Did Brother Bernard and the others make it back here?" Simon asked.

"Aye," the abbot replied. "Bernard lives. The healing baths helped with his deep wounds, but he remains weak."

"Praise the saints," Simon breathed.

The abbot's features darkened. "The other knights told us about de la Roche. He took the Grail and the sword of Charlemagne?"

"He's murdered so many of us. We must stop him." Kaden said, sliding onto the bench beside Simon.

"What about the rest of the treasure, is it safe?" the abbot asked.

"Simon managed to seal off the treasure before that monster could send his men back for more." Kaden sat forward, concern etched into his youthful face.

The abbot nodded and his gaze met Brianna's. "Is that why you brought Brianna back into this battle?"

"Aye," Simon replied. "Her visions must lead us to de la Roche before…" His words died off.

"I understand. But perhaps it is best to pray instead of demand Brianna's visions reveal the things we need," Brother Kenneth said with a lift of his brow.

His voice was gentle, understanding, and brought a lump of emotion to Brianna's throat. "I've been trying to dream, but sleep suddenly seems to elude me at every turn."

The abbot stood and slipped away from the bench on which he sat. "Perhaps I might be able to help." He moved to the far side of the refectory and returned with a mortar containing several dried herbs, and pestle. He ground the herbs together and reached for her untouched mug of ale. He sprinkled the powder from the mortar into the golden liquid. "My sleeping draught should aid you in finding sleep." He held the mug out to her.

"What are the herbs?" Brianna asked as she stared down into the dark liquid.

"Dried valerian, lavender, passion flower, chamomile flowers, and lettuce."

Hesitantly, Brianna brought the mug to her lips and took a sip of the bitter liquid. She shuddered.

"It tastes terrible, but it works, believe me." He laughed.

She nodded and downed the rest of the mug in a gulp. "Then let's hope it works soon." She set the mug on the table and drew a long, deep breath, fighting the bitter taste that lingered on her tongue.

"You should not be alone this night, however, in case the draught brings you nightmares instead of the dreams you seek."

"I'll happily sit with Brianna," Abigail said, setting her spoon alongside her bowl as she finished her portion of stew. "I've dealt with her nightmares—"

"Nay," Simon interrupted before he realized what he was saying. "Abigail you need your rest. We've all seen how weary this travel makes you. I can get by with much less sleep. I'll stay with her here in the refectory. We can build a pallet for her next to the fire. I will stand guard in a chair."

Abigail frowned. "That would not be proper."

"Nor is it necessary," Brianna interjected. How would she ever be able to sleep with Simon watching over her? Just the memory of him had kept her up last night, despite her exhaustion. His nearness would not serve her well at all.

Simon stood, facing the older woman. "We are in a monastery, Abigail. Her virtue is safe among my brothers and me." He turned to Brianna. "Are you frightened to be alone with me?"

Brianna narrowed her gaze as she straightened her spine. He knew her so well. He knew she could not argue the point now that he'd thrown out that challenge. She would not allow him to best her with a sword or with anything else. "If you must stand guard, then so be it."

The corner of his mouth quirked as though to smile, but he held himself in check as the others finished their supper then cleared from the room. Abigail was the last to leave.

"Are you certain you'll be all right ... alone with him?" she asked, her voice laced with concern.

"I'll be well." Brianna smiled and drew her sword from its scabbard. "As long as I have this nearby, there is no need to worry."

Abigail's eyes widened and shifted to where Simon now stood near the hearth. "Perhaps I was worried about the wrong person."

Brianna laughed and returned her weapon to its sheath. "I promise not to harm him. All will be well." She took Abigail's arm and led her to the doorway where Brother Kenneth waited. "And I shall see you in the morning."

Abigail's soft gray eyes searched her face for a moment before she sighed. "May you rest well, and dream well, my child."

Once Abigail was gone, Brianna turned back into the chamber. No longer needing to pretend for Abigail's sake, Brianna's smile faltered and fatigue consumed her as the abbot's draught took hold. She wobbled on her feet, suddenly unsteady, and reached out.

Simon was there, holding her arm. "Steady, my warrior."

Brianna shook her head, trying to clear her senses. Had Simon said what she'd thought he'd said? The tables in the room suddenly swam before her eyes. Nay, 'twas only her mind playing tricks on her. "I'm suddenly quite tired," she said.

"Your pallet awaits you." Simon guided her across the chamber toward the fire. There, he turned her toward him. His hands moved to her waist.

She gasped as the warmth of his touch permeated her spiraling sense. She closed her eyes and leaned slightly forward. In an instant, his warmth was gone, along with her scabbard and sword.

She snapped her eyes open and swayed where she stood. "How dare you remove my sword?"

He was close enough that she could make out a rather fuzzy frown on his face. "Your weapon will only be in the way once you lie down." He took her in his arms once more and guided her down as though she were a rag doll, down to a soft woolen blanket atop a pallet of sweet-smelling heather. "Besides, you will harm yourself if you try to draw that weapon in your current state."

She allowed him to position her atop the bedding. He was right, but she still did not like the fact he'd made the decision for her. "Place the weapon by my side."

"I'll be at your side. You've no need of a weapon."

She lifted to her elbows and tried to focus on Simon's face. "With you at my side, I'll need every weapon available." She frowned as he knelt down beside her, bringing his face closer.

"Even under the effects of a draught, you are as prickly as ever."

"I am not prickly." A frown came to her lips as she closed her eyes. She had to stop looking at him and remembering how it felt when those lips were pressed against her own. Her heart was beating too fast. A hot flush crept up her cheeks. Nausea pinched her stomach and a slow, thudding started at the back of her skull. She wrenched her eyes open and stared at Simon as she struggled to sit up.

He stood away from her, near the fire. "Simon, I don't feel—" The word feel became thick and stuck in her throat.

She swallowed. At least she tried to swallow. Her throat was dry and her tongue felt thick. She tried again. "I don't feel well." Her hands started to shake. She stared at them with rising panic. A spark in the fire popped, sounding like an explosion. She clamped her shaking hands over her ears. What was wrong with her?

Simon turned toward her. He took a step that seemed slow and exaggerated, then another. Brianna's heart thundered in her chest as she watched Simon become a shifting, dancing kaleidoscope of shadows and movements that blurred together. Panic swelled inside her, swamped her, pulled her into a black whirling eddy.

Far away a voice called. "Brianna…" The word echoed through the long, dark tunnel of her mind. She reached out with flaying arms and captured something solid. She clung to it.

"Steady now … my warrior."

She concentrated on the words, clinging to them like a lifeline as the world around her continued to spin out of control. Simon.

He took her in his arms. "Must be … the herbs." His voice sound far away and strained.

She clung to him as a huge beast charged forward, bearing a dark-skinned Moor. The thunder of hoofbeats filled the space around her. A hooked sword flashed high in the air. A scream lodged in her throat as she reached for her sword. Where was her sword? Simon had taken it away. The sword came down and the scream forced itself past her lips, echoing all around her, resounding in her ears like thunder.

"It's all right, Brianna. You're hallucinating." Simon's words filtered through her thick mind.

Aye. This wasn't real. She grasped the word as she would her weapon. "You're not real!" She challenged the Moor.

He vanished, leaving in his stead an empty chair.

She turned her face into Simon's chest. She didn't know how long she remained there with him, wrapped in his arms, her face buried in the soft linen of his shirt. But it seemed like forever.

Gradually, her headache eased and silence descended over the chamber. Her heartbeat slowed and her tongue moved with ease as she swallowed against the dryness that had settled in her throat. Her shaking eased.

"Brianna?"

She looked up into Simon's comforting gaze and felt an overwhelming sense of relief. Her body relaxed as true exhaustion took hold. "Hold me, Simon. Please, just hold me as I sleep."

He framed her face with his hands, tilting her gaze toward him. "I will be right here, Brianna."

He was so close. Close enough to kiss. She shifted forward, bringing her lips in contact with his. He kissed her quickly, then pulled back. "Kiss me, Simon, like you did last night."

His lips brushed hers, hesitating. "I promised to keep you safe."

"I am safe with you."

His arms closed around her and a groan escaped him. His lips caressed hers in a hundred kisses that robbed her of breath and sent shivers tingling through her.

She inhaled sharply as she pulled back to stare into his face. His features were taut with strain. She blinked up into his eyes and saw something she hadn't seen there in years. Hope.

Her tongue came out to moisten her lips. She tried to speak. She had to tell him she felt it, too — a surge of something light and wonderful and pure. Her breath came out in a rush as her body felt suddenly heavy and weak. "So ... tired," she whispered.

She heard a low sound as Simon laid her back on the pallet and shifted beside her, watching her face. "You should sleep and dream. The abbot's potion seems to have passed."

"Stay ... with ... me."

"I'm not going anywhere," he whispered near her ear.

Brianna tried to focus on Simon's face, but her vision blurred; her thoughts scattered as her eyes drifted closed.

Had it only been a dream? Had Simon's lips upon her own been something she'd only imagined, as much a fantasy as her hallucinations had been?

That was it. That had to be it. Why else would she give herself over so easily to the man who had taken everything she wanted away from her?

But he'd also promised to give it back.

In the next heartbeat, her mind went blank. Sleep claimed her and the mists of her dreams began to rise.

Chapter Ten

She knew she was dreaming because she recognized the mists shrouding the blue-black Cullen Hills and the dales covered in a purple blanket of sweet-smelling heather. She could hear the sound of softly falling water as it rippled down the hillsides, flowing into streams in a journey to the coast and the ocean beyond.

She could feel herself floating, moving through time and space as the sun reached its zenith only to be replaced by the moon. Darkness hovered. The lush green landscape vanished, replaced with shadows of silver streaked light that whipped her to yet another image.

A light appeared in the distance, a twisting yellowish orange that blossomed into red. Brianna shuddered as the color grew more intense. Her heartbeat thudded in her chest as the image of an abbey came into her vision, an abbey that seemed to grow up from the dark stone near the Scottish shore. Her vision sharpened until she could clearly see a square building with a bell tower. The image shifted. Shivers prickled her flesh as she felt the enemy approach.

So quickly the enemy came, without preliminaries beyond the single shout of challenge and the violence of his charge. A horse, followed by hundreds of others, burst into the scene with the sunset at their backs. The animals advanced, mouths agape, nostrils flaring, shod hooves striking sparks against the granite of the stony Scottish hillside where Simon and his men gathered near several small campfires.

"You'll die this day, you bloody savages!" a voice cried out as his silhouette drew closer. The sound of hoofbeats thundered all around punctuated by the bellow-bark of breath expelled through equine lungs.

The Templars scattered, drew their swords, and prepared to face the enemy. Pain rippled through Brianna's mind as she tried to focus her sight on Simon alone. Where had he gone in the melee? She had to find him amongst these men because she was certain the man who engaged him would be none other than de la Roche.

Then she saw the Frenchman as he came off his horse to engage on foot. He battered Simon's broadsword to cut away his defenses and make the fatal strike. But Simon held his own as the screech and clangor of steel rang in the air. The Templar anticipated each move his enemy made. He forced the man back as he held the ground around them and the advantage. As the Frenchman hesitated, she caught an impression of a man above medium height with a square, hard jaw. His eyes were arresting. They were fierce, light-colored, the eyes of an old man in a young man's face. He wore a mail and armor that did nothing to disguise the monster beneath.

De la Roche.

"The Scottish Templars have a strong will to survive," he taunted as he thrust his sword. "But I am stronger."

Simon blocked, then blocked again as the Frenchman suddenly found a source of strength deep within himself. A flash of steel, a sparkle of a gemstone, and Brianna knew it was the power of Joyeuse that had turned this battle around. The sword of Charlemagne would triumph as it had for generations.

Simon used all his power and struck the sword. He stumbled as the mystical steel deflected his blow. He went down to one knee, tried to bring up his weapon even as he wavered. In the next heartbeat, de la Roche struck Simon's weapon away with a sharp blow. The sword spun to the ground.

Simon was unweaponed, awaiting death at this enemy's hand. He knelt there on one knee, empty hands outstretched, chest heaving, but there was no fear in his face. Instead of death, the will to live blossomed in his eyes.

The Frenchman laughed and swung his sword.

Brianna's eyes filled with moisture as she gasped. Pain spiraled through her and she quickly drew the mists of numbness around herself. She knew she was dreaming; knew she couldn't watch Simon die in her dreams or in reality. She had to run from the image of Simon's beheading.

She pictured herself running, panting, until the image in her mind shifted, but instead of seeing anything she smelled the salty stench of rock exposed to the sea. She searched the darkness, praying her mind would show her where she now was.

A tall, slender shadow detached itself from the darkness. Gradually, her eyes became adjusted to the gloom and she discerned the walls of a cave. They were the most unusual she had ever seen. Black basalt columns stretched from the base of the cave to the ceiling overhead. And several fractured columns made stepping stones from the water to where she stood. She could hear the rush of water in a rhythmic cadence and knew they were near the ocean cliffs.

Moonlight streamed through the cave's arched entrance now and she could see a man she didn't recognize more clearly. He wore a long white tunic with a bloodred cross on the front, but the garment was tattered and stained with both dirt and blood.

"Nay, I will not tell you any more," he cried as the sound of a lash rippled through the salty air and connected with flesh and bone.

Brianna froze. She watched with her heart pounding in her chest as a man emerged from the shadows behind the Templar. De la Roche. "You will tell me everything I need to know and more," he said in a silken tone as he came around the man to peer at her.

Nay! He could not see her. This was a dream, a vision; she was protected from those she saw, from the dangers. She swallowed and remained still. The eyes staring at her were eerily translucent. It was as though he could see through to her soul.

Brianna couldn't help herself. She closed her eyes, her lips forming the silent words of prayer. "Sweet Jesus, deliver us from evil." Blood thrummed in her temples. The darkness pressed in around her, taking her breath.

A sound shattered her senses. Her eyes flew open even though she was still in the grips of the dream; she was no longer staring into the face of evil, but at the inside of an inn. She stood in the center of the common room. Over the hearth hung a sign. She couldn't read the words, but could clearly see the outline of a Saracen's head carved into the wood. The scent of roasted mutton and onions pervaded her senses. She took a step back as a serving maid dashed in front of her and her hip collided with the solid wood of a table behind her.

Brianna spun around and her breath stilled in her lungs. Sitting at the table before her was de la Roche once more. This time he wore a monk's brown robes. Before him on the table was a tin chalice.

As she stared at the cup, it changed from gold to silver and back again. A sense of peace came over her for a moment until she suddenly noticed the Grail was filled to the brim with a dark red liquid. The liquid smelled sickeningly of copper.

Blood. He'd filled the Holy Grail with blood.

She gasped.

"I drink this night to the victory of those I've triumphed over." He reached for the Grail and took a drink. Then he raised the cup to her. "You'll join me in my celebration?"

Brianna screamed.

Drenched in sweat and shaking uncontrollably, Brianna jerked out of sleep into brutal wakefulness. Her body trembled. Her heart pounded. Her lungs labored, and her flesh was stippled with gooseflesh.

He hadn't seen her. He couldn't have.

Breath rasped in her throat as she expelled air, expelled the dream. A heartbeat later, warm hands tightened around her.

Simon.

She reached out and touched his jaw, his throat, where de la Roche had severed... His flesh was warm, his pulse leapt beneath her touch. "You're alive," she whispered.

"You're safe," Simon countered.

By the pink light that filtered through the shudders, she knew dawn blossomed on the other side. Yet she felt as though she'd hardly slept. Brianna shivered.

A heartbeat later, Simon moved away then returned to settle a cloak around her shoulders. "This should help to warm you." She was starting to warm already where his body pressed against hers.

"I take it you had a vision?"

Brianna pulled back and looked at the curiosity in his dark eyes. "Not one but three visions. I must think on them and try to make sense of them, but..." Her gaze moved to his neck. Her fingers followed her gaze. She stroked the side of his neck where the sword had struck. He drew a startled breath at her touch.

"Tell me."

She swallowed against the sudden tightness in her throat. They were both warriors. They both lived by their swords, and knew what could happen during any conflict. It was the reality of their lives. "You died at de la Roche's hand."

"If that is what must come to pass." His voice sounded distant, yet his gaze grew more intense. "What else did you see?"

"The first vision was of the battle, the next took me to a cave, then to an inn room where I saw de la Roche along with the Holy Grail." She shuddered at the memory.

"What is it? What aren't you saying?"

"The Grail was filled with blood. I suspect it was Templar blood." Her gaze caught his. "Simon, why is he doing this? What sort of reason could there be?"

Simon smiled bitterly. "What always drives men like him to such extremes … power. The French have wanted the Templar treasure for many years to help repair their country's financial woes. The Templars, who escaped France's persecution years ago, brought the treasure to Scotland to keep it safe."

"But the treasure is not safe any longer thanks to de la Roche, is it?"

Simon shook his head. "Our troubles are worse than they've ever been."

"I saw the Grail. Can we not find the inn and take it back?"

"We could if we knew where to look."

Brianna smiled. "I think I know where. In the course of my dream I saw an image over the inn's hearth. That of a Saracen's head. Is there not an inn on the Isle of Mull with that very same name?"

Simon nodded. "Then that is where our journey begins. Should we wake the others?"

"Aye. We cannot risk further delay." He rose lithely to his feet.

Brianna stood and remained there, studying him a moment longer. Power and strength. That was Simon. De la Roche could not, would not take this man from the world while she was near. Brianna's fingers reached for her sword only to realize the weapon was not there. It lay alongside the pallet where Simon had placed it last night. She scooped up her weapon and secured it at her waist once more.

"Brianna?" Simon asked. The light of dawn behind him streaked his hair with gold, and lit his normally dark eyes with a brilliant luminosity. His expression looked softer this morning, not so stark or severe as when he'd come to the inn to find her. "You mentioned a cave in one of your visions."

"Aye. I saw a Templar, bound and hidden in a cave, the likes of which I've never seen before."

"Could you see who this Templar was? That man must be who de la Roche is impersonating within the Order."

She shook her head. "I only had brief glimpses of his face as de la Roche tortured him for information about the Templars."

Simon walked to the hearth to stare into the flames. "That's how he did it. He's torturing the information he needs out of one of us."

She should be thinking of the poor Templar who was caught in de la Roche's net. Instead, her thoughts filled with Simon as he stood in the odd mixture of light and shadow from the flickering flames. She'd always been fascinated by Simon's strength and his dark good looks. Even while she'd been disguised as a Templar she'd found herself staring at him. He was exerting that same fascination now.

She not only wanted to keep looking at him, she wanted to reach out and caress the harsh planes of his cheek. But that could never be. She had to stay alert to the dangers around them if she were to keep Simon from becoming the victim she'd seen in her dreams.

She tore her gaze away from him. "I won't let you die."

"Brianna." Simon's tone was serious as he stepped away from the hearth and to her once more, his dark eyes probing as they usually did. "My death does not frighten me."

She lifted her chin with defiance. "I lost my brothers because you kept me from acting upon my dreams once before. I refuse to allow that to happen again." She strode forward until she stood sword to sword with him. "You can order me away, chain me to a tree, whatever you like, but I'll find a way free. This time I'm not going anywhere, Simon Lockhart. Until you die or we both die or we defeat de la Roche, we are in this together until the very end."

Before he could reply, she stepped back and said, "Wake the others. If we are to leave soon, I'll need to inform them about my dreams."

Chapter Eleven

The sun had barely crept over the eastern horizon as the occupants of Crosswick Abbey gathered in the refectory to listen to Brianna's recounting of her dreams. The men no longer looked at Brianna with suspicion as they had upon their arrival yesterday. Instead, they appeared now to accept that she was one of them, despite her gender. They leaned toward her, waiting attentively.

Before Brianna could begin, Brother Kenneth bustled into the chamber and placed a mug of clear liquid before her. "My most sincere apologies, milady." Lines of worry bracketed the abbot's dark eyes. "I don't know what went wrong. I know my herbs well. Yet someone managed to switch the dried lettuce for belladonna. 'Tis a miracle I did not kill you!" The abbot grasped the cross that hung about his neck and clamped it between his fingers until his knuckles turned white. "I have burned the tainted herbs so no one else might be affected. It was so dark, and I only wanted to help you dream…"

Brianna stood and moved to the abbot's side. She reached for his fingers, gently unfurling them until she clasped them with her own smaller hands. "I do not blame you, Abbott. It was a mistake. I am fine, thanks to Simon. And, I did manage to sleep and then dream thanks to your potion." She smiled and some of the worry left the abbot's face.

"Please accept this healing tonic I offer you now. It will purify your blood and make certain none of the belladonna remains inside you." He offered her a sheepish smile. "It's quite safe, I promise. I drank some of it myself just to be certain."

"That was very kind of you." Brianna's gaze shifted from the abbot to the cup. She reached for the wooden mug and brought it to her lips, drinking deeply. When the contents were gone, she handed the mug back to the abbot. "Very reviving. Now I feel certain we can get on to my dreams with clear thinking."

Brother Kenneth nodded. "Aye, tell us all about what you saw," he said waving Brianna back to her seat, then settling down on the bench beside her.

"The man I saw in my dreams was dressed as you all are — in monk's robes. He is of average height with dark hair that is cut close to his head, and he has eerie light blue eyes. He still walks with a bit of a limp as well."

"Tell us of your dreams," Brother Kenneth prompted.

Brianna nodded. "With the help of your draught, I had three distinct dreams, revealing three locations. Simon has been trying to identify them on the map for some time. Perhaps the rest of you might help us there."

Simon looked up from the parchment scroll containing the monastery's only map. The map had been fashioned by Brother Bernard after one of his journeys from the abbey to the western isles. The outlines of the coast, the isles, rivers, and harbors were reflected in bold ink, but the parchment also bore the image of Christ rising over the top of the map with angels on either side that were surrounded by stars and celestial bodies.

It was more a work of art than a directional tool, but perhaps if Brianna could describe the inn or the cave in detail, one of the monks might recall a specific location.

"In one of the dreams I saw a cave. The cave was unusual." Brianna frowned as she struggled to put words to the image in her memory. "This might sound odd, but the landscape looked as though rocks in the form of pillars exploded upward from the depths of the sea, to remain that way for all eternity."

Brother Kenneth's eyes widened. "I know this place. It's off the coastline of the Isle of Mull. You speak of Fingal's Cave on the small isle of Staffa." The excitement in the abbot's dark eyes faded. "That isle is difficult to reach, even by boat. The Atlantic swells may very well crush you against the rocks before you can find purchase to land."

"If de la Roche can accomplish the task, so can we," Simon said as he returned his gaze to the map. Only small circles represented the places where the Inner Hebrides were located. He rolled up the parchment and set it aside. "If this isle is as distinctive as you say, Brianna, we shall have no trouble finding it."

"I agree with Simon," Brianna said. "We must try, no matter the risk."

For once he and Brianna were united in their goal. The thought would have made him smile had the situation not been so serious. "How many men can you spare, Brother Kenneth?"

The abbot sighed. "We are so few now, thanks to de la Roche's attacks." His gaze moved about the table to each of the knights present there. "Brothers Thomas, Jacob, and Alaric are skilled warriors all."

Simon nodded to each man. "We also welcome Benton, Kendall, Iain, and Cameron, Sir Alan's men. With Brianna, Kaden, and myself, that makes ten."

"Don't forget about me," Abigail interrupted. "I might not be a warrior, but I can take care of myself."

Brother Kenneth frowned. "I shall never get used to women in battle."

Simon sent Abigail an apologetic smile. "Like it or not, abbot, it seems to be something you and I cannot object to." He turned his gaze to the abbot once more. "That makes eleven of us."

The abbot frowned. "Eleven against a hundred Frenchmen. It will be Teba all over again."

"Nay." Simon and Brianna said in unison.

Simon closed his eyes as the image of the battlefield filled his mind. His brothers' bodies lay everywhere. So many dead, so many maimed and wounded. Simon opened his eyes, burying the memory deep inside himself. "That will never come to pass again." He crossed himself. "We will find more men to fight with us. By all that is holy, I will never allow that to happen again."

"We will never allow that." Brianna came to stand beside him.

Simon nodded. "Let us be on our way. We have wasted too much time here already." He turned to Kaden. "Take Benton and Kendall and saddle the horses. The rest of us will gather the supplies we need."

The men scattered to do Simon's bidding. Brianna remained where she stood. He could not look at her. He couldn't allow her to see the moment of doubt that had flashed through him. God's teeth! For the first time since Teba, he had allowed the slightest bit of fear to sink in.

Nay. They would win this battle. They would rid Scotland of the Scottish Templars' greatest enemy. Then life could return to normal once more. They would journey this day to a place he had not been in a very long time. Perhaps, if he were fortunate, he would find the help he needed.

Simon shook his head, clearing his thoughts and his emotions before he turned to face Brianna. "We should join the others."

Brianna remained still and brought a hand up to his chest as though wanting to console him when she knew from their shared experience that nothing could. His skin warmed beneath her tender touch. For a heartbeat he let the reality slip. There was something unreal about the moment that he longed to hold onto. Something peaceful. Familiar. It awakened a foreign part of himself, a part that desperately craved moments like this in the past, but had never had them, moments when someone cared for him.

"You do not always have to be so strong," she said, her voice a silken caress.

"I am a warrior."

She let out a long breath. "As you reminded me not too long ago, even warriors have weaknesses."

He knew what his weakness was becoming. He put his hand over hers and stared into her eyes, wrapping the peacefulness of the moment around himself. He would need all the serenity he could gather in the days ahead if her dream of his death was what lay ahead for him. "I'll do whatever it takes to win this battle against de la Roche."

"Simon—"

He tore his gaze from hers and twisted toward the door. "We will speak of this no more." He strode from the chamber, leaving her to follow in his wake.

Outside, his men had the horses saddled and waiting. The beasts moved restlessly, their breath pluming in the cold morning air. They prepared to ride out, then waited as Brother Kenneth approached the group.

"Godspeed," the abbot said.

"And may He be with you, Abbot, and those who remain here," Simon said with a respectful tilt of his head.

The abbot blessed them, then sent them on their way. Simon took the lead, while Brianna and Abigail rode side by side, with the men fanned out in twos behind them.

Silence hovered over them as they rode hard throughout the morning, barely stopping until the sun was at its peak. They came to a stop near a rambling stream, allowing the horses to rest.

Simon sat down beneath a tree and let his eyes slide shut. His eyelids had barely settled before he felt someone standing before him. "What is it?"

"When do we eat?" Alaric asked.

Simon cracked one eye open. "Whenever you'd like to."

Food. Simon's stomach growled on cue. They hadn't eaten anything but oats this morning in their haste to leave.

Something hearty would be wonderful. "Are you offering to cook?" Simon opened both eyes to see Alaric and Benton stood before him, frowning.

"Nay, we thought maybe, since she's a girl, that Brianna could cook something for us."

Brianna sat on the ground near the horses. She held her sword in one hand and a sharpening stone in the other. Sharp slicing sounds filled the afternoon air as she ran the stone along the blade. "You want me to cook?"

"We'll start a fire while you cook us something to eat," Benton said hopefully. "We're starving."

Brianna stood and sheathed her sword. "You're not hungry enough to eat my cooking."

"Oh, yes we are," Alaric said, his eyes widened and his tongue darted out to lick his lips. "Anything would be fine. Truly."

Brianna looked to Simon. "Do you expect me to cook just because I'm a female?"

He shrugged, not wanting to get in between Brianna and his men. They had a long way to go on this journey together. They needed to come to terms on their own. "Perhaps just this once, you and Abigail could…"

"Abigail needs to rest." Her gaze strayed to where Abigail lay on a soft patch of grass, her eyes closed, asleep. "You'll have to deal with me." She grunted and turned toward the horses that stood quietly, their heads bowed low to the ground as they munched on grass. "Don't say that I didn't warn you."

Alaric and Benton set a fire and soon orange-yellow flames snapped and hissed in the afternoon light. Brianna had gathered water from a nearby stream to fill the iron pot they carried on the pack horse. He watched her slice chunks of salted pork with her sword and tossed them into the broth.

Plumes of mouth-watering steam rose into the air, and his stomach rumbled loudly. Perhaps this was a good idea.

Brianna's cooking might help to make amends to the men who still resented her participating in Templar business.

Simon smiled with satisfaction. One way to a man's heart was definitely through his stomach. He watched as she tossed in a few handfuls of oats, then a handful of onion chunks before she stirred the contents together.

Sometime later she announced, "Food's ready." The men hurried to the fire's side with their wooden bowls extended. Brianna cast a surreptitious glance at each man as she spooned the chunky liquid into each bowl. Simon watched as Benton eagerly dug into his bowl with his spoon, bringing the steaming stew to his lips. His eyes widened as he chewed. "What is this?" he asked Brianna.

"Your meal."

His face puckered as he continued to chew and chew.

Simon took a bite from his bowl of the partially burnt, brown mush. He swallowed thickly then cast a meaningful glance at his men. "Perhaps we should believe her the next time she tells us she can't cook."

Brianna shrugged and lifted her own spoon to her mouth. "I did warn you."

The men finished their meal in silence and it didn't take long for them to repack the horses and get underway once more. Dusk was fully upon them when they finally reached the village of Lee. It was an ordinary village of thatched-roofed cottages in the shadow of Lee Castle.

Brianna brought her horse alongside Simon's. "Abigail is not used to riding this hard. May we please stop in this village for tonight?"

"Nay," Simon said. His gaze shifted in the fading light to the castle nestled in the Clyde Valley below. A place he had not seen in ten long years. "We will stay at the castle."

A frown came to Brianna's lips. "Do you know the owner of this castle as well? Is it another Templar brother?"

He brought his horse to a stop and turned to face her. "This is my home."

"Your home?"

He nodded as he waved to the guards that dotted the towers. A shout went out moments before the sound of the portcullis raising filled the air. "I'll return for good someday when the Templars no longer need me."

"I've never seen a castle this large. There are ten towers!" Brianna's eyes widened. "My father's Rosslyn Castle looks tiny by comparison."

He kicked his horse into a gallop. "Come, there's only a short while until nightfall is fully upon us."

It wasn't long before the eleven of them rode over the drawbridge and cleared the open gates. They came to a stop in the bailey. Simon slipped from his horse only a moment before a familiar voice sounded behind him.

"Welcome home, milord!"

Simon smiled as a bent man rushed up to him. His family's steward was older than he remembered, but Simon was certain time and many battles had changed him as well. "Gillis, I should have known you would be the first to greet me."

The old man came to a stop and started bowing as he lost his balance.

Simon caught him by the arm and brought him back to standing. "None of that, Gillis. You and I need no formalities between us."

The old man's gray eyes filled with tears as he stared at Simon. His gaze lit on the small scar at his temple, and Simon subconsciously reached up to cover it with his fingers. "'Tis nothing to worry about, Gillis. I was one of the lucky ones to come away with only this."

Gillis brought his bony hands up to bat the moisture away from his cheeks. "Does yer presence here mean ye've come back to stay?" Hope brought a crack to his voice.

"My duty continues." Simon sobered at the reminder. "Allow me to introduce my guests." He gestured to the men and women behind him.

Gillis's watery eyes filled with hope. "Ye've brought a wife home." He shifted his gaze between Simon and Brianna. "She's a beaut, if I do say so meself!"

"Mistress Brianna is not my wife."

The old man's eyes narrowed. "Yer betrothed?"

"I'm a monk. Or have you forgotten?" Simon clapped the old man on the shoulder. "None of that talk now. If my sisters catch wind of such talk…" He let his words die off before he asked the question that had burned in his chest since the moment the castle came into view. "How are my mother and the girls?"

"Lady Lockhart is off visiting her sister in Edinburgh. And of the girls, only Bella and Caitlin remain. All the others are settled with their husbands."

"As it should be," he said through the travel dust that suddenly clogged his throat. A pang of remorse shot through him. He should have been there to see his sisters safely settled, but the Templars and the Brotherhood had needed him. "May I see them?" Would they even recognize their brother after so long?

A look of sadness brought shadows to Gillis's eyes.

Simon frowned. "What is it, Gillis?"

"'Tis Bella. She's been ill fer a while now."

A chill rippled down Simon's spine. He had been gone too long. "What's wrong with her? Has anyone sent for Lady Lockhart?"

"We sent a message tae her yesterday, but it's two days of hard riding tae reach her. As for Bella's condition, I dinna know, but she's very bad."

Abigail came forward. "Take me to her. I am no great healer, but I have learned a thing or two in my years. Perhaps I can help."

"I might be able to help as well," Brianna said.

Simon nodded to the two women. To the others he said, "I will send someone down to see you inside. Until I return, make yourselves comfortable." A cold gust of wind followed Simon, Brianna, Abigail, and Gillis into the castle as Simon retraced the steps he had taken as a young man through the great hall, up the stairs, and down a long corridor to where his sisters' rooms had always been. Gillis led them into an overly warm chamber at the end of the hall and pointed to a slight form in the center of a large bed.

Simon's chest tightened as the flickering candles revealed his sister's dark hair as it framed the gray pallor of her face. She looked as near to death as any warrior he'd seen on the battlefield. Bella was young, not long past her fourteenth year. She'd been only four when he'd left. She'd changed so much during that time. Now, instead of a child, a young woman lay before him. Her body was slim and lithe and should have been brimming with vitality. The vise of terror gripped his chest. "What's wrong with her?"

"She's been violently ill and unable to keep anything down since yesterday," said a young maid who stood by the large, curtained bed.

Abigail moved across the chamber and knelt beside the bed. Brianna moved to the window and opened the shutters to let fresh air into the room.

Bella's eyes were closed and she appeared asleep.

"Bring me some hot water and some dried mint if you have any," Abigail said.

"We do, mistress." The maid bobbed a curtsey and hurried from the chamber.

Abigail placed a hand on the girl's forehead. "She has a fever and chills at the same time. It's almost as if..."

"If what?" Simon asked firmly, preparing for his worst fears to come true.

Abigail's soft gray gaze met his. "I've seen this combination before when the afflicted had been poisoned."

"Saints above," Brianna whispered as she came to the bedside near Abigail.

"Brother? Is that you?" a soft voice beckoned from behind him.

Simon turned to see Caitlin framed in the doorway. During his absence his sister had blossomed into a refined beauty. Gone were her girlish curls, replaced by a sophisticated swirl of black locks highlighting her country-fresh features and sparkling eyes. "Caitlin."

The sixteen-year-old flew into his arms and he held her tight. "My dearest sister, good to see you again," he said past the tightness in his throat. "We have much to discuss, but for now I must ask you how long has Bella been ill?"

"Only two days." She released her tight hold on him. "I'm scared, Simon. She became so ill so fast. She cannot die."

A familiar guilt knotted his gut, but he pushed it aside. "She will not die." He moved to the bedside with Caitlin and sat at the edge of the bed. He lifted Bella's cold hand in his and did the only thing he knew to do in this situation. He prayed. He begged God to hear his prayers, hoping, willing that Simon had not been forgotten. After all he'd suffered, he only asked this one thing…

He was still praying when Bella groaned, and her eyelids fluttered open. She gazed around. Confusion knit her pretty brow when her gaze lit on his face. "Simon?"

The vise around his chest eased. He squeezed her hand. "Shh, don't try to talk now."

She tried to sit upright, then released a groan and collapsed back against the bed. A moment later her eyes opened and she cast him a weak smile. "We knew you were coming."

Simon frowned. "How did you know when I did not even know myself until just yesterday?"

Caitlin sat on the bed beside him. "The man you sent ahead of you told us."

"I sent no messengers."

Caitlin's frown matched his. "But the man… He said you would be here and left us a basket of apples that you'd sent as a greeting. We were waiting until you arrived to eat them."

What little blood remained in Bella's cheeks vanished. "I ate one. They were too beautiful not to, and I was so very hungry."

Swallowing the sudden dread that clogged his throat, Simon asked, "The basket of apples, where are they?"

Caitlin stood. "They are in the kitchen belowstairs. I'll go get them from cook."

"Make certain to ask if anyone else has eaten from the basket."

She nodded and hurried from the chamber.

The maid returned with the hot water and herbs. Abigail busied herself with steeping the mint in the water. When she was satisfied with the color and scent, she spooned small amounts into Bella's mouth.

Brianna came around the bed to stand by Simon's side. In a low tone she said, "You suspect de la Roche, don't you?"

"I should have foreseen this event. The man will strike at me any way he can." Simon swallowed to ease the aching tightness in his throat.

"You could not have known he would go after your sisters."

He remained silent a moment. "De la Roche has tried to kill anyone and everyone associated with the Templars. That I forgot about the family I left behind is no one's fault but my own."

"You are with them now, Simon. That's what matters." Brianna turned her gaze to Bella. "She'll be well soon."

He frowned. "How can you say that? Did you have a vision?"

She shook her head. "Nay, I just ... feel it."

Simon's gaze returned to his sister's face. The faintest shade of pink had returned to Bella's cheeks. He stared eagerly at his sister, hoping for some other sign of her improved health.

Nothing.

"We both know how fast life can fade away." Simon clenched his fists at his sides, fighting his sudden feeling of helplessness. It was his custom to shape events in the way he wished them to go, not to surrender and do nothing at all.

This situation would not last. His sister would heal and he would once again be in control. De la Roche might have fooled him again, but it would be the last time.

Simon Lockhart was never a fool twice.

Chapter Twelve

Brianna crept through the silent hallways of the castle until she came to the great hall. Simon was still abovestairs with Bella and Abigail, and for that she was grateful. She wanted to speak to Kaden, alone.

She found the knight at one of the long tables with the others knights. "Kaden, might I speak with you?" she asked as she approached.

Kaden stood and excused himself from the other knights. "Has Bella taken a turn for the worse?" he asked, his expression solemn.

Brianna shook her head. "I need to speak with you about something else entirely." She paused as she signaled for him to follow her to the wall near the tapestry bearing four knights returning from a victorious battle. Brianna frowned at the familiarity of the scene, the knights, until she recognized her own dark red hair escaping from her helm. Her breath caught at the sight of Simon, Alan, William, and herself as they left the battle of Teba behind. Simon carried in his hands the heart of Robert the Bruce.

"One of Simon's retainers made the tapestry for him after he and William returned to Scotland. She was quite grateful her lord had not been taken from her in a land so far away," Kaden said, breaking into her thoughts.

"That's not how it happened," she said, her tone grim.

"I know." Kaden studied her face. "What do you wish to speak with me about, because I doubt it is the tapestries?"

"Simon."

"Why?" A note of surprise colored his voice.

"I need your promise to protect him, no matter what."

Kaden frowned. "From what?"

She dropped her gaze from his face. "I dreamt about his death at de la Roche's sword. There was a battle with the ten of us and hundreds of them. Simon was disarmed and the Frenchman cut off his head." She swallowed against the sudden tightness that entered her throat. "I cannot allow that to happen. Promise me that you will stay with him, protect him."

Kaden expression softened. "It was only a dream, Brianna."

She shook her head. "My dreams are different. They have a way of becoming reality."

Kaden reached out and placed his hand on her arm. "I promise you, with my life, that I will protect Simon from that man, no matter what."

She drew a sharp breath as emotion once again tightened her chest. "Thank you, Kaden, for your friendship and your loyalty." She placed her fingers on his hand. "I am relieved, sharing my dream, and the burden of protecting Simon with you." She offered the knight a weak smile. "To a different future than the one I saw."

"To a different future," he echoed.

Brianna was grateful when after her meeting with Kaden, Gillis led her to a candle-lit chamber down the hallway from Bella's sickroom. Exhaustion had suddenly made her weak and she needed sleep.

"Shall I send someone with food, milady?" Gillis asked from the doorway.

Brianna was too tired to correct his assumption she was a lady. "Nay," she replied with a wistful look at the large, canopied bed in the center of the chamber. "I require only sleep."

With a bow of his head he shut the door, leaving her to silence. She walked to the bed made from a foreign dark wood. It was so dark it appeared almost black. She reached out and ran her fingers over the carved edges. The workmanship was exquisite, featuring the trailing leaves of ivy branching out from a heart, with a crown rising above it. She'd never seen anything like it. From the canopy, a rich green cloth hung that was embroidered with darker green ivy, flowers, and the same red heart. She sat on the edge of the bed and searched the chamber. Hanging from a hook on the front of an overly large armoire was her finest green gown and a fresh chemise. Someone had unpacked her travel sack while they'd been attending Bella.

Brianna looked around the chamber at the fire that had been lit in the hearth. A bucket of water, a sheet of linen and shavings of soap waited nearby. She leaned back against the thick bedding, staring up into the canopy overhead. The soft scents of rosemary and cloves tickled her senses. The scents of a well cared for home.

But who cared for this castle? Simon's steward and his staff, or was there someone else? Brianna suddenly realized how little she knew about Simon on a personal level. She knew his likes and dislikes, she knew he dropped his left shoulder as he tired during a battle, and she knew how stubborn he could be at times, but outside of the things she'd learned about him in the Templars, she knew nothing at all. And suddenly, that fact bothered her more than it should.

She lay there on the bed, staring into nothingness, too exhausted to move, but her mind whirled with thoughts of Simon. When he'd kissed her she could sense both his hesitation and his passion. She understood that about him at least. He was a monk. She was a warrior. Passion had no place in either of their lives, and yet...

Brianna forced herself off the bed. She had best keep her mind from such thoughts. With renewed strength, she unfastened her belt and sword and laid them on the bed. She withdrew her dagger from her boot and placed it beneath the pillow, then smoothed the fabric back into place. She had no doubts she would be safe in Lee Castle, but old habits died hard. She would sleep better knowing her dagger was within reach.

Loosening the laces of her dirty gown, she pushed it over her shoulders, allowing it to slide down her body to the floor. Her chemise followed. She undid her boots, removed her stockings, then left them at the foot of the bed before she folded her discarded clothing and placed them over the back of a chair by the hearth.

When she was done, she knelt before the bucket of water. Cupping her hands she drew out lukewarm water to rinse her face. Freed from the travel dirt that had coated her face, she longed to free the rest of her body from the same. She dipped the cloth in the water and washed. The soap carried the scent of heather, and the fragrance, combined with the sensation of being clean, brought a sigh from her lips.

Reaching up, she loosened the ribbon holding her hair back and let if fall freely around her shoulders. She ducked her hair into the bucket before lathering it with the remainders of soap, then rinsed the long strands. She squeezed the water from her hair back into the bucket, and tossed her hair back to fall down her back, feeling the remnants of water slide down her flesh. She reached for the soft sheet of linen beside the bucket just as the door creaked open and the soft rap of boot heels sounded on the floorboards.

She clutched the linen against herself with a gasp.

Simon froze in the doorway. He was wearing only breeches that clung to his muscular thighs. Droplets of water rolled down his chest from the damp tendrils of hair brushing his neck. "What are you doing in here?" he demanded.

"Gillis brought me here."

One hand rested on the door latch, the other hung at his side. His posture was not rigid, in fact he seemed almost relaxed, yet he radiated a tension that reached out and touched her with its barely leashed power. "To my chamber?"

"Your chamber? I'm certain it was a mistake."

"It was no mistake," he said haltingly.

She moistened her lips nervously with her tongue, trying to think of what to say that would rid the atmosphere between them of that disquieting emotional charge.

"Don't do that!"

Her gaze flew to his face. "I beg your pardon?"

He drew a harsh breath, his hand clenched the door latch and his other hand balled into a fist. "Never mind." He watched her with an intentness that made her heart pound and her mouth grow dry. He came into the room and stopped beside the chair. His fingers gripped the wooden backing so tightly his knuckles turned white.

She pulled the linen sheet more tightly around herself. "I did not mean to intrude. I'll get dressed and leave."

"Stay here if you wish."

"But this is your room."

"I shall find somewhere else to sleep this night."

She didn't know what to say as he headed for the doorway. She hurried to the armoire and with lightning speed slipped her chemise over her head. She let the linen fall to the floor. "Simon?"

He paused and turned to look at her. His gaze moved from her feet upward. Raw hunger burned in his eyes.

A shiver tingled through her as she met his gaze. What did he want from her? He was in need of something…She tried to tear her gaze from his and failed. Instead she took a step toward him but paused as his quick intake of breath filled the suddenly silent room.

His pulse beat wildly at his temple. "If you know what is good for you, you'll stay where you are, Brianna." His words were soft, yet conveyed the tone he used when ordering her about.

"When have I ever been good at taking orders, especially from you?"

He closed his eyes. "I am tired, pushed to my limits, and slightly drunk."

She took two more steps closer and could smell the honeyed sweetness of ale, sandalwood, and musk. The seductive mix lured her closer until she stood less than an arm's length away. "If you wish to sleep I could get you some—"

Simon snapped his eyes open as the scent of heather enveloped his sense. He knew he should take a step back, hasten for the door, put aside the memory of Brianna standing by the armoire in the sheerness of her chemise. The fabric did nothing to conceal her from him. Instead, the fabric clung to her full breasts, delineating her nipples.

He was hardening, almost to the point of pain, just looking at the seductive image she portrayed. He clenched his jaw, fighting the overwhelming desire, and lost as his hand drifted up to slip beneath her wet hair. His fingers coiled in the silken curls at her nape and he gently urged her forward. Brianna lifted her head and he couldn't stop himself, he captured her lips. She softened in his arms and she filled his senses completely. Her skin was like velvet as he brushed his hand over her back. Her wet hair, silky and smooth and cool to his touch, did nothing to cool his need to touch her, to taste her, and hold her near.

His emotions warred inside him as he tasted her sweet innocence, wrapped himself in her touch. It had been far too long since he'd last been with a woman. Far too long since he'd been unsettled by anything.

And Brianna unsettled him in every way. She'd bewitched him from the moment they'd first met. He'd been assailed by unfamiliar emotions and feelings, half of which he could neither name nor identify. She filled him with more than simple desire or lust. She did something to him he couldn't comprehend. Part of him wanted to hold her, to kiss her, and the other part wanted to run as far and as fast away from her as he could.

He broke the kiss and stared down into her face. Her gentle green eyes searched his, but it was the concern there that touched him deep in his heart. Simon reached out to lay his hand against the flush of her cheek. The softness of her skin never failed to amaze or warm him. No matter how much he might deny it, she was a part of him in a way no one had ever been before. No matter their conflicts, Brianna was a deep and integral part of who he was.

Then let her go. But he could not find the strength. He couldn't turn away from what had started between them years ago. She watched him so intently that it made his throat tight. There was so much emotion in those green eyes of hers: the same desire that coursed through him reflected there.

As though reading his thoughts, she lifted her face to his and laid a soft kiss upon his lips. He drew her to him and with a groan raided her mouth. He tasted her thoroughly, leaving no doubt that he wanted more.

Against his lips she said, "Is this wise?"

"Nay." The word ripped from him as he smoothed her chemise over her shoulder.

"The two of us have never been wise, only passionate." Her fingers fumbled for the laces on his breeches.

Heady with desire, he pushed her chemise over her arms, past her waist until it pooled at her feet and she stood naked before him. He brushed his fingers gently over her breasts, then came back to engulf the tender fullness to find her nipples peaked and straining with a need that etched itself plainly on her skin. When he brushed his thumb across her nipple, she gasped her pleasure.

Simon bent his head and his mouth hovered over one breast while his hand cupped the other. Brianna bit back a cry as she arched her back, pressing herself more fully into his sensual caress. His teeth bit gently on the nipple he'd brought to full arousal.

She groaned and her hands coiled in his hair, urging him closer. His limbs were trembling and he knew they could not hold back the storm that surged through them both. Scooping her into his arms, he carried her to the bed and set her gently in the center. He pulled the bed curtains closed around them, creating a private chamber that was only theirs before he followed her down.

In the golden light seeping through the bedcurtains he looked down at the woman in his bed. Her red hair spilled across the pillow with the lure of a seductress. His gaze moved over her body, her rounded curves, her smooth flesh free of the battle scars that marred his own back and sides. He prayed he could keep her that way despite the coming conflicts. She need not suffer the way other warriors did.

As though sensing his hesitation, Brianna inched her fingers up his back, holding him to her. "Don't think, Simon. For once in your life, just feel what's inside you and give yourself over to it."

Her words were the salve he needed and he knew he had to be a part of her. Need threatened to overwhelm him with its fiery intensity as he tasted the honeyed sweetness of her mouth once more. No other woman had ever held this kind of power over him. Ever.

Her lips moved along his jawline, down his neck, across his collarbone. Her lips left fire against his flesh as they trailed along his chest and down across his abdomen. "I want to be one with you."

He gazed into her eyes and could see no fear, no regret, only desire. Fire seared through him, and the muscles of his stomach clenched. He could have her. She wanted him. This was right, the two of them together. Here and now, as they both lived for the moment.

Her hands were trembling, Brianna realized.

She had known this moment would come since she'd dumped hot stew in Simon lap when he'd erupted back into her life. That's how it had always been between them. They were like fire and ice. But there was no ice in his eyes right now. Nay, his expression had become blindly sensual and his eyes filled with silken fire, and she wanted to be devoured by the heat.

His hands moved over her breasts, her abdomen, and lower to tease the soft curls at the apex of her womanhood. Indescribable sensations shot through her. His fingers slid lower, deeper, until two fingers gently entered her core and began a rhythmic stroking. She cried out as the hot throbbing inside her built almost to the point of pain, yet it wasn't. Only an odd emptiness remained as he pulled his fingers away to shift over her. He cupped her buttocks and lifted her gently. "Wrap your legs around me." His tone was guttural.

"Why—"

He plunged inside.

She gave a low cry and clutched him with her thighs and hands as his big palms held her, sealed her to him. She felt stretched at first, then the tension eased, to be replaced with only a desperate hunger.

He slid out and back into her with slow, deliberate thrusts that grew harder, deeper, as flesh met flesh. She tried to choke back the unbidden cries of pleasure each measured thrust produced, but it was impossible. Instead of fighting Simon as she always did, she joined him. Arched up again and again, meeting each plunge of his hips with an eagerness that took her breath away.

A groan lifted him up on his arms. She gazed at Simon, as raw and unfettered as he had ever been in her presence before. She knew in that moment she had never seen anything so beautiful as the gleaming, sculpted perfection of his body. Her gaze lowered to where her hands grasped his hips, how she coaxed him closer and closer with each bold thrust.

The sight of him, the feel of him, even the musky scent of their joining sent a flood of pleasure through her. She cried out as she neared the edge of some incredible precipice. She twined her legs more tightly around him, fusing their bodies together as she rushed headlong over the brink of erupting passion.

His cry of release joined hers, mixed, and melded in the hazy golden darkness as he gave to her again and again until the two of them were shaking with the force of the ecstasy that rippled through each nerve, vessel, and fiber of their being. He shifted beside her, and they lay there panting as incredible spasms continued to wrack her body. The intense need from moments before was gone, replaced by a warm and soothing sense of peace. Her arms tightened around his shoulders.

His breath was as labored as her own. He lifted his head and looked down at her. A lock of dark hair fell over his forehead and she reached up to smooth it back. "That wasn't supposed to happen."

"But it did." And she liked it very much. She would not mind sparring with Simon at all if every argument could end this way. Yet she knew that was impossible. As soon as they left the peacefulness of Lee Castle, they would be in the presence of others, always, as they searched for the meaning behind her vivid dreams.

"This was a stolen moment, wasn't it?" she asked as her breathing settled into a more normal cadence.

He nodded and bent to kiss her lips once more before he turned away and grasped the bedlinens, tucking them around her. "We must follow where your visions lead."

"About that." She lifted up on her elbow to look at him. "I've been thinking."

He chuckled. "You've been thinking during all this? Perhaps I need to see if I can distract you more? I suddenly have the urge to see if I cannot wipe all thought from that active brain of yours." He leaned down and ran his tongue over her nipple.

Heat stung her cheeks as her body responded immediately. She felt herself readying, warming once more at the very thought of him hard and hot within her. She inched back and clamped her hands into fists so she wouldn't be tempted to touch him. "Let me say this first."

He smiled. "You like the idea then?" He reached for her and pulled her against him.

"Simon!"

"Talk quickly." He turned onto his back and lifted her on top of him, sliding inside her. His hips moved upward and she gasped at the fullness and the pleasure.

His face was flushed, his eyes glazing with an expression of primitive pleasure.

She couldn't talk, she couldn't think as he thrust deep, quickening the rhythm. This joining was incredible, basic, elemental. In only moments, wave after wave of pleasure washed over her.

An instant later she could feel Simon spasm again and again within her, shuddering helplessly as he poured his seed into her body.

She collapsed on top of him. His hips still moved yearningly, as if he couldn't stop even though he had reached his satisfaction again. A moment later he lay still, breathing heavily, his hot flesh nestled against her own.

Sweet heavens, the passion between them was nothing she'd ever imagined and better than her innocent hopes. They loved as hard as they fought. The thought brought a smile to her lips.

"You're thinking again," he said, his voice still uneven. His breathing gradually steadied and slowed.

She pulled back to look at him. "We need to go after de la Roche and the Grail first. The inn I saw in my vision is farther away than the isle, but if we attack the Frenchman there, we can accomplish many things. The Grail might be used to release your sister from the grips of this poison, and we might put an end to de la Roche's terror before he can torture that poor Templar any more and..." She couldn't say the rest. The image of Simon losing his head was still too fresh in her mind.

She rolled off of him and sat up. "I will never let that happen to you. I lost my brothers because of one of my visions. I refuse to allow that to happen again." Emotion clogged her throat.

Simon sat up, facing her. "Brianna, your dreams did not bring about their deaths in any way."

She shook her head. "I saw what would be. I could have stopped it."

His features lost their softness. "You were not to blame. I ordered you away."

"I should have ignored you," she whispered.

"I did not give you the chance. I wasn't about to let you die alongside your brothers."

She nodded. "It took me a long time to forgive you for that. But this time the situation is different. It's one mad man against us, not thousands."

He reached out to gather into his arms until she melted against his bare chest. "The reason I involved you and your dreams in this madness is so that we are forewarned. Because of you, we know how and from whom de la Roche received his information about the Templars. We know where we might be able to intercept the man, and if it comes to a battle to the death, I will be prepared."

She pulled back to look into his face. "We will be prepared. I will be beside you. You promised me." He wouldn't go back on his word when the moment arrived, would he?

"That I did." His quiet voice had a steely undercurrent. "I don't want to endanger—"

"Not this time." Her heart skipped a beat and her muscles tensed as anger swept through her. She scooted off the bed. "I'm not going anywhere, Simon Lockhart. You swear by all that's holy that you will uphold your end of our bargain."

Simon came off the bed and took an impulsive step toward her. "Brianna—"

"Nay." She took a hasty step back. "I want no other words from you but your promise never to send me away again."

"There is nothing I can do or say to change your mind?"

"Nothing."

His lips set in a grim line. "Then you have my oath that we battle together until the very end."

"I feel my place is here, with Bella. Can you forgive me for that?" Abigail asked as she clasped Brianna's hand. In the courtyard around them, the men readied the horses for their departure from Lee Castle.

"There is no need to apologize. You are doing the right thing. Bella needs you."

"Then why do I feel so guilty about abandoning you?" Abigail said haltingly, her gaze on Briana's face.

Brianna squeezed Abigail's hand and released it. "With her mother gone, you are all she has."

"But our adventure?" Abigail's gaze wandered to the horses.

In all the years she'd known Abigail, first as her nurse, then as her friend, she never would have guessed that the woman yearned anything other than the lot this life had given her. Brianna smiled. "This is just one of many that lay ahead for us all. There will be many others."

A faint smile touched Abigail's lips. "You promise?"

"I promise. When this adventure is through, Simon and I will take you anywhere you wish."

Abigail's eyes misted and a single tear ran down her cheek. "I will hold you to that promise, and now I demand something of you."

"Anything."

"Do not fall beneath that evil man's sword."

"Not if I can help it."

A second tear joined the first on Abigail's cheek. "Promise me."

Brianna knew she could not guarantee her return. She'd seen too many battles, watched too many men fall to make that hollow promise. But she knew what Abigail needed to hear. "I promise to do everything in my power to return here and to spend the rest of our days living out one adventure after another."

Abigail drew Brianna into a quick embrace before stepping away. When she pulled back, her eyes were filled with both sadness and hope. "Then I await your return."

Chapter Thirteen

The warrior woman would have to die.

Pierre de la Roche set down the tin cup that was the Grail on the table before him. With his hands free, he lifted from beneath his brown monk's robe the small pouch he wore extended from a long length of string about his neck. He opened the silken pouch and withdrew the thick lock of fiery red hair he kept there.

He smoothed the strands of hair through his fingers. A smug sense of satisfaction rode through him. Lockhart would howl with pain at the sight of her dismembered body. Hearing that sound alone would be worth the extra time it would take to find the girl and abduct her. If he could snatch her right out from under Lockhart's nose, all the better it would be. The man's sense of duty and protection would be his ultimate downfall.

De la Roche smiled at the thought of how frantic Lockhart would be when he couldn't find the girl. He would search the countryside, taking him away from his true purpose of finding him and protecting what was left of the Brotherhood of the Scottish Templars.

"Monsieur, we must leave now. One of my scouts has sighted the Templar and his men crossing the Firth of Lorne. They will be here before nightfall," Philippe Batar said as he seated himself at the small wooden table in the corner of the Saracen Head Inn's common room.

"Do not call me monsieur. I shall be known as Excellency." De la Roche glanced coldly at his captain.

"As you wish, Excellency." The man swallowed roughly. "I must still advise you to leave here as quickly as possible."

"How can I leave when I am the trap?"

Philippe frowned. "I do not understand. You've been avoiding the Templars for weeks while you healed. Does this mean you are better now?"

"I am healed." And he was, thanks to the Grail. His leg was still not straight and he walked with a definite limp, but his muscles were stronger than they'd ever been. He was ready to take on Lockhart and to exact his revenge upon the man through the girl's youthful flesh.

Simon and Brianna and the men they'd gathered on their journey here would come to him like sheep to the slaughter. And this time, he'd be ready and waiting.

Philippe's brow knitted with doubt. "You still seem weak at times, Excellency."

The doubt in his captain's face suddenly filled de la Roche with fury. "I am not weak!" Did the man think he wanted to lie there helpless in this hell-hole of an inn for days on end? He muttered an obscenity and saw terror replace the doubt in the captain's eyes. De la Roche smiled. That was better. Philippe had to realize who was in control here.

If de la Roche had learned anything over the past few weeks, it was the intoxicating feeling of being in control of another human being. He took great pleasure in subjugating Philippe and all the members of his army. That was why they remained loyal to him. They feared what would happen if they were not.

That fear would see him triumph over these Scotsmen once and for all. He'd have everything he ever desired: he'd rid the earth of the vileness that was the Scottish Templars, and he'd have their Templar treasure to fund a new life and a new empire for himself — Scotland, England, then France. It was only the beginning of what was to be.

De la Roche tucked the lock of hair back into his pouch and slipped it inside his robe once more. "Bring me my sword."

Philippe's eyes widened nervously. "Your sword?"

"Joyeuse. Hurry!"

He moved quickly across the chamber, grabbed the sword that lay with the rest of their gear, and brought it to de la Roche. "What do you intend to do?"

He gripped the hilt of the sword in his hands and felt the power of the ages rush through him. The Grail had healed him. Her hair had given him some sort of strange connection to the Sinclair woman. The sword, Joyeuse, would see that the coming battle turned his way. How could he fail with all those things in his favor?

After two long days of travel, Simon, Brianna, Kaden, and the other warriors reached the eastern shores of the Isle of Mull. The hazy light of dusk settled over the land.

"We ride for that hill." Simon motioned off into the distance as he led Brianna's horse to her. "We'll set up camp there for the night." Simon handed her the reins of her horse, but he did not move on to help as the others pulled their horses from the wooden barge that had ferried them across the Firth of Lorne.

Instead, he leaned forward until his eyes were even with hers as though to kiss her. Would he kiss her here in front of the others? She tried to muster up a sense of indignation, but found she could not. All she could think about was being wrapped in his strong arms, and how his lips parted as he moved even closer. She cared only how his mouth would feel against her own. She held her breath and waited.

She could feel his breath caress her cheek, could smell the soft scent of soap as it lured her into his sensual spell. "Thank you," he whispered.

"Excuse me?" She went still. The sensuality of his tone and the proximity of his lips warred with his unexpected words.

"Thank you for allowing Abigail to stay behind to nurse my sister." His eyes darkened.

She clutched the leather reins in her hand, forcing herself to keep from reaching for him. If she shifted forward she would bring their lips into contact. "You're welcome." She must not touch him, or she'd be lost.

Clearing her throat, she stepped back. "The others appear to be waiting for us."

Disappointment flickered in his expression. "Then we should be on our way." His hands grasped her waist and he lifted her onto her horse, despite the fact he knew she could mount the beast on her own. He stood there, looking up at her. "Later, you will not escape so easily."

She swallowed. She didn't want to escape him any longer. What had flared between them two nights ago was now a burning need. The muscles of her stomach knotted at the thought. How quickly could they ride to the hill and set up camp?

A smile came to his lips as if had understood her thoughts. He mounted, and with a flick of his reins, set off toward the hill. Brianna followed, leaving the others to wonder what madness had possessed the two of them.

A thrill of delight moved through Brianna as she and Simon disappeared over the hill away from the others. She followed Simon as he sped toward a small copse of trees. They entered the shadowed area below a large acacia tree. He dismounted and strode over to her.

"Simon, I can…"

"Allow me, please?"

He reached up, his big hands encircling her waist, and lifted her off her horse.

Her breath caught at the raw desire she read in his eyes. His expression held the same intense hunger she'd seen there when last they'd made love. The hands at her waist kneaded her flesh through the soft fabric of her gown. The heat of his body reached out to her, claiming her.

"Simon." The word was a whisper and a promise as he backed her up against the giant tree.

"I need you." His voice was hoarse as he smoothed her gown and her chemise from her shoulders to reveal her breasts. She gasped as his mouth enveloped her left nipple. He sucked avidly, possessively, while his hand cupped her other breast and began to squeeze rhythmically. The same liquid burning she'd experienced before tingled between her thighs.

She closed her eyes and leaned her head back against the tree. "I need you, too," she gasped, giving herself over to the urgency of the moment. It was so unexpected, and so delightfully decadent. "What about the others?"

"We must be quick." His hand left her breast to release himself from his breeches. His arousal sprang free. His large hands slid down her thighs, and a raging fire neither she nor Simon were able to deny sparked until they both knew there was no going back.

He lifted her skirts and chemise to her waist and set his hand to her firm flesh. She arched into him and sighed. So did he. For one long moment they savored the feel of each other's flesh — one against the other — until desire became a scorching heat that threatened to possess them both.

"Follow my lead," he said, his voice raw.

The sound of his need fueled her own. She arched back against the rough bark, releasing the pungent scent of earth and leaves. She drew in the heady scent, letting it wrap her in the primitive sensual plane they'd entered.

Brianna released a soft cry as Simon's palms cupped her buttocks, raising her, adjusting her body against his manhood.

"Put your legs around my waist."

She obediently encircled him and released another cry as need flared deep inside. He entered her with one urgent stroke. Her head sank back against the rough bark of the tree as she felt every ridge, every inch of the length of him.

He cried out and stopped, flexing inside her. His face held a pleasure and a relief that was nearly unbearable. "Brianna," he whispered, bringing his face to rest against her cheek. "I have never wanted anything more than I want you at this moment."

She was trembling with her own unspent desire. "Then give us both what we want," she breathed into the graying light.

The words were the catalyst he needed, or the permission he sought. A heartbeat later he was plunging, driving inside her with a force that rocked through her. Her shoulders were pushed back against the tree as she reveled in the sensation of him — so rigid and heavy, so incontestably male, moving within her. She met him and matched him, wound her legs more tightly around him, drawing him deeper still.

She relinquished control of the battle between them and simply urged him on. She wanted only to touch the pinnacle they had reached before — that incredible, flaming peak they would soar over together, until finally they were one.

Brianna cried out and arched up to him as wave after wave of pleasure radiated through her as his own release followed hers.

She drew a shuddering breath and leaned back against the tree once more. She raised her hand to his hair and tenderly pushed a wayward lock behind one ear. A quiet tender moment passed between them as her heartrate slowed and his breathing eased.

He stroked her back with one hand as he held her to him with the other, even now that their passion was spent, refusing to let her escape his possession. After another long moment, he slowly stepped back and lifted her off of him. "I did not mean to be so rough," he said haltingly.

"You weren't." She smiled up at him. "I think we have unleashed a new sort of challenge between us. One that is infinitely more pleasurable than swordplay."

"Agreed." His lips quirked a moment before he sobered. "I want you to know I have no desire to remain a monk any longer. It's not just because of you, or this," he said, stroking

141

the exposed flesh of her shoulder and arm. "I miss the worldly ways of man, and I want so many more moments like this in your arms."

"You like our new war games?" she asked with a smile.

"'Tis a game you can win over me every time." He matched her grin. "I hate to bring this moment to an end, but we must get back to our true purpose for coming here." He adjusted his breeches before straightening her gown, setting them both back to rights.

Heat filled her cheeks. She hoped when the others caught up to them they would assume it was merely the excitement of the moment that colored her features so. "To the horses, then?"

"Aye. Let's go see what lies over that hill."

At the top of the hill Simon brought his horse to a stop.

Brianna skidded to a halt beside him. "What is it, Simon?" she asked, peering out at the darkening gloom.

"Just below us." Simon couldn't say if he was pleased or disappointed at the sight of lamps hanging outside an inn that bordered the edge of a forest.

"Do you think it is that inn? The Saracen Head from my vision?"

"There is only one way to find out."

They waited at the crest of the hill for the others to catch up before proceeding into the small town. The abbot had warned him about the thieves and outlaws that haunted the forested areas of Mull. The inn yard was bare of grass and the dirt was rutted and well-worn. Many travelers had been here before them, most likely because of the barge that shuttled travelers from the mainland to the isle.

The ten of them and their horses filled the inn yard leading to the stone and thatched structure. Simon dismounted and stretched, then stepped up to the board that hung from iron hooks above the inn's door. The name of the inn was almost wiped away by years of wind and rain, but the image of a dark-skinned man with a white turban on his head left no doubt about where they were.

"It is the Saracen Head," Brianna said from behind him, her voice taut with disbelief.

He turned to see her staring at the sign, her eyes narrow with concern. "It appears so."

She met his gaze. "That was too easy."

"Perhaps someone is looking over us, and guiding our way."

"Or perhaps it is a trap."

He drew his sword. "Are you prepared?"

The whisper of steel against leather was the only answer he needed.

"Kaden." Simon motioned with his hand that the warrior take two men and go around the back while the others entered through the front.

Kaden nodded and silently disappeared through the darkness around the side of the stone building.

Someone was watching them. Simon's warrior instincts flared as he searched the thick underbrush at the edge of the inn yard. Nothing. No sign of anyone. Perhaps the abbot's words were playing tricks on his mind. Regardless, he tightened his grip on his sword.

A soft rustle.

God in heaven, it was not his imagination. Someone was there. "Brianna, whatever happens go into that inn and get the Grail."

"And leave you?"

"You must get the Grail. It must be here, just as your vision revealed."

"Simon, I—"

"Promise me, Brianna."

He would have things no other way. "I promise." Brianna held her sword at the ready. She could be inside the inn and back out again in a heartbeat. Simon would not be alone for long.

She turned to face the woods, Jacob, Alaric, Benton, Kendall, and Iain turned also, as they too sensed the presence of something in the woods.

Shouts suddenly sounded all around them. A dozen men broke through the trees to surround them, their drawn swords glistened malevolently in the lamplight cast from the inn. A dark-haired man stepped forward and regarded them with a satisfied smile. "You were a fool to come here," the man said as he swaggered toward them. His words carried a heavily accented lilt. His tunic was stained with what might have been ale, as that scent wafted around him.

"We are but travelers, searching for a place to rest," Simon said.

The man's smile broadened as he leered at Brianna. "I know who you are, Brother Simon. My master de la Roche described you and the woman in perfect detail."

A chill ran through Simon. "Is de la Roche here?"

A bark of laughter filled the silence. "The man is everywhere. There is no stopping him. You are fortunate you deal with me and not him and his sword of death."

Joyeuse.

Both the Holy Grail and the sword of Charlemagne were here. They had to take advantage of the moment. Without the aid of the treasures, de la Roche would be easier to overcome. If they could only get the sword and the Grail away from him.

"Brianna, Iain, stay together and make your way into the inn while the rest of us keep these men busy. We need those artifacts."

Brianna and Iain nodded and positioned themselves at the back of the group of warriors, closest to the inn's doorway.

The dark-haired man faced Simon, his features illuminated by the flickering light of the lanterns. Forcing his mind to clear, Simon held his sword at the ready and ducked into position. If it was a battle they wanted... Out of the corner of his eye, he could see the other men with their swords and targes, as every instinct, every muscle, waited for Simon to signal the strike.

In the next instant, Simon's throat vibrated with the roar of a battle cry as savage and old as his Highland ancestry itself. The air echoed with the sound of the cath-ghairm as the warriors flung themselves into battle.

The moment the fighting started, Brianna motioned for Iain to follow her through the doorway of the inn. Inside, golden light cast from rushlights hung on the walls at the front and the back of the chamber. The room was devoid of patrons except for one man who sat at a table near the hearth.

"So nice of you to join me," said the man dressed in the brown robes of a monk. But he was no monk. He was the monster de la Roche she'd seen in her dreams.

Brianna's heart skipped a beat as she clutched her sword and took a step toward him.

"You'll not be needing that weapon in here. Put it down and join me for a drink." He picked up a tin vessel from the table and took a long drink.

"Thanks, but I'll pass." While she moved slowly forward, Iain slipped through the pale gold light at the edges of the chamber. Movement at the back of the room caught her eye, revealing Kaden and two of the warriors as they entered through the back. "We have you surrounded. We can do this peacefully if you will hand over the Grail and the sword."

De la Roche stretched out his legs before him and gave a long, mournful sigh. "I've no intention of surrendering anything. In fact, before this night is through, it will be you who will take orders from me." Heavy lids veiled his eyes.

Brianna edged forward until she stood within striking distance from the man. One swing of her sword and this would be all over. Yet she'd never killed anyone without provocation before. "I have no wish to kill you."

De la Roche's lids lifted to reveal icy blue eyes glinting sharply in the rushlights. "And I have every intention of killing you." He sprang from his chair and came up with a sword in hand. With a quick and unexpected upswing, he knocked the weapon from her hand and pulled her back against his chest.

Suddenly, the room erupted in chaos. De la Roche's men lunged from the shadows, weapons drawn to engage the others. The clash of steel upon steel broke the stillness of the chamber.

Brianna braced herself for battle and drove her foot backwards into de la Roche's knee. At the same time she brought her fist down on his wrist and sent Joyeuse flying.

The Frenchman shrieked in pain and released her.

She grasped the Grail from the table and tossed it to Kaden who had just felled his opponent. "Take this to safety."

He caught the Grail and tucked it into his belt. "I will not leave you." The knight remained where he stood, staring at her across the fighting.

"Kaden, it's our duty to see the Grail safe. Once you do, come back and help us."

After a moment's hesitation, he turned and fled.

The rigid tension in Brianna's body eased. The Grail was safe. Before she could turn around, she found herself slammed against the table. Pain radiated through her chest as her breath left her lungs. The room danced before her eyes.

"You fight like a woman," de la Roche snarled from behind her. He jerked her hands behind her with one hand and pressed a dagger to her throat with the other.

"Perhaps, but a woman who's bested you this eve."

He jerked her from the table. Her flesh stung as the dagger pierced her flesh. "You'll pay for taking the Grail from me."

Brianna tensed, preparing for the worst. She should have been more careful. Too late for should haves now…

His pitted cheeks creased as he smiled down at her. "I won't make this easy for you. I want you to suffer before the end comes. Lockhart will wallow in misery at your death." The dagger vanished as he slammed her head against the table once more.

Her dreams had been wrong about one thing. De la Roche did want to kill Simon, but not before he had squeezed as much torment as he could out of the people closest to Simon. He would torture Simon into that ultimate sacrifice of his own life. Brianna shook her head, trying to clear it of the ringing pain of the Frenchman's blow. "Simon will never capitulate to you over me."

He bent down and brushed his cheek against hers. "You underestimate your appeal, my sweetling." His voice was seductively gentle. "He'll do anything I ask to see you safe." His smile faded and agony rocked her as he slammed her head against the table once more.

"Then you don't know Simon at all," she whispered hoarsely.

Pain exploded in her head again and she hurtled down into welcome darkness.

Simon cleared his mind of all else except survival as he brought down his sword, slashing, blocking, slashing again as he battled foe after foe.

Only a few moments had passed since the first clash of swords and already the ground was red underfoot, the air choked with dust. Simon dashed a hand across his brow to keep the sweat from rolling into his eyes. He vaulted over two bodies, then ducked as a blade hacked down in an arc across his shoulders. He regained his balance and came up with his sword slashing, cleanly severing the attacker's arm from his body.

He whirled and lunged out of the way as the dark-haired man charged. Simon turned to face him as he regained his ground. Brianna should be inside by now with Iain, Kaden, Cameron, and Kendall. Simon had to defeat the dark-haired man, then join her.

Simon's sword flashed in the lantern light as he brought his blade up to block a powerful thrust by the experienced warrior. At the blow, the sharp ringing of steel filled the air and it took Simon a moment to recover his momentum to strike again. His sword arm was aching, his body bruised, cut, but despite the pain he pressed the attack. His sword clashed against the Frenchman's once, twice. The man's eyes filled with wild rage as he gasped for breath, watching the last of his men fall to the ground beneath the Templar onslaught.

Simon clutched his sword. He balanced on the balls of his feet, prepared to lunge forward when a door slammed open behind him.

"It's over, Lockhart." The voice seethed with hatred.

Simon stole a quick glance at the door and froze. A man in a brown monk's robe staggered forward with Brianna tossed over his shoulder, motionless.

It was the man Brianna had described, the icy-eyed devil responsible for murdering so many of his brothers. "Let her go, de la Roche."

"Give me the Grail!"

"I don't have it."

De la Roche shook his head. "You have something I want. I have something you want."

"Let her go!" Simon's voice trembled with the same rage that coursed through his body. He took a step toward her; he wasn't being reasonable; he was only feeling. He would die before he let that bastard hurt Brianna.

A sword crashed down against his blade, sending it spinning out of his hands at the same time he was jerked backward. His arms were seized. He broke the hold, fighting his way to her.

Brianna.

He was jerked off his feet. Rage, acid hot, tore through him. He kicked out with his feet, contacting something. A heartbeat later, pain exploded at the side of his head.

Simon tried to shout her name. The words filled his mind, but could not form on his lips. He writhed against the hands that grasped him with bone-crushing force.

A flash of pain came again and again, until there was nothing more.

Chapter Fourteen

"Wake up," a voice from somewhere beyond her called.

Brianna slowly opened her eyes. Images whirled, blurred around her.

Pain throbbed at her temple. "Wake up!"

Her cheek stung as she turned her gaze toward the source of her pain. De la Roche stared down at her.

"You're awake. It's about time. I was tiring of waiting. We must get started."

"Started?" Brianna struggled to raise her head before she realized she was strapped at the wrists, ankles, knees, waist, and shoulders to a hard surface. She glanced wildly around her, but could see only the wooden table to which she was bound and the man standing beside her.

The man was of medium height with a barrel chest and torso that seemed too thick in proportion to his long legs. One of those legs was straight, the other appeared bent below the knee, and his weight was shifted onto his right side as if he'd been injured. Brianna raised her gaze to his ice-blue eyes glittering in the light of the torch he held. "What do you intend to do to me?"

The man smiled, but there was no joy in his gaze, only anger and malevolence. "I intend to use you in a way that will bring me far more pleasure than I've had in a while." De la Roche smoothed back the hair from her temple. "Poor little warrior. You are frightened of my intentions, aren't you?"

He yearned for her fear. She could see it in his eyes. "Where am I?"

"Where you are is of no concern. All that will matter is what Lockhart does. We will see very soon if he thinks you are worth fighting for." His fingertips drifted over her cheek. His touch was light until he reached the bruises he'd caused. Pain followed in the wake of his touch.

Brianna pretended nonchalance. "What would you have me say? I cannot predict what the man will do."

A twisted smile came to his lips. "I think you know him very well, sweetling. Very well, indeed."

"He is a warrior. He will do only what is logical. Coming for me is not worth the risk of his men." She said the words boldly, but inside she trembled at the thought of being at the madman's mercy.

"I'll get what I want from Lockhart, and from you. It's only a matter of time." His fingers reached her hairline and he reversed the direction, retracing the painful caress.

Brianna forced herself not to show her fear. She had to be strong.

De la Roche's gaze narrowed on her face. "I see you are a brave little warrior. Perhaps we should put your bravery to the test?" He frowned. "What could I do to you that would be a fitting punishment for stealing the Grail from me?" His tone was suddenly as hard as the pressure he exerted on her bruised and battered skin.

Her throat tightened as she looked into his light-colored eyes. "The Grail was not yours."

"It was mine because I wanted it." He reached for her hand, squeezed it brutally.

She bit back a cry as pain radiated up her arm.

"I will have the Grail again. I will have all the treasure soon. When Lockhart comes after you, my men will be waiting."

He leaned over her. As he did, a pouch slipped from inside his robe to brush her face.

Brianna turned to look and saw a wisp of her own hair protruding from the opening. Her eyes widened at the sight. He had come to her that night and taken a lock of her hair. With her teeth, she reached out and bit down hard, seizing the pouch. She twisted her head, jerked hard, and snapped the silken string from de la Roche's neck.

He gasped at her sudden movement. "What are you about?" De la Roche raised his hand and brought it down against her cheek.

Biting back the pain that exploded in her head, Brianna used the force of the blow and her own breath to send the pouch flying into the darkened corner of the tent.

"Damn you!" de la Roche growled. He gripped her cheeks with his fingers, drawing her face back to his furious gaze. "I don't need your hair any longer. I have you. And soon I'll have everything I ever wanted — your death, the Templar treasure, and Lockhart."

"He won't come for me." She bit out the words.

"He'll come, but not before I have a little sport at your expense." He released her face and turned to reach for something behind him. When he turned back to her, the glint of a knife appeared in the torchlight. "So how shall I punish you that will leave a lasting impression?" His thin lips pulled down in a pout.

Brianna braced herself for whatever pain he would inflict on her next. "You could let me go and spare yourself the sting of my blade."

His bark of laughter filled the silence. "Brave to the last, just like a warrior." He shook his head. "I was going to punish you as a thief by taking your hands. But that will never do." He pursed his lips as if in thought. "Perhaps I will treat you the same way I shall treat Lockhart. I will not take your hands, but I'll destroy your fingers instead. You'll never be able to hold a sword again once I'm through with you." He laughed again. "A warrior who cannot fight. What a fitting end it will be."

He brought the knife down with violent force.
Brianna screamed.

Simon came awake. He became chillingly aware of the darkness surrounding him, the odor of the damp earth, the smell of horses. The inn yard. He was still there. Why? Why had de la Roche left him behind?

Why should I slice you down when I can make you suffer? De la Roche's words came back to him.

"Damn you, de la Roche," Simon cried out into the night as pain ripped through him. How could he have been so stupid as to send Brianna into the inn alone?

But he hadn't sent her alone. Simon gained his feet. He searched the ground for his sword. He found it several paces from him. Gripping it tightly, he glanced around the moonlit inn yard. He could make out the bodies of his fallen men. Were any of them still alive?

He found Jacob, Alaric, Benton, and Thomas lying strewn about the yard. All still lived, though Benton and Thomas had been seriously wounded, one in the chest, the other on the leg.

Sick to his stomach that he hadn't been able to stop de la Roche, Simon staggered inside the inn to check his men there. His gaze fell on Kaden at the doorway. His face was covered in blood from a beating, and it was obvious from his injuries that the warrior had fought valiantly to try to save Brianna.

Simon bent down, fully expecting his friend to be dead.

A finger to the side of his neck revealed a soft beat. "Kaden," he said softly, realizing then that the knight was still breathing, although very shallowly.

Kaden's eyes blinked open.

"Rest easy. I'll find a healer if it's the last thing I do."

Kaden lifted his hand to Simon's shoulder. "On the side of the inn. Under a large rock. The Grail. Brianna saved it." Kaden's gaze filled with agony. "I tried to stop him."

"It's not your fault, Kaden. It's mine."

Kaden struggled to sit up, but collapsed back against the ground, his breathing ragged. "Nay, de la Roche is to blame."

Simon nodded as words failed him. Pain and anger clashed inside him. He stood. "I'll go get the Grail. Perhaps it will help."

Grabbing a torch from the wrought iron holder just inside the doorway of the inn, Simon moved to the side of the inn. There he found a large boulder and set his sword and the torch down as he bent to roll the rock over. Buried beneath the rock was a shroud of linen that appeared to be part of Kaden's shirt. Simon opened the linen to expose the shimmering metal of the Grail. He sheathed his sword and gripped the torch and the holy vessel and hurried inside the inn to fetch a skin of water.

He dropped to his knees at Kaden's side. He poured water into the vessel and brought it to Kaden's lips. As the cup made contact with Kaden's flesh, the cup changed from silver to green to gold and back to silver again. A warmth moved from where his fingers touched the cup, up his arm and into his chest, as though the cup were not just healing Kaden, but Simon as well.

Simon drew in a startled breath. The magic of the Grail was real. For the first time in a long while, Simon actually felt as though God might not have abandoned them after all. He'd given them this moment of healing, and for that Simon was grateful.

When Kaden's features appeared more at ease, Simon left him to attend to his other men. Jacob and Alaric responded immediately to the liquid from the Grail and helped him administer the healing liquid to Benton and Thomas by propping the men up so that they might more easily swallow. Jacob and Alaric stayed beside Benton and Thomas while Simon headed inside the inn to check on Cameron, Kendall, and Iain. All three men were merely unconscious. The liquid from the Grail brought them to their senses almost immediately. It did not take long for all the able-bodied men to gather in the inn yard close to where Thomas and Benton still slept.

"We need to regroup and follow whatever trail we can find that will take us to Brianna," Simon informed his men.

"If she still lives," Iain said, his tone solemn.

Agony twisted inside Simon, but he forced the pain aside. He had to stay focused, or the pain would overwhelm him. "De la Roche won't kill her outright. He's trying to wound me through her."

Benton roused from his sleep. "Nay! You cannot follow her," he said, his voice barely above a whisper. "The dark-haired Frenchman left me alive to tell you if we don't retreat, he'll kill Brianna."

"He'll kill her anyway," Cameron said ominously.

Benton tried to sit up. With help from Jacob, he managed to prop himself up on his elbows. "De la Roche wants you to give yourself up, Simon. In three days he wants you to meet him at Pennyghael Abbey to surrender yourself to him."

Alaric and Iain erupted into curses.

"He'll kill her no matter what you do," Jacob said as he strode back and forth across the inn yard, giving vent to his own nervousness.

"I say we follow the trail he left behind," Kendall growled. "We've all seen what he's capable of. We have no guarantee that she lives."

"I agree," Kaden echoed. "He's setting a trap for you, Simon. Whether he's killed Brianna yet or not, we must keep you safe."

"No doubt the man is capable of murdering Brianna, but he needs her to get to me. That's ultimately what he wants. So I very much doubt he's killed her yet." Simon's thoughts whirled as he considered what their options were. "I agree we need to appear as though we are following the man's orders in case he has set men to watch over us. But nothing prevents us from following Brianna's trail as well."

"How can we manage such secrecy? The land here is too flat and open for us to conceal ourselves. They'll see exactly what we are doing."

"And if this night's attack has taught us anything, it is that we need more men if we are to defeat de la Roche's full forces. We only met a small contingent this night and look what they were able to do to us," Thomas said with a frown.

Simon exchanged a knowing look with Kaden as an idea came to mind. "We can use secrecy to our advantage to make it appear as though I'm travelling to Pennyghael Abbey alone, while someone else steals off to Lee Castle with the Grail, and the rest of us rescue Brianna."

One corner of Kaden's mouth quirked up into a smile. "Brown robes?"

Simon nodded. "How can you truly tell one monk from another when concealed within our robes?"

"'Tis impossible," Kaden agreed.

Each man's eyes widened as understanding dawned. Without words, they each knew what must be done.

"Since I am most like you in height and coloring, I volunteer to head to Pennyghael Abbey," Iain said as he stepped up to Simon, his mail gleaming in the moonlight.

"You're a good man, Iain." Simon clapped him on the shoulder. "Gather your robe and prepare to leave. I will change out my horse for yours. De la Roche will suspect no foul-play if he recognizes my horse from a distance."

"Good idea." Iain turned to go, but Simon stalled him with his hand. "Know this, Iain; we will not leave you alone for long. We will all meet you there in three days."

"I pray you will, or otherwise, I'll be dead," the knight said before turning to head for the stable.

"We'll be there." Simon's voice held a note of finality as the knight strode away. After a pause, Simon turned to Jacob where he knelt beside Benton. "I ask the two of you to take the Grail to Lee Castle. See that my sister and anyone else who may have fallen ill from de la Roche's poison are treated;

then join us in three days' time at Pennyghael Abbey. Benton, use the Grail as you see fit to make yourself ready for battle in that time."

"With pleasure," he replied.

"The rest of you will travel with me. We will follow the trail left by de la Roche until it leads us to Brianna. Dead or alive, we will see her returned to the Brotherhood." His heart pounded as the fear he tried to keep at bay took root inside him and grew to monstrous proportions.

Brianna was not dead.

He knew from the very depth of his soul that she was alive. He sensed her presence in this world. It made no sense to believe such a thing. But he did. He clung to the thought as he and his men donned their mud-colored robes.

Brianna was still alive. She had to be.

Chapter Fifteen

Brianna's right hand throbbed, waking her. Was she bleeding again? Or had something else woken her? Did she hear footsteps outside the tent where she remained strapped to the table? Was de la Roche coming for her again?

Her heart hammered as terror gripped her. He would do that to her again. He'd already smashed two of her fingers and cut open a third. She'd never hold a sword in her right hand again. Her dreams of being a knight were over.

Fury burned away her fear and despair as she struggled against her bonds for the hundredth time. The rope cut into the skin at her wrists and ankles. She'd worn the flesh raw with her efforts to escape.

But she couldn't.

And even if de la Roche was not outside the tent in which she lay, he would be soon. The torture would start again, and no one would stop him. Not even Simon. She prayed with everything inside her that he wouldn't come for her and find himself in a similar trap.

Damn de la Roche for this!

How could a man so evil continue to thrive?

It wasn't fair. But she'd learned from her father's abandonment when he'd learned of her brothers' deaths that little in this life was fair.

As her fury ebbed, she realized that de la Roche had not stripped her of everything. She still had complete faith that in the end goodness would prevail. God would see to that.

No sooner had the thought materialized than she heard the shuffle of footsteps outside the tent. She tensed, every muscle becoming rigid. God help me make it through this next round of pain.

The flap of the tent flew up and de la Roche's silhouette was outlined by the early morning light.

He strolled toward her with that malevolent smile tugging at his lips. "Are you ready for some more, my sweetling?" He stood above her, stroking her battered cheek, drinking in the pain his fingers caused with those cool, unfeeling eyes.

He reached for her crushed fingers and squeezed, wringing a yelp of pain that she could not hold back. If she could just free her hands, she would fight back. She would find a way to do that eventually; then de la Roche would have a taste of her vengeance. She would find a way to gain control in this situation. Until then she would have to endure the pain and agony.

Eventually ... she clung to the thought as he reached for a small iron hammer.

It took until sunset the next day for Simon to track the trail of broken branches and partially hidden footprints left by de la Roche's small contingent to the campsite below. Four tents were arranged around a campfire that burned low and darkness fell over the land. The darkness would cover their movements, but also made it harder to see where de la Roche and his men were stationed. In the distance, Simon could discern three men moving about the campsite beneath the light of the moon.

Simon and Kaden left the other men behind as they crept, half-crouched, closer to the campsite. They hid behind a rock and peered out. "I see only three men, but with four tents, there must be more," Simon whispered.

"Perhaps they are guarding the campsite in shifts. It's what we Templars would do," Kaden said, his voice low.

"Then we will have to get in closer to see just how many we are up against."

Kaden put a hand on Simon's arm, stalling his progress forward. "You do not intend to fight them, do you?"

"Not if I can help it. It would be best for Brianna's safety if we could sneak in and take her without them knowing."

"Agreed."

Silently, they crept forward until they were no more than a hundred paces from the first tent. Kaden took a step and something snapped beneath his heel. Simon froze. Kaden did the same. Every muscle in Simon's body tensed as the harsh tenor of his and Kaden's breathing scored the silence.

After a moment, Simon forced himself to relax. His fingers unfurled. He cast a glance at Kaden in the silvery darkness. No one had heard. Cautiously, they continued forward until they reached the first tent. Soundlessly, Simon lifted the edge and peered inside to see four men asleep.

He signaled for Kaden to go to the next tent on the left, while he moved to the one on the right. Once again, Simon barely lifted the edge of the fabric. Inside, he could see one man near the doorway carrying a bucket of water toward another man who sat in a tub in the center of the tent. The man's back was to him, but Simon knew without seeing his face that it was de la Roche who reclined there, awaiting his bath.

As silently as possible, Simon shifted away, and like the shadows of the night, moved on to the next tent. Kaden met him there. With a shake of his head, Kaden communicated that the other tent he'd searched had not held Brianna. This tent had to be the one.

Simon's lifted the edge of the tent and a silken string coiled about his fingers. He followed the string and saw that it was attached to a silken pouch that lay discarded in the shadows. He tugged the string, bringing the pouch closer and noticed a fiery-red lock of hair protruding from the top.

Brianna's hair?

Simon clutched the pouch in his fist as he peered beyond the shadows into the interior of the tent. A single candle set on the dirt floor cast a pale golden light about the manmade room. His heart accelerated then stopped as he saw Brianna inside. She was strapped to a table where she lay with deathlike stillness. Blood dripped from the tabletop onto the floor from where her hands rested.

A flash of fear raced through him. His heart thundered to life in his chest, driving the sensation away. He drew his knife and cut the fabric of the tent enough so that he and Kaden could steal inside.

Brianna.

Her name gave him strength as he surged forward and with precise movements, cut the ropes that bound her to the table. He stared down at her battered and beaten form. Blood caked the side of her face and bruises dotted both cheeks.

Simon curled his fist around the hilt of his dagger, praying de la Roche would find them now. The need for revenge twisted inside him.

"You'll have your turn when the time is right," Kaden whispered beside him.

"How could he do this to her? Merciful heavens!"

"She's still alive," Kaden said. He kicked dirt over the sputtering light of the candle, pitching them into darkness.

"Merciful heavens!" The words echoed in her brain. Brianna kept her eyes shut. She must be dreaming. It was a pleasant dream, yet there were no images to fill her mind as they usually did with her visions. Only sound came to her. It was Simon's voice, yet it wasn't. He sounded odd, hoarse, and strangely broken.

"She's still alive," another voice broke through her reprieve of darkness. Kaden?

Brianna allowed the voices to wash over her, comfort her. She pulled the blanket of darkness she'd created closer about herself. She couldn't open her eyes or the torture would start again, the pain that rippled though her fingers and up her arm would overwhelm her senses as it had earlier today. Was that today? How many days had she endured the madman's company? Time seemed endless now.

"For God's sake," Kaden said. "Don't just keep staring at her. Let's get her out of here before de la Roche or his men return."

"She's so … battered and broken," Simon whispered.

"You've seen worse. Now pick her up and let's go!"

She was gently lifted and cradled next to a warmth that seemed so familiar. The scents of soap and musk surrounded her. Simon's scents. Perhaps she wasn't dreaming. Had Simon come for her? Did he know about de la Roche's men?

She had to warn him. She struggled to open her eyes, to will the darkness away, but could not find the strength. From deep inside she pulled up reserves she didn't know she possessed. "Danger." The word was nothing more than a whisper of sound.

"You're safe, Brianna. De la Roche's men are asleep or distracted." Simon's words were thick with emotion. "We are taking you away from here."

"Danger," she said again, more forcefully this time. Slowly she lifted her lids and her eyes focused on the face above her.

Blue eyes glittered with a moist brilliance. Simon's eyes. "We are taking you home."

"I have no home."

"We'll see about that," he whispered near her ear. As gently as butterfly wings, he pressed a kiss to her bruised and battered flesh. There was no pain, only a soft tingling warmth.

Was she truly free of the nightmare? Simon had come for her after all. He shouldn't have, but he had. Tears sprang up behind her eyelids as gratitude filled her chest.

A noise sounded off to her left.

Brianna jerked awake. She jumped to her feet, reached for her sword. Her hand came up empty. Her sword was gone. Pain shot through her right hand. Memory returned.

The room dipped crazily before her eyes, only it was not from dizziness. The room literally dipped and swayed as though rocking with the sea. The faint scent of salt permeated her dulled senses.

The door opened.

"Brianna?" Simon entered the dimly lit room and hastened to her side. "You're trembling." He took her arm and helped her to a chair near a small table.

"Where am I?"

He pulled a second chair up to hers and sat. "We are on a ship enroute to Staffa."

"Staffa," she echoed. Her eyes widened. "We are going to Fingal's Cave."

He nodded. "'Twas all you talked about after we found you. You kept telling us we must rescue the other knight you saw in your dreams. You were adamant about us going to Staffa. You feared the knight had suffered as you did at de la Roche's hand. You wanted him found and returned to the Brotherhood."

"I did?"

He nodded, searching her face. "You don't remember any of it?"

"I remember enough." She looked away, unable to bear the echo of pain she saw in his eyes. "You should not have come. If he'd caught you, he would have tortured you as well. Perhaps he did. It's all such a blur."

"I will always come for you. Look at me, Brianna. Do I look tortured?"

She looked at him. He looked strong and whole in spite of the lines of grief and weariness she saw in his face. "No, you are as you always were."

He smiled and some of the weariness vanished from his eyes. "You will be as you always were again, too."

Her gaze dropped to her bandaged right hand. During the last hours of torture, she had pretended that the limb no longer belonged to her; that it was a distant object that could not cause her pain. A sense of that same remoteness still remained. "It doesn't hurt any longer."

"Kaden and I splinted the two crushed fingers, and put the other three back into their sockets."

She frowned. "I remember blood. There was lots of blood."

Simon nodded. "One of the bones had pierced the flesh. We managed to put the bone back in place and sewed you up. There will be a scar, I'm afraid."

She closed her eyes, blocking out the sight. Aye, there would be a scar on her hand and on her soul.

"Brianna, you will be whole again, I promise you." The passionate tone of his voice almost convinced her that he could will that very healing he demanded with his words. Suddenly, he held her in his arms; his fingers tangled in her hair as he rocked her back and forth. "The Grail will see you healed."

The Grail. "Kaden was able to hide it?"

He pressed a kiss to her temple before he pulled away. "Thanks to you, aye, he hid it from that monster and we were able to use it to heal the men. I've been using it to heal you as well."

"But you were to send it to Bella..." Her words faded at the thought that Bella would now suffer because of her own injuries.

"The Grail has been to Lee Castle already. Now it is back here with you."

Brianna tensed. She had to ask the question burning in her heart. "Does she live?"

"Aye," Simon reassured. "Bella improves daily. The Grail and Abigail's care have seen her through. And now, it is your turn."

"To heal?" She gazed at her damaged hand and her throat tightened. "My fingers are too badly damaged."

"You will heal, and you will fight."

She shook her head. "Nay. I'll never—"

"How many hands do you have?" Simon's words were strong, his voice hoarse. "How many?"

She choked back a sob. "Two."

"I've seen you fight with your left hand before. We'll perfect your technique and build your strength in your left hand. Many great warriors use both. You are a great warrior, Brianna. Not many men could withstand what you did. It proves what we already knew; you are strong, and brave, and special."

Brianna's gaze met Simon's and the faintest smile touched her lips. A warm sensation filled her. How strange after what she'd endured to feel the essence of hope blossoming within her once more. But she did. "Thank you, Simon, for believing in me."

He nodded, then stood. "You should rest. Soon after that, we shall arrive at Staffa. Our first goal is to rescue the knight abandoned there. Once we complete our mission, we shall begin your lessons."

She nodded.

"One more thing. I need you to drink once more from the Grail. Just to be certain…" He moved to a chest that rested on the floor near the foot of her bed. He lifted the hinged lid and withdrew a tarnished tin chalice. After filling it with water from a bladder that hung on the wall, he returned to her side and handed the Grail to her.

Brianna took the cup in her hands and brought the liquid to her lips, drinking deeply. The cool liquid flowed past her lips and down her throat, warming her as it moved through her. The chalice shifted from silver to blue, then green, then gold beneath the lamplight that warmed the darkest corners of the cabin, all while remaining cool to the touch. "How odd. I've never seen any metal do that before."

"I thought the same thing when it changed colors on me." Simon motioned for her to finish the contents.

She stared, mesmerized, at the ever-changing color. "It's almost as if it draws on the life of the person who holds it to return life."

"If that is true, then allow me to hold the Grail for you," he said, taking the chalice from her hands as it continued to shift from silver to gold. "I owe you so much."

Brianna finished all but one swallow, and placing her hand on the cup, pushed it back toward Simon. "Heal yourself, Simon. You are not to blame for de la Roche's actions, not with me, not with the other people he's hurt. Do not lose faith that good will overcome evil in all things."

She raised the cup to his lips. "Do you share this belief with me?"

He drank the remnants of the cup, then smiled. "I do."

Simon looked up from the document he studied to see Brianna standing a few paces away from him on the deck of the ship. The emerald green of her gown contrasted magnificently with her skin and unruly dark-red curls, which seemed to shimmer while her eyes sparkled. He had been keeping his distance from her over the last few hours until he was certain she was healed. They'd been moored off the coast of Staffa for that long as well. He had no intention of going forward on this journey without her. He had to prove to himself and to her that she was still as able-bodied as she'd ever been.

Looking at her now, with the wind in her hair and color blooming in her cheeks, he'd say she was more than she'd ever been before. It was as if what she'd endured at de la Roche's hand had strengthened her. Her sheer vitality sent a sensual shock through him. Every muscle tensed as he fought for control.

Brianna's gaze shifted from him to beyond him. "The cave," she said as her gaze fixed in compulsive fascination on the darkness beyond the opening. "It's exactly as I dreamed it."

"And that surprises you? Everything is always as you dream it."

Her face paled. "Nay, never say that."

Instantly, he knew she was thinking about the battle ahead where he was beheaded by de la Roche. He stood and moved to her, taking her hands gently in his own. "You are a different person than the woman who had that vision. The future is already changed."

She nodded, but her gaze didn't leave the dark entrance. She moistened her lips. "Will we go for him soon?"

"As soon as you're ready. The tide is low which gives us our best chance for entering the cave." He studied her face, saw a slight hesitation reflected in her green eyes. "I could go alone if you'd prefer."

She shook her head. "I'm going."

"I'll tell the others."

From somewhere far away came the high, screeching cry of a seagull as Simon helped Brianna from the boat. They slipped onto the one area of flat rock on the entire island of Staffa. Simon cradled her against his side so as not to touch her hand, and she liked the feel of him there. Close. Intimate.

And there was something else, something even more fragile building between them: trust. She realized with a sense of awe that she trusted him and received trust in return. He was the first person aside from Abigail with whom she could simply be herself — the warrior and the woman.

Sunlight kissed her skin as she and Simon, Kaden, and Jacob headed for the opening of the cave still some distance away over the slick basalt rock. The air smelled of salt and a breeze lifted the ends of her hair, tossing them about her face. She pushed the unbound strands back out of her eyes with her injured hand. At least her hand was good for something. The thought brought a smile to her lips.

"What are you smiling about?" Simon asked as they headed toward the jet black opening in the side of the rock.

"No matter what we find inside that cave, it feels good to be out of doors … with you."

He reached for her left hand. Together they clamored over the volcanic rock toward the opening. Darkness greeted them. Brianna squeezed Simon's hand, trying to quell the infinitesimal shaking in her hand. But whether she was scared of what they'd find or excited at the prospect of rescue, she couldn't honestly say.

He let go of her and rustled around in the knapsack he wore over his shoulder. He produced a flintstone and the makings for a torch which he quickly wound together. He drew a dagger from his boot and struck the steel to the stone. On the third strike, a spark settled on the fibers he'd wound around the wood. He picked up the torch and encouraged the embers with his breath. Soon flames glowed brightly to send golden fingers of light threading into the darkness. The cave funneled into a long strip of black ahead of them.

High overhead, seagulls squawked as they dipped and weaved, chasing the ever present wind. "Ready?" Simon asked.

Her heart sped up as excitement wedded with fear. "I'm ready."

"I'll go first. Stay right behind me."

Her breath quickened as the four of them felt their way along the broken pillars that created a stair-stepped walkway. The entire island was made from hexagonal pillars thrust up from the depth of the sea in what she could only assume was some sort of volcanic eruption centuries ago. The ocean cooled the rocks quickly, leaving fingers of stone stretching for the sky.

As they moved along the naturally-formed path, the temperature dropped and the hiss of the waves mingled with the harsh tenor of their own breathing, echoing against the cathedral-like ceiling overhead.

The torch created a golden kaleidoscope of twisting, dancing light on the cavern walls as they made their way deeper into the cave. Cold dampness seeped into her bones and plastered her dress to her legs as they inched forward along the stair-stepped path.

Simon stopped.

"What is it?" Brianna stopped and peered around him. Light from the torch splashed across the walkway and landed on a human skeleton a few feet away. She gasped.

"This skeleton has been here a while." Simon shuffled forward. "We have to walk past it. They are just bones. Don't be afraid."

They are just bones. Brianna kept the words in mind as she inched forward along the path. The pale, gray bones reclined against the damp stone wall, the skull angled so that it appeared to watch bypassers with its eyeless sockets, almost daring them to pass deeper into the cave.

A shiver moved along her spine.

As though sensing her emotions, Simon took her uninjured hand and gave it a gentle squeeze. "We'll find him."

"I hear something," Kaden said from behind them.

The four of them stopped. Silence fell over the cave except for the deep rushing of the waves as they swelled and receded against the rock.

A groan. "Help … me." The words were faint.

"The sound came from just ahead, off to the right beyond the curve in the rock wall." Kaden's voice bounced off the walls and rang back at her as did the sound of steel against leather as the men drew their swords.

Simon turned and handed Brianna the torch. "Be prepared for anything."

Brianna's breath jammed in her throat as they hurried around the bend. Light from the torch slipped across the body of a man chained by his hands and feet to the slick stone wall. He was suspended from the rock, his feet dangling down. His clothes were in tatters and hung from his emaciated frame. Blood-brown streaks marred his face, legs, and arms, but did not hide the glittering moisture that welled in his eyes.

"Jacob and Brianna, stand guard while Kaden and I get him down," Simon said.

Brianna didn't move. She couldn't. All she could do was stare at the man she'd seen in her vision. He was alive, at least, even though he'd been abused and tortured more intensely than even she had been. Her gaze moved to his hands. They were whole. Her breath rushed from her lungs in a painful sigh of relief. At least he had been spared from that ordeal.

She turned around, finally able to do as Simon had asked. She watched the entrance of the cave for movement as the sound of Simon and Kaden's daggers ground against the rock, no doubt loosening the chains that held the man in place.

Shuffling sounds came from behind her. "He lost consciousness." Kaden's voice held a note of concern.

"He's free." Simon's voice assured her moments later. "We can assess the damage later. For now, let's get him out of here."

Jacob took the lead, his sword at the ready, while Kaden carried the limp man in his arms. Simon offered Brianna his hand. She took it, reveling in the warmth as together they began the journey back along the pathway to the boat and out of the bowels of Fingal's Cave.

Chapter Sixteen

There were rainclouds on the horizon. Pierre de la Roche frowned as he brought his horse to a halt at the rise of the hill overlooking a valley below. Scottish rains always put him in a bad mood. Mostly because the rain washed away all signs of the brown-cloaked man he'd been following since he'd discovered Brianna gone from his lair.

How dare they come and steal her away from him just when he was starting to enjoy stretching out her pain, watching her agony as he slowly destroyed her fingers? There were so many other bones he could have mangled. And they'd robbed him of the pleasure.

But who had come for her? Lockhart was on his way to Pennyghael Abbey alone. He'd seen the evidence of that with his own eyes. Perhaps it was his friend, the unshakable Kaden Buchanan. De la Roche frowned. It mattered not; without Brianna to distract him, he'd had no choice but to follow Lockhart as the Templar made his way to the abbey as instructed. He'd force the Templar into the ambush that awaited him near the woodlands a few miles from Pennyghael Abbey. The familiar excitement that always preceded a kill swept through him, warming him against the chill winds that had picked up intensity in the past few moments.

He'd toyed with Lockhart long enough. It was time to gather his full army and demolish the Brotherhood of the Scottish Templars. He'd kill them all, then take their treasure and forge a new empire of his own. He looked expectantly at the sky overhead. Rain was coming, and soon. He and his men would try to make it to the next inn or farmhouse. Even a crofter's cottage would suffice before the rain came.

Then he would wait out the storm and sit before a roaring fire and dream of the pain and the carnage that would come at the end of his notorious sword, Joyeuse. The forced reprieve would give him time to savor and anticipate the killing to come.

It would take more than the Grail's healing powers to set the man they'd found in Fingal's Cave back to rights. They'd learned the man was a Templar named Roinald Brown. He'd confirmed Brianna's dream, telling them he'd been captured by de la Roche and hidden in the cave. He'd suffered torture far more severe than what Brianna had endured.

The man was half-starved and brutally beaten. What he needed was the healing that could come only in the healing waters found at Crosswick Abbey and the ministrations the brothers there could provide.

"We need to separate," Simon said to Kaden and Jacob as they set sail for the isle of Mull. They laid Roinald on a pallet that rested in the protected area below the forecastle.

"If we separate any further, we will all be at risk." Kaden frowned.

"I don't see any other way. Roinald is too weak to go into battle. Having him among us will only slow our progress. It would be safer for all of us to send him back to Crosswick."

"I will take him," Jacob said, his gaze straying to the man on the pallet.

Brianna knelt by Roinald's side. She brushed the sweat-dampened hair from the injured Templar's head with a cool cloth. Fever had set in. "You will be well, Roinald. The Grail will help you heal as it did me." Her voice held a note of calm reassurance.

Simon only wished he felt that same way about the man's chance of survival. When they'd found Brianna, she was physically battered, but she'd retained much of her health and strength. Roinald's emaciated body might not be strong enough to recover.

Simon moved to Brianna's side and laid a hand on her shoulder. "You should rest, too. You are still not fully healed."

Brianna shook her head. "I am much improved. And I agree. It would be best for us to separate. Although, I think we should send Kaden along with Jacob and Roinald. It will take one of them just to hold him upright. The other will have to offer protection in case…" She let her words trail off.

Kaden's frown increased. "She is right. I will gladly go, but that will leave you and Brianna in a similar situation. She's not ready to fight yet."

Brianna stood and faced Kaden. Before he could react, she whipped her sword from her scabbard with her left hand and brought the tip of the blade to rest beneath his chin. "What was that you were saying?" she challenged.

Admiration shone in his eyes. "I take that back. The two of you will do excellently on your own."

Simon did not share Kaden's amusement. He took the hilt from Brianna's hand and returned her sword to her scabbard. "Brianna is quick with a sword, right or left handed, but drawing a sword is not fighting a battle." He turned to Brianna. "I mean that with no disrespect."

"No offense taken," she said. "You are correct. I am healing, but my full strength has not returned."

He nodded. "If we are to defeat de la Roche, we still need more men. Kaden and Jacob, after you leave Roinald at Crosswick Abbey, you will ride for the nearest clans. Brianna and I will do the same once we reach shore. If we are to crush de la Roche, we must have the help of the Highlanders. And we have two days only to gather our forces and meet on the rise above Pennyghael Abbey."

"Agreed," Kaden and Jacob said in unison.

Simon looked toward the sky. Blue-black clouds rolled across the western horizon and the afternoon wind carried with it the bite of cool moisture. He drew a deep breath, letting the pungent dampness flow through him. "A storm is closing in. Once we reach shore, we will go our separate ways

173

and make as much progress as we can before the rain and sunset force us to stop."

"Until then, Brianna, can I interest you in a little left-handed sword play? We must build up your strength for the coming battle."

"On the deck of the ship?"

"Does the idea scare you?"

Her eyes narrowed. "Is that a dare, Simon Lockhart?"

He allowed the hint of a smile to tug at his lips. "Think of it however you like. You say you are hale and hearty. Prove it."

In the blink of an eye, she turned to Kaden. "May I borrow this again?"

"Borrow away." He handed her his sword then stepped back toward Jacob.

She advanced on Simon with a laugh. "I'll prove I'm well, you over-eager barbarian."

He drew his sword and a sense of rightness came over him at the sight of Brianna acting much as she always had. De la Roche might have damaged her fingers, but he had not damaged her spirit.

"Come, Jacob, let's be away from here before the Grail has even more healing to do." Kaden scooted the two of them farther back until they were against the rails.

Brianna tucked her injured hand behind her back as she balanced Kaden's sword in her left hand. The animation left her face and she flicked her wrist slightly as though testing her own strength.

"Does that feel comfortable?" Simon asked, studying her closely.

She lunged forward with another laugh. "Never let your guard down. Isn't that the first thing you ever taught me?"

He brought his sword up to meet her stroke. "Nicely done." He pressed his attack, holding himself back as he advanced.

She met each downward thrust and countered with movements as precise as she ever had. Yet a frown marred her face.

"What is it? Are you in pain?" he asked though he did not drop his guard.

"You are holding back. Come, Simon. De la Roche and his men will show no such mercy. Or is it that you don't have the stomach to fight me as you have so many times before?"

He knew she was needling him. And it worked.

Simon struck Brianna's sword, hard. She took the blow with an upward thrust and for a moment, she staggered beneath the onslaught. Then something flashed in her green eyes and she pressed her own attack, forcing him back along the long, narrow deck.

There was no holding back as they perfectly parried each other's movements. Back and forth they went along the deck, until time seemed to stand still and there was only the two of them: breath for breath, stroke for stroke.

The wind ruffled through Brianna's hair, sending it into wild disarray around her face. She reached up with her injured hand and tucked the errant strands behind her ears. No pain lingered in her gaze, only warmth and excitement and hunger. Simon's heart slowed to a snail's pace and then sped up.

He lowered his sword and felt every breath he took like a whisper of promise against his lips. Cool fingers licked along his spine and made him shiver. He had a strange feeling that he was close to something magical, something he'd waited for his entire life…

Her features softened as desire lit her eyes. She lowered her sword. "Is this battle at an end?"

Transfixed by the slow, sensual movements of her lips, it was a moment before he realized she was speaking to him. He shook his head, clearing his thoughts, and took the three steps that separated them. "We are done. You've proven you are a powerful warrior left- or right-handed."

She smiled.

"And a beautiful woman." He leaned toward her. To his delight, she swayed toward him. Her eyelids fluttered closed.

He reached for her left hand, his touch a caress.

A soft whisper of breath escaped her.

He swallowed hard and forced his thoughts in a different direction. He couldn't kiss her here, not in front of the others, no matter how desperate he was to feel the softness of her lips against his own. He lifted Kaden's sword from her fingers.

Her eyes snapped open.

"Land, just ahead," he warned, stepping back and handing Kaden his weapon, feeling suddenly cold and alone. "All of us should prepare for our arrival. We have not a moment to spare."

Brianna and Simon rode hard for what remained of the day. As soon as the sun went down, the rain began to fall. Sporadically at first, then huge drops as Simon had predicted. The heavens opened and rain poured down with stunning force. Brianna could hear the drumming of water on the makeshift lean-to Simon had created out of sticks and ferns. Surprisingly, few drops managed to pierce the foliage above them.

The fire Simon had built was small, but it provided adequate warmth and had allowed them to cook a trout he'd caught in the nearby stream. The fresh meat tasted good after so many days of dried fish and oats.

Gazing into the fire, with nothing else to do, Brianna became suddenly aware of the nearness of Simon's body. She could see the rise and fall of his chest, imagined the tension of his hands as they clenched the hilt of his sword, and his eyes...

Simon jerked his gaze away and shifted restlessly. "It appears as though we'll be stuck here until morning," he said, his voice tight.

The scent of the rain mixed with that of burning acacia wood, surrounding them. The earthy scents melded with the musk and soap of Simon's fragrance. She breathed deeply, pulling the scents deep into her body. She wanted to hold on to his scent forever.

But that wasn't all she wanted to hold on to forever. The thought sent a ripple of awareness through her. She wanted so many things when it came to Simon. She wanted his trust. She wanted his companionship. And, if the feverish heat warming her limbs were any indication, she also wanted to be joined with Simon in the same searing fashion she had known before. She wanted to look at him in the evening light. She wanted to touch him. She moistened her lips and experienced a hot, melting sensation between her thighs.

A gasp tore from her lips.

His gaze shot to her face. "Is it your hand? Does it hurt?"

"Nay." She inhaled sharply and remained still, looking helplessly at him.

"Then what is it?" he asked.

She could not bear this. It was time to be brave. "I want you to touch me. I want you to kiss me."

He leaned back as far as their small structure would allow. "I can't touch you, Brianna." His voice was choked. "If I do I might not be able to stop and I have absolutely no desire to hurt you any more than you've already been hurt."

"You will never hurt me as he did." Her gaze was on his face and she smiled. If she wanted to be near him tonight, she would have to show him just how healed she was. "The Grail has done miraculous things for my fingers. Would you like to see?"

Before he could object, she loosened the bandages from her hand and slowly unwound the thin sheets of linen he'd placed there, until her fingers were freed. "My smallest finger sustained the most damage. I still cannot bend it, but it appears almost normal." She bent the other two fingers near the thumb. "You can still see a scar where you sewed me up, but other than that, they are working better than I ever dared to hope."

He reached for her hand and cradled it in his larger one. With his thumb he stroked the renewed flesh up and down with a feather-light touch. "Truly, I would not have believed this was possible if I hadn't seen it myself." His brow creased as a frown came to his face. "The man should have been dead after his fall from the castle tower. But somehow he managed to survive and kidnap Brother Roinald. Only Roinald could have revealed the location of the Templar treasure. Any good health de la Roche enjoys now is because he stole the Grail and used it for himself."

Brianna slipped her fingers from Simon's hand to frame his face. "We have back one of the treasures de la Roche stole. And we shall find a safe home for the rest eventually. Only finding the help we need to oppose the Frenchman stands in the way of our triumph over him."

"Will we find that help?"

"I believe so." She offered him an encouraging smile that suddenly shifted to something more passionate.

"Brianna," his gaze clung to her face and she saw an echo of her own desire. "You must stop looking at me in that way."

The beauty of his lips held her spellbound. She wanted to reach out and touch his lower lip with her tongue, to taste him as she had before. "In what way?"

"As though you want to devour me."

"But I do want that." The sound of the rain pelting the top of their shelter mixed with the scents of damp earth and the warmth of the fire, wreathing them in a mystical world of sensation. "I feel as though we are alone in a wild secret garden at the beginning of time, when anything is possible and nothing is forbidden."

Simon groaned and turned his head and kissed the palm of her injured hand where it touched his cheek. "Is anything possible?"

A shiver of sensation rippled through her fingers and up her arm. "Yes."

He pressed kisses down her palm to her wrist. His lips lingered on her flesh just long enough for her to feel their heat before he moved toward her forearm and elbow. Her pulse leapt at the touch of his lips.

He lifted his head, holding her captive with his eyes as he pulled her closer until she could feel the heat of his body against her own. Everywhere he touched burned. A shudder ran through her as he brought his lips to hers. "If anything is possible, then I don't want to think about my vows, the brotherhood, de la Roche, or anything else at the moment. Only you. Only us."

"Is there an us?" The unexpected words came out in a breathy rush.

"I wish I could say aye." He looked as though he'd been slashed with a sword. And she knew why. He was thinking about Teba. Their failure there would temper both their lives forever. "Neither of us knows how a battle will go. In two days' time, we will triumph or we will fail."

She nodded. "I don't want to think about the future either. I only want to feel."

Raw, unveiled passion lit his eyes — an almost animal intensity that stole her ability to breathe. He looked at her as he never had before — as though he wanted more than her touch, more than her kiss, more even than access to the secret passageways of her body. He looked as though he wanted her soul.

And she would give it to him. The realization sent a white-hot bolt of desire careening through her. He brought a hand up to caress her cheek and pushed his fingers back through the thickness of her hair. The sensation of his fingers on her scalp set her afire as he drew her near. "I think I shall—"

"Please, Simon, don't think. Thinking always leads us into trouble. Just feel."

He smiled. "As you wish."

An earthy, fresh scent surrounded her as he slowly let her hair slide through his fingertips. She found she was holding her breath as one hand left her hair to cup her shoulder then slide down her arm to the laces of her gown. The garment left her body, followed by her chemise as though they had melted away. When nothing covered her except her shoes and hose, his hands ran down the length of her legs to remove her boots. Then slowly, sensually, he rolled her hose down one by one, and caressing the bottom of her feet as he went, he freed her from the last remnants of her clothes.

With a seductive smile that warmed her all the more, Simon pulled back, and sitting on his knees, he removed his shirt and his boots and breeches until he was naked before her.

Despite the rain, the air was not cold in the private little shelter he had built for them. The fire flickered, sending its warming rays through the small space, illuminating his body in pale shades of orange and gold. She could only stare at him, enchanted by the hungry passion in his eyes.

Desire uncoiled deep within her body, sent frissons of warmth sliding through her blood. Her heart thundered in her chest as she watched him watch her.

"You're so beautiful," he whispered as he leaned over her to plant a kiss on her right nipple.

Brianna gasped at the unexpected contact, but before she could become accustomed to the sensation, his hands slid down her sides, forming against her thighs, gently urging her legs apart. Moving between her knees, he leaned forward. She strained upward to kiss him. His mouth slanted over hers and he forced her back onto the ferns.

He settled urgently between her thighs. Naked flesh pressed against naked flesh. She felt the thudding of his heart against her own chest. His hardness probed the wetness between her legs, but he did not enter. Instead he teased her with small circular motions until desire flared beyond her control.

She cried out with almost painfully throbbing need. His lips captured hers and moved in a gentle, sensual rhythm that left her breathless as he trailed kisses from her lips to her throat, each one like a spark against her heated flesh. He explored the pale curve of her throat, her collarbone, past her breast and to her nipple.

He flicked his tongue over the sensitive bud. Her breath came in hot, harsh gasps as he continued his slow seduction, laving one nipple then the other. She arched upward, craving his touch, as need such as she'd never experienced before washed through her in waves.

When she thought she would die from wanting, his tongue left her nipples to trail flames of desire down her tingling, burning flesh. And as he nipped and tasted, his fingers explored her flesh, finding places she'd never realized were sensitive to the touch: the inside of her elbow, the back of her knee, along the inside of her thigh.

He touched her until her skin fairly vibrated with tension; she grew hot and wet and desire was an insatiable need that threatened to tear her apart. Shamelessly, she opened herself to him. She clutched at his hand and guided it over her head where she held him captive. "Please, Simon, now. I must have you now."

She coiled her legs around his buttocks and guided his hardness toward the core of her womanhood. The warmth of the shelter wrapped around her as his hardness slipped inside her.

She gasped at the pleasure of it. The fullness. The rightness of this moment.

He moved slowly at first, allowing her to catch the rhythm, then he moved harder. In. Out. Long. Short. The ferns overhead were a blur of green above his shoulder, with every breath she took in the rich scent of earth and fresh green. The rustling of the leaves beneath the ferns was as sensual as his harsh breathing in her ear.

Her body tightened as a slow-burning desire built, higher and higher, bringing both desire and desperation. Her body quivered with each erotic sensation. She strained toward that cusp that would send her into splendor. Simon plunged inside her deep and hard, again and again, until she arched upward. She cried out her pleasure. Tears stung her eyes, blurred her vision as spasm after spasm tore through her.

His smile was savage as he moved harder, faster. He stiffened and then groaned. His body went taut as he released a cry that was both primitive and earthy into the night. A smile, the likes of which she had not seen before on Simon's face, touched his lips as he settled beside her on the ferns, rolling her with him so that they remained intimately connected even after their love-making was through.

His breathing was as ragged as her own as they lay there, listening to the sounds of the night. Her arms instinctively tightened about Simon's massive shoulders.

He lifted his head and looked down at her, his breathing labored. "Merciful heavens. You make love with as much passion as you fight."

"I hope that is a good thing?"

"Very good." He leaned down and kissed her, wrapping her in a cocoon of warmth to shelter her from any chill that might follow the storm overhead.

"Then shall we continue our battle?"

He threw back his head and laughed. "Not now. I think it best if we both rest for a while." He lifted her off him, curling her against his side. His lips brushed her temple as he settled her head on his shoulder. "I hope your hand was not hurt. We were very vigorous."

She nestled her cheek on his shoulder, running the tips of her fingers down the muscles of his chest in a loving caress. Drowsiness was already tugging at her as she murmured, "You didn't hurt me. I feel more at peace than I ever have before."

Simon gently stroked Brianna's hair back from her face as her breathing became even. He shouldn't have done this. He shouldn't have taken what she offered, but he couldn't have stopped himself. Brianna meant so much to him — so much more than he ever dared admit before. And now that he had taken her again, he knew he could never let her go.

He tightened his arm around her with yearning. But how could he commit to something so precious when it could all be taken away with the stroke of a sword? If Brianna's vision of the future came to pass, he would die. He could not offer her anything until after that battle came to pass, but he could make her happy in the moments they had left — however few or however many that might be.

Time was their enemy now.

In two days, they would either rest in eternal peace, or in each other's arms.

He knew which option he preferred.

Chapter Seventeen

"Brianna."

It was Simon's voice, but something was different. His voice vibrated with an unusual sound of eagerness and laughter. She opened her eyes. His face was different, too. He was laughing down at her, his eyes alight with a newfound joy she had never seen there before. In the moments between sleeping and waking, something had changed within him. Something that had been taken from him long ago had been returned.

"The rain has stopped. We must keep going if we are to make it to Pennyghael Abbey as planned."

She was naked beneath the cloak he'd spread over them last night. He was as gloriously naked as he had been when they'd made love. Early morning light filtered through the opening of their shelter, bathing Simon in a peach-colored glow that glinted in the darkness of his hair and turned his skin to a warm bronze. "You seem eager to go into battle when you are not even clothed yet."

He smiled. "I can dress faster than you can." He leaned down and kissed her with infinite sweetness. "And it's not the battle ahead that woke me from my dreams. It was you. I have never been this happy, Brianna." He pulled her into a sitting position. "But we must also remain vigilant. Complacency has injured many a knight."

She instantly sobered. "Do you think de la Roche is out there even now, watching us?"

The smile did not leave Simon's eyes as he lifted her hand and placed a kiss on her re-bandaged palm. "He's out there somewhere, of that we can be certain. Because of that, I want you to do something for me." He released her hand and turned to the saddlebag he'd set near the shelter's opening. He fumbled around inside the bag before he withdrew the Grail and handed the vessel to her. "I want you to carry this with you."

"The Grail?" She gently touched the satiny smoothness of the ancient cup. She frowned as the morning light gilded the artifact, turning it silver, then gold. She felt captured by the Grail's ever-changing color. "It appears as though it is a humble vessel one moment, then a glorious treasure the next. Do you see the same thing?"

"Aye, perhaps because it was the cup of a carpenter and a king." He shrugged. "All I know is that I am grateful it healed you and Bella and so many of my men." He placed his hand over hers against the cup. "I want you to carry it."

"Because of my dream?"

He kissed her again, quick and hard. "I want you to carry the Grail because I trust you to keep it safe."

The vessel warmed beneath their joined hands, filling her with a sense of peace and hope that they would not only triumph over de la Roche, but they would return the Grail and Joyeuse to the Templar treasure hold, keeping them safe for all time. "How close are we to Pennyghael?"

"I'm not certain. Maybe a day's journey until we get through these foothills. Another half day across the open land."

They were close. So very close to either success or failure. "Then that leaves us only half a day before de la Roche's army should arrive to scout the location and gather more men." Brianna scooted from beneath the cloak he'd laid over them. "We must get started if we are to have the best advantage in this battle."

He smiled mischievously. "Not just yet," he pulled her to him until the warmth of his breath brushed her ear and his arms formed a deliciously secure haven around her. "We have time for this." His teeth gently nibbled at the lobe of her ear.

A tingle of heat ran through her. "What about vigilance?"

His hands cupped her breasts. "As I said before, we need to enjoy the moments between now and then." His thumb and forefinger plucked at her sensitive nipples. "Do we have an accord?"

An aching fire throbbed between her thighs at his touch. "In all things."

His hand slid down from her taut stomach, then further down to tangle in her soft curls. While his fingertips delicately circled and rubbed, his thumb pressed skillfully against her core. He opened her legs and lifted her into the air, then slowly slid into her, filling her.

"Hold me tight," he said as breathlessly as she felt.

She did and forgot about leaving. She forgot about de la Roche. She forgot about everything except the feel of him. She closed her eyes, arched her head back as she moved up and down, feeling a slow, sensual caress that stoked her desire.

She could feel Simon's heart pounding against her breasts, feel the rising and falling of his chest with each labored breath. He brought her closer with a groan and she could feel the hair surrounding his manhood brush against that most sensitive part of her. He moved beneath her, matching her rhythm, driving deeper.

Brianna clutched at his shoulders, feeling something coiling inside her, wanting to be let out.

Simon arched her against him, bending his mouth to envelop her breast, nipping, suckling, until she sobbed at the exquisite sensations building inside. The sensation was too hot, too hard, too intense to hold on any longer.

She gave herself over to sensation and a savage cry tore from her lips, followed by Simon's, mixing their voices, pleasure, and release.

She collapsed against Simon, her head cradled on his chest, struggling to catch her breath. He cupped the back of her head with one hand, her buttocks with the other and held tight. As soon as she could breathe again, she lifted her head to find him as breathless as she was. He smiled down at her with that same laughter she'd seen earlier. "I think I will enjoy the moments between now and then very much."

He laughed softly. "So will I, my beautiful warrior."

The smile faded from her lips. That was the second time he'd called her beautiful. But she knew the truth. "You do not have to say such things to me, Simon. I need no pretty compliments. My father taught me to be honest about myself."

He stared at her with astonishment in his eyes. "He taught you what?"

"That I'm no beauty."

With a finger beneath her chin, he returned her gaze to his. "Do you know what I see when I look at you?"

She shook her head, suddenly breathless again at the fire in his eyes as he studied her face, her hair, her body still intimately pressed against his.

He tugged at a lock of her hair that had fallen over her shoulder. "Your hair shimmers in the light when you move your head. In the sunshine, your tresses turn to radiant fire." His finger stroked the curve of her brow. "Eyes so green, they remind me of the velvety hills of Glencoe in the spring. So beautiful." He stroked the side of her cheek with the back of his forefinger. "Your skin is as soft as the down on a bird's wings and it makes me long to touch you every time you draw near." His hands went to her shoulders and slowly caressed their way to her hands. He took both hands in his own and brought them up to his lips. He placed a kiss on the back of each hand. "Your hands, no matter their condition, are an extension of the warmth and honor and grace inside you. Aye, they wield a sword, but not for personal glory, only to aid those in need and to protect those you love."

She could feel tears burning behind her eyes and she quickly closed her lids to hide them. His words touched her, but it was the sincerity in the eyes looking into her own that sent a spiral of joy rippling through her, and the warmth of something else, something special that she did not want to name.

"Open your eyes, Brianna. Look at me."

Her eyes opened to find him smiling down at her.

"When I look at you I see beauty and strength. Your father was mistaken about so many things."

This time she could not stop the tears that came to her eyes. Her throat tightened. "You have no idea how much that means to me."

He gazed at her with surprise and anger and something else... "I need to ask you something that has been weighing on my mind for some time now." He hesitated a moment before he continued. "When I stopped by Rosslyn Castle to find you, your father talked about you as though you were dead. His steward, Judson, was the one who let me know where I might find you." His voice was silky smooth, almost a whisper. "What happened after you returned home from Teba? Your father used to dote on you. That he would say cruel things to you and cut you out of his life makes no sense."

Brianna tried to smile, but found her lips were trembling. Her heart pounded jerkily with a queer sort of panic. "I can't talk about my father. I won't."

Simon nodded. "When you are ready to talk about it, I am here to listen." He leaned forward and brushed a kiss against her cheek with velvet tenderness.

Her throat tightened all the more. Not once during the past several days in Simon's presence had she thought about her father's abandonment. She'd thought only about living life with a purpose once more. The purpose Simon had given back to her. She frowned and brought her gaze back to him. Perhaps she did own him an explanation.

"Perhaps someday I'll tell you what happened between us, but not now."

He nodded and offered her a gentle smile. "We can both focus on the 'between now and then' moments for a while."

"Agreed." The pressure in her chest eased and she leaned her head against Simon's chest once more.

"Rest for a few moments, then we will prepare to ride out." He settled her beside him and drew her into his arms. A breeze that was cool but not chill swirled through their private shelter, touching her cheeks and tugging at her hair, bringing with it the heady scent of greens and rich damp earth. Instead of pain, she suddenly found herself filled with hope — the hope that they would triumph over de la Roche and his army, that she could put her father's anger behind her, and for a future with the man who held her so tightly in his arms — if only her dream of Simon's death did not come true.

Simon!

Brianna's eyes flew open, her heart pounding with terror.

Blood. Simon. Death.

Nay!

Then as she came fully awake, a shudder of relief ran through her. A dream. It was only a dream.

Simon lay cradled to her in the small shelter, breathing the deep, even cadence of sleep. His arms were around her in a loose embrace as she stared into his face. Peaceful. Calm.

Then the image came again. Simon dropping to his knees. De la Roche standing over him, his sword held as to strike. The sword coming down toward his neck…

She drew in a harsh breath. Her dreams did not always come true. She'd only had the dream because she'd been thinking of Simon before she'd slept as well as her father and her brothers. 'Twas her own pain and anger that had no doubt tricked her into this nightmare.

But what if these images were a true vision? What if Simon were to die in such a barbaric manner?

The pain that tore through her was unbearable. She gasped.

Simon's eyes flew open. "Brianna?"

Her trembling hands reached out to touch his face. Warm, vibrant, filled with life.

His gaze filled with concern. "What is it?"

She did not want to speak of it, to give it any hook into either her or his reality. She had to forget the images. Bury them deep inside her.

"Was it another dream?" he asked.

She nestled closer to his warmth. "Aye, but it's gone now."

"By your trembling, I'd say it still lingers. Do you wish to discuss it?"

She nestled deeper into his shoulder. "Nay. The dream is gone."

He chuckled. "Because you willed it so?"

She looked at him then. "Exactly. If I give it no merit, it will never come to pass."

"You dreamed of my death again. Didn't you?"

"Nay," she lied. Destiny could be fought just as any other battle. The things she saw did not necessarily have to happen, not if she were careful. Had she not changed her own fate once before? Her father had sent her to the forest to die. That had not come to pass because she had refused to die. It had been her strength of will that had taken her from the forest and the dangers lurking there, to Abigail and the home they'd shared together.

She would meet fate head-on this time as well, not for herself, but for Simon. Simon would be safe. She would give him everything she had inside herself — her strength, her determination, her love.

She startled at the thought. Love. She did love him, had loved him for years. Joy cascaded through her, rippling, forming circles of radiance. It didn't matter what horrible darkness had brought them back into each other's lives.

Simon made her forget all that and see only the good things, remember the good times.

Love.

She bit down on her lip, studying Simon. Should she tell him? Not yet. It was too soon, too fresh in her own heart. And she didn't want to discuss anything that might bring forth even more of Simon's already over-protective instincts. She had to stay beside him as they confronted de la Roche. It was the only answer to changing the fate she had envisioned.

They had to stay together.

Blood. Simon. Death.

He would not die at de la Roche's hand. Not if she could still hold a sword in either one of hers.

Chapter Eighteen

They were still half a day's travel from Pennyghael Abbey. But he wanted this conflict to happen here, deeper in the forest where no one could help Lockhart if they witnessed his time of need.

No Templars could help him. No Highlanders could intercede. The man was all his.

De la Roche pulled the hood of his monk's robe up around his face as his nervous horse danced beneath him. The beast could sense his anticipation. His prey was so close now. The horse he recognized as Lockhart's and a rider crested a hill, emerging from the trees, before the land dropped away into the valley.

Simon Lockhart was concealed within the folds of those mud brown robes. De la Roche knew that bastard anywhere.

Satisfaction warmed his chest as he clutched the sword hidden within the folds of his robe. He'd managed to ride ahead of the Templar under the cover of the forest and appear at the head of his army, ready to take the Templar down — a hundred soldiers to one. The Templar would never survive. The conflict was hardly a fitting test for the power of Joyeuse, de la Roche admitted to himself with a flicker of regret. But it would have to do until the rest of the Templars arrived to avenge their fallen brother.

De la Roche rubbed his pitted cheek and watched the man on the lone horse ride closer. His hand tightened on the hilt of his sword. He would be the one to sever the man's head from his body. He'd send the head back to the Brotherhood as a challenge; then he'd burn what was left of the body.

The Templars would rise to his challenge. They always did.

Lockhart came closer. He could hear the footfalls of the fool's horse against the damp earth.

He paused as another sound came to him, a soft rumble, growing in intensity with every heartbeat. Suddenly, the sight of a hundred men rose above the ridge behind the Templar. Fury seethed inside him at the sight of additional men. How had Lockhart managed that feat? Had he gathered more forces to him while de la Roche had maneuvered around him in the forest?

Fury shot through de la Roche. Lockhart had been told to come alone. "Philippe!" de la Roche yelled to his captain.

"I see them, Your Excellency. What are your orders?"

Frustration and rage churned within de la Roche and he desperately fought to keep his temper. "My orders are to attack, you fool! What else? Attack! Leave not a one of them alive. But Lockhart is mine. Understand?"

Philippe nodded and returned to the men.

De la Roche narrowed his gaze and leaned forward on his horse. With a supreme sense of satisfaction, he drew Joyeuse from his robe and leapt forward to greet his prey.

Iain had felt his enemy even before he cleared the ridge. Looking down on de la Roche with his army fanned out behind him like a blanket of evil only proved it. They had come for Simon. A hundred Highlanders would meet the French army instead. Iain felt his muscles go taut and he reached for his sword, careful to keep his hood in place until the very last.

Death was inevitable in this life. That his own death would spare another's brought him a small sense of justice. He might live if he were very lucky. The odds, however, appeared to be against them. A thousand trained warriors, armed with France's finest weapons would greet a rag-tag group of

Highlanders that he'd managed to scrape together as he rode toward the fate that awaited him.

He prepared to engage his enemy. "For Scotland!" he shouted as he surged forward.

So quickly the enemy came. The violence of their charge left carnage in its wake as the first volley of arrows found their targets in the bodies of the first charge. A barrage of men came at them with swords draw, flashing in the sunset at their backs.

Iain had eyes for only one such warrior. De la Roche bore down upon Iain on the back of a white horse. The beast appeared as fearsome as the rider with its mouth agape, eyes bulging, shod hooves striking sparks against the granite of the hillside. The hood of the man's robe slid back, revealing Iain's enemy — enemy to all the Templars.

De la Roche.

"I'll have your head, Simon Lockhart!" the Frenchman cried. "I'll have it off your shoulders and delivered to your precious Templar brothers, you bloody savage!"

Iain released a harsh breath along with a prayer as he met the whoosh of the man's sword, feeling the power of the strike clear to his bones. He tumbled over the back of his horse and to the ground. He clenched his fist around his hilt. With his other hand he clutched the hood of his robe against his face and prepared for another strike.

De la Roche turned his horse and came at him again, bearing down on him with furious speed. Iain was up on his feet in time to duck beneath the whistling slice of de la Roche's sword as it passed over his head. The blade dipped further down. Iain threw himself against the earth to avoid the blow and came up instantly, his feet planted against the earth he loved. He drew breath and prepared himself as de la Roche came off his horse.

There was no speech between them. No sound but the screech and clangor of steel as their swords met, as Iain tried to hold his own, but de la Roche's strikes were too powerful, as though something aided him.

The Frenchman's sword sparked in the setting sun as it came down at him again and again, draining him of strength. De la Roche held his ground, forcing Iain back, further and further into the melee around him. He slipped on the bodies of the fallen Highlanders and their blood as it turned the green grass red. Time slowed as he countered de la Roche's strikes. Around him he heard the cries of the dying, saw the blood-stained faces and bodies of his countrymen, and smelled the acrid taste of blood, fear, war, and death in the very air he breathed.

His lungs were afire and pain riddled his body. He retreated further into the fighting, staggered, stumbled. His hood came down.

De la Roche's eyes went wide as he stared at Iain's face. Iain took advantage of the man's shocked disbelief and thrust his sword into the Frenchman's abdomen. A deep red stain blossomed like a hideous flower across de la Roche's lower half. De la Roche's eyes bulged and his face paled, but he did not fall. Instead, he drew back, freeing his body from the weapon.

"Damn you, Lockhart!" he growled to his non-present enemy. "Damn you to hell!"

Fear fluttered in Iain's stomach as a look of hatred darkened de la Roche's face.

"You'll pay for his insolence!" De la Roche charged, wild and undisciplined, fueled by his rage. He brought his sword up then down against Iain's, slicing his weapon clean through.

Iain tossed the blunted weapon aside and drew his dagger. He tried to toss the blade at de la Roche's chest, but the man struck it away with a clean, sharp blow of his own sword, sending the smaller weapon spinning to the ground.

De la Roche charged.

Iain struck out with his fists, connected with the man's nose a heartbeat before the man's weapon sank into his chest. Flame bloomed near his heart. Blood spilled from the wound, drenching his robe. Iain staggered, went to one knee. His chest heaved as he tried to catch his breath, to fill his damaged lungs with precious air.

He bled. He hurt. He prayed it would be over soon. If he could not win, he wanted to die swiftly and with honor. He straightened his back and forced his gaze to his enemy's.

De la Roche's face twisted with triumph. "I'll take down every last one of you before I'm done. Joyeuse is too powerful a sword, and with it I am invincible."

"No one is invincible," Iain forced the words past his pain.

"We'll see about that." De la Roche's sword came down, arcing out of the red sky of sunset; a blinding slash of steel bit deep into Iain's neck.

A wild rustle of wings shivered through the air as birds suddenly left their trees for the sky.

Brianna stared into the sunset over the water of the Firth of Lorne. Something didn't feel right. There was an emptiness suddenly that filled the fading night sky, as though some form of goodness had been taken from the earth. Her throat tightened as a soft gasp escaped her.

"What is it, Brianna? What's wrong?"

She shook her head, still staring out at the sky. "Did you feel anything different a moment ago?"

"Different how?" Simon came up to stand behind her and looped his arms around her waist.

"I can't say exactly." The birds returned to the trees, she noted with a sigh. The odd sensation lingered, but she brushed it aside and pressed her head back against Simon's shoulder. "One more day and we will be at Pennyghael Abbey where we will meet up with Iain and the others."

Simon turned her to face him. "It will be good to put all this behind us. De la Roche has been terrorizing this land for far too long. Perhaps we shouldn't stop here for tonight, but ride for the clans MacDougall and Maclean of Mull. We'll need as much help as we can get to take back Joyeuse."

This time a sensation of rightness came over her as she met Simon's gaze. "Gathering the clans, involving them in what happens next, gives all of us, Highlander and Templar a chance to protect the country and the people we love." At the word, an aching, loving tenderness filled her heart.

"Are you ready to ride out before we lose the light?"

When she nodded, he leaned down and gave her a long, slow kiss that spoke the words he did not say aloud. It was enough for now. Perhaps someday in the future he would tell her what she longed to hear.

The horses were saddled and ready in the distance. Simon waved her ahead of him, then joined her, matching his longer stride to hers. A giggle worked its way up inside her as they strode toward the horses.

His stride grew longer. She matched it.

He glanced at her and a mischievous grin tugged at the corner of his mouth. He walked faster and faster. Brianna kept pace until they were both running for the horses. A leap and they were both on their animals' backs, sprinting forward into the hazy light of dusk. As they raced across the open land, their laughter merged, floating upward, once again sending the birds from the trees.

Brianna smiled as a bittersweet joy filled her. Their situation was dire, their destiny unknown, but some things never changed no matter what. And she and Simon would battle it out with swords or sticks or on the back of a horse for the rest of their lives.

She looked to the sky and said a silent prayer that their time together would be longer than just a few more hours. If they survived the coming conflict, then they could look forward to many heated battles in the future.

Nothing would make her happier than to battle it out with Simon for the rest of her life.

The next morning, De la Roche led his men onward, along the shoreline toward Pennyghael Abbey. He rode at the front of his army. His men would follow him wherever he led, and they would give him his dreams.

Last night he and his army had set up camp after they'd killed the false Lockhart and his band of men. De la Roche had needed Philippe to attend his wound. The Scottish knight's sword had pierced his flesh, but not his organs. Oh, how he wished he still possessed the Holy Grail. With the artifact, he would have healed in no time, and not had to endure the pain that riddled him now.

Angered by the ordeal he'd had to endure, de la Roche had sent a powerful message to Lockhart along with one of the Macleans that he'd left alive. The Highlander headed for Duart Castle, his home — a home that would not be his for much longer. Now that the Highlanders were involved, de la Roche would show no mercy to anyone. Lockhart's deception and his involvement with the Highlanders had only strengthened de la Roche's resolve to succeed, to conquer.

He could feel victory like a fire in his bones. In that moment, de la Roche felt the hand of destiny close about him. He would take Scotland. Scotland would become a warrior nation, his warrior nation. He would lead those who followed him through England, France, and through the entire continent, until he had gained the empire he deserved.

He would build an empire such as the world had never seen. He who had begun his life as an insignificant bastard tossed away with all those who carried the pox. He would show them all.

His army had not been marching long when smoke rising from a village greeted them. De la Roche narrowed his gaze on the site. His men would strike the sleepy little village. He had no illusions that this would be a worthy battle, but his men needed something to whet their appetites for what was to come. He needed them to feel the same hunger that burned in his soul. They would feel the power and the rewards of being his army.

He drew his sword, raised it. Behind him the others did the same. They charged. They slaughtered, until the smell of blood was heavy in the air.

When they were through, they moved on toward Pennyghael Abbey, leaving a conquered country in their wake.

Chapter Nineteen

Simon and Brianna reached Duart Castle, home of the Clan Maclean, at dawn the next day. Deep into the night, growing as weary as the horses, they'd stopped for a few hours' rest. Simon knew he was pushing Brianna hard, but they had to keep ahead of schedule if they were to gather the men they needed and arrive as he'd arranged with his men.

Outside the castle walls, Simon announced Brianna and himself, and the gates came up to allow them access into the bailey. Lachlan Maclean and five of his men waited there with swords in hand. If the stony looks on their faces were any indication, the Macleans were not eager to see them. "Brother Simon," Lachlan greeted them with a slight bow as they dismounted. "What can the Templars want from us now?"

Simon frowned, puzzled by his strange words. "Why do you say such things? What has happened?"

Lord Maclean's gaze narrowed. "You do not know?"

Simon's anger rose. "We just arrived. What am I to know?"

The head of the Macleans signaled his men to sheath their swords. "Your man, Iain, stopped here two days past, searching for warriors to help him. Over a hundred of my men left here with him."

Simon relaxed, pleased to hear Iain had already been so successful in gathering the forces they needed. "All is well. Iain is waiting for me to arrive on the morrow before we go into battle."

"All is not well." Lord Maclean motioned impatiently for one of his men to come forward with a rough cloth sack. The man opened the cloth and reached inside to pull out Iain's severed head.

Brianna gasped and her eyes widened in alarm. "Iain…"

Anger and pain rushed through Simon. "What happened?" he asked, his voice pinched.

The battered-looking Maclean bowed his head, but not before Simon saw agony fill the young man's gaze. He'd been at the battle with Iain. "The Frenchman … his army … they killed them all. The man you are after, this de la Roche, he has the sword Joyeuse. He is invincible."

"No one is invincible, not even de la Roche with that sword," Simon said with deadly softness. "If you and your men follow me, I will show you just how wrong you are. My men are gathering other clan members and all will converge on Pennyghael Abbey before sunset this eve. We will take de la Roche and his men down. Scotland will be freed of his tyranny once and for all."

"Nay!" Lord Maclean's eyes blazed down at him. "We have sacrificed enough already. How many more of us would you have slain at that monster's hand?"

"He will continue to terrorize this land if we do not stop him."

Lord Maclean's body went rigid. "My clansmen cannot risk any more lives."

"And if de la Roche lives, not just your men, but your wives and daughters will be at stake."

"I am willing to take that risk."

"I am not." He turned to Brianna. "Come. We will continue on our way."

She stepped toward Lord Maclean's men. "Not without Iain. He was a good man, and he gave his life for what he believed in. We might only have this small part of him left, but even that part deserves a proper burial."

With a look of sorrow, the man replaced Iain's head in the sack and handed it to Brianna. "All righteous men deserve a proper burial."

"Then we will see to the proper burial of your slain men as soon as we are through with de la Roche."

He nodded, but did not meet her eyes. "We thank you."

"Come, Brianna, we have much to accomplish before this day is through," Simon said, reaching for the cloth sack. "I will ride with Iain." They mounted silently and he kicked his horse, sending the beast cantering down the path from which they had come.

"Where do we go now?" Brianna asked when they'd cleared the gates of the castle.

"Our last hope is to gather men from Lord MacDougall at Aros Castle farther up the western coast."

"Will they help us?"

He shrugged. "Only one way to find out." He encouraged his horse into a gallop. They had to keep up their frantic pace if they were to arrive at Pennyghael Abbey before nightfall.

The sun continued its slow, inexorable trek into the sky. Quickly, warming rays slid across the ground, casting the lush, green landscape in morning light.

A seagull glided effortlessly through the cloudless blue sky, then down along the sea cliffs off to their left. Simon turned his face toward the morning sun. A sigh-soft breeze ruffled his hair, caressed his cheeks. The normal joy he might have felt in the moment was gone, as Iain's head bumped the side of his horse with each step the beast took.

Simon reined his horse to a stop.

"Why are we stopping?" Brianna asked, as she came to a stop beside him.

"We are going to bury Iain here."

"This is nice," she said, surveying the view out across the water. "Iain would like it here."

He forced a smile. She always found something hopeful in every situation. "Aye, he would." Simon slid off his horse and strode to the edge of a cliff. He set the sack down so that Iain's sightless eyes faced the view. "Let's build him a cairn. Help me collect rocks?"

With Brianna working silently at his side, it did not take long to build the cairn to serve as Iain's resting place forever more.

Simon took a shuddering breath as he knelt down beside the gravesite as he set the last rock. Iain had given up his life pretending to be Simon. He tightened his fists as he tried to think of something else, tried desperately not to let himself wallow in despair. He needed to remain strong and in control for the battle ahead.

Brianna touched his shoulder.

He jerked at her touch, then stilled, trying to silence the hammering of his heart.

"It is just to mourn him." She rubbed his back in soothing circles.

"He was a good friend to do what he did for me." He looked up at her. Their eyes met. Empathy drew her brows together and tightened her mouth. She leaned closer. The familiar scent of heather surrounded him, wrapped him in familiar warmth. She pushed back the unruly lock that fell over his brow, all while offering him her silent strength.

She extended her hand. "And you will always remember the sacrifice he made."

He took her hand and allowed her to pull him to his feet. "I fear others will sacrifice their lives if we cannot convince the MacDougalls to join us. I know of one MacDougall from my early days with the Templars. Let us pray he is still amongst his kin. He will be crucial in helping me convince the others that our cause is a worthy one."

She did not release his hand, instead squeezing it affectionately and offering him a smile. "Then let us hope your friend is there."

"Hector can be persuasive when offered the right motivation."

"What can we offer him that might motivate him to help us?" Brianna asked. "We cannot give him the Grail, and we have nothing else of value."

"We won't need to offer the man anything that is of this world. All we need offer is the chance at battle. The man craves excitement. No doubt these last years of the Templars' disbandment have been a sore test to his patience. Let's go offer that motivation, shall we?"

Brianna and Simon arrived at Aros Castle later that morning. The gates were opened at their approach and a large well-muscled man with a Scottish claymore strapped to his back rode over the drawbridge to greet them. His gaze narrowed on them as he approached. "Stinger?" he said gruffly. "Is that you?" he asked in a thick, accented voice.

"Aye, 'tis I, Hector."

The man laughed as he slid off his horse. He came toward them with his arms outstretched. "God's blood, Stinger, it's been too long."

Simon dismounted. "Indeed, old friend."

Hector's gaze shifted from Simon to Brianna. "You are keeping different company than you have in the past."

"More pleasant than your company," Simon said as he signaled for Brianna to dismount and come join them. "Allow me to introduce Brianna Sinclair."

Hector raised one dark brow. "Are you still a Templar, man?"

"Aye, my friend. That is why we are here. I need an army."

"Sounds serious."

"It is," Simon agreed.

"Then we'd best do this inside the castle's walls." He let out a shrill whistle and two young boys came forward over the drawbridge to gather the horses. "Sam and Tate will care for the animals. Follow me." As he turned back toward the gatehouse, he clapped Simon on the shoulder. "Truly, 'tis good to see you, Simon. I've heard rumblings from other clans that things are not going well for the Templars in this land at present."

"You've heard right." They crossed over the drawbridge and entered the square bailey where forty men stood in a single line, awaiting orders from someone.

"Hector, are you in charge here?" Simon asked.

The man smiled. "Aye. I had to do something to pass the time. I've been organizing not just the MacDougalls, but the MacKinnons as well."

Brianna's eyes went wide. "Are these all of your men?"

Hector laughed. "Nay, these are just a few of the knights. We have nearly a hundred and ten knights, three score of archers, as well as squires and servants to tend them all."

Simon paused as he took in the numbers. "You never did do anything in a small way."

Hector laughed again. "Why do you need an army?"

"To battle a Frenchman named de la Roche."

Hector nodded. "I've heard of the troubles he's caused the Templars recently."

"He's attacking more than the Templars now. His army slaughtered over a hundred men yesterday — Templars and Highlanders both."

Hector's gaze turned dark, dangerous. "Then my army is yours. I'll need a day to get them ready to move out."

Brianna frowned. "We don't have a day. We must meet our enemy tonight at Pennyghael Abbey before he slays the other Templars who await us there."

Hector looked to Simon for confirmation. At Simon's nod, he frowned. "Getting the men ready will take some time, but we can do our best to have the company ready in a few hours." He turned to his men. "Prepare for battle, men, and with all due haste!"

The men turned to do his bidding.

Simon nodded. "Thank you, my friend."

Hector turned to Brianna. "While we wait for the men to prepare, would you like to have something to eat?"

Brianna looked to Simon. "Do we have time? I am truly famished and your kindness would be most appreciated."

"We have time," Simon agreed.

"Then you can also meet my other guest." Hector's smile slipped as he turned to Brianna once more. "I didn't consider it before ... when you were introduced ... are you by some chance any relation to Lord Henry Sinclair? He arrived yesterday morning, seeking warriors for hire to protect his estate. I have a few I can spare him and still have plenty for our battle with de la Roche."

Brianna's face paled.

Simon went to her side and slipped his arm around her waist, steadying her. She trembled beneath his touch. Pain blazed in her eyes, turning them glassy and overbright.

"Lord MacDougall," a thunderous voice boomed from across the bailey. Anger darkened the older man's expression as he strode forward. "What's this about you going to war?" He stopped before them. A ruddy flush came to his cheeks.

At her sides, Brianna's hands curled into tight, white fists.

"Brianna, what's wrong?" Simon asked, his own voice tight at the pain and anxiety he read on her face. "Is it him?" Simon reached for his sword.

Brianna reached out and stayed his movement as the older man's gaze met hers.

Dark, deep-set eyes widened, then narrowed as though measuring her. Lips which hinted at an intense, silent pride were drawn into a taut, disapproving line. "You should be dead."

She straightened. "As you can see, I am not."

"I suppose God has been merciful where I was not."

Brianna's breath expelled in a gust of pain. "I did not know you were here or I would have spared you from thinking anything other than what you choose to believe."

"Brianna." Simon's expression hardened. "Is this man your father?"

She gave Simon a look that sliced right through him. "Aye, Lord Henry Sinclair is my father."

Chapter Twenty

"Why are you here?" Brianna asked her father. She couldn't believe it was him. She'd never expected to see him again. He looked as he always had — stern and angry, yet he'd aged as well in the last year since she'd seen him. Gray streaks peppered his once dark hair and lines wreathed his eyes and mouth.

"My business matters not to you." His eyes filled with their usual disappointment. "You are nothing to me anymore."

Brianna swallowed against the familiar pain that lodged in her throat. She took a step back, trying to pull a veil of numbness around her. But the pain of his rejection forced its way through.

You'll never be a knight. You're a failure. You murdered your brothers with your ruse of being a knight. You are worthless to me. Leave now, before I kill you myself for your treachery.

A suffocating feeling swamped her at the memory of her father's painful words. "I am glad to see you well, Father. Now if you'll excuse me, I must—" She never finished her sentence as she turned and ran for her horse. She kicked it into a headlong gallop over the drawbridge and into the valley beyond.

She heard Simon call her name, but she didn't stop until she was well away from the castle. Then she slipped from her horse, staggered a few feet, and was violently sick.

A failure. A murderer.

"God's blood!" Simon dismounted beside her and drew her into his arms.

"I will not go back there—"

"No one is asking you to go back," Simon said softly. "If you'd told me about him … I don't understand. God's blood, Brianna, what happened between you and your father?"

She staggered away from him to lean against a tree. "I tried not to think about him, about how he hurt me."

Simon gripped his sword. "You know I would never allow him to harm you."

She closed her eyes and leaned her head back against the trunk. "He doesn't harm me physically, Simon. If he did, I could hold my own against him." The bitter hint of a smile pulled up her lips at the thought. "Nay, he hurts me with his disapproval and with his vicious tongue. I have never been the daughter he wanted. He wanted a sweet docile thing who would do as he bid. Instead, he got a daughter who longs to carry a sword and to fight for the injustices she sees in this world. And then there are my dreams…"

She opened her eyes, looked at Simon. "He thinks I'm mad." She wrapped her arms around her stomach.

"He dismisses your visions?"

"He's always told me my visions are the work of the Devil. That I must repent and turn from my own folly." She started to shake. "When I was fifteen, he sent me away from Rosslyn Castle to a convent so that I could exercise the demons from my mind. He didn't understand that I couldn't stop the visions. They have always been a part of me."

In a heartbeat, she was in his arms, her head pressed against his chest. "Tell me all of it, Brianna. For I know there is more."

She couldn't stop the tremors wracking her body. She pressed herself against Simon, taking the warmth and security he offered her. He curled his hand around the nape of her neck and anchored her to him. His eyes fastened on hers. Now was the time to tell him the truth. The awful, humiliating, painful truth. She swallowed hard. Although she wanted to, she didn't turn away.

"At the convent, the abbess was the first person to truly see my gift for what it was. She was the one who sent me to Brother Kenneth and the Templars. Her prayers had told her that my destiny was somehow linked to that Order, not to the nunnery."

"What about Teba? What happened after I sent you home?"

Anguish reflected in Simon's gaze, mirroring her own. "He blamed me for William and John's deaths. He sees me as their murderer."

"They died alongside hundreds of others," Simon whispered. "There is nothing you could have done to save them."

"I could have fought with them," she said softly.

He drew a sharp breath. "I sent you away. I see now why you were so upset with me when I first came for you at Abigail's inn. Had I not sent you away, Brianna, you would most likely have died along with your brothers."

"I know that now." She sighed. "I knew that then. I just felt so helpless."

"We all did."

She nodded jerkily. "When I came home, my father was filled with rage, then sorrow for the loss of his sons, and I became the focus of his anger once more. He disowned me, forced me to leave with only my sword and a horse. That's when I made my way to Abigail's where you found me."

"Do you want revenge against your father? Revenge can be very sweet."

"Nay! I could never do such a thing."

"Then you are a better woman than he is a man."

"The only thing I want to do is leave this place and him behind." She dropped her gaze to the earth at her feet.

"We can leave now. I had a feeling that would be your preference. Before I came after you I told Lord MacDougall to follow with his men when they are ready."

She looked up at Simon, at the understanding in his gaze. He bought her gaze to his with a finger beneath her chin. "Not all men are as your father, Brianna. I will never hurt you like he did. I respect your visions just as I have always respected your skill with a sword. It is not something that comes from the Devil. It is divinely sent. Never forget that."

The pain in her chest eased. "Thank you, Simon."

"Don't move," he said, going to his horse.

She didn't think she could move if she tried. Never in her life had she felt this lifeless and weak.

He returned a moment later with a cloth and a bladder of water and washed her face as if she were a small child. He offered her the water to cleanse her mouth. "Better?"

"Much," she replied.

He helped her sit on the ground and drew her back into his arms, cradling her. "What happened to your mother?"

"She died when I was very young." A smile came to her lips at the memory of her mother. "Even as a child I wanted to be a warrior. Each time I picked up a stick and used it as a sword, my father punished me. My mother, on the other hand, encouraged me to toddle after my brothers with that stick. Even then, I knew how to best them." Brianna drew a deep breath. "Had she lived, my life would have been very different."

She could feel the muscles of his chest tense. "Brianna, had I known about your father, or even your brothers, I might have treated you differently myself."

"You mean you would have let me stay in the battle?" Her throat tightened with unshed tears.

"Never." He frowned down at her, but his eyes were soft. "But I would have treated you more kindly after I discovered you were a girl in the midst of the Templars."

"I deserved no kindness for my deception." Tears burned behind her eyes.

"You deserved understanding," Simon said. "I have seven sisters. Growing up, I saw them long for things they could never have in this world of men." His jaw tightened. "I did what I could for them at the time. Just as I tried to do what I could for you with the Templars."

"I know you did." At his words, the last vestiges of her control shattered. A single tear slid down her cheek. Another tear fell, then another.

She was crying, for goodness sake. She never cried. She wiped the tears from her cheeks, but they kept falling, faster than she could wipe.

"Let them fall, Brianna. I'll take care of you." He gathered her closer.

The sentiment made Brianna's breath catch and her tears fall harder. She cried for it all: she cried for her mother who had died too young; for the father who had thrown his daughter out into the world without remorse. She cried for the uncertainty that lay ahead of them, for her own unfulfilled dream of being a knight.

"It's all right," he whispered the words over and over, making her feel something she hadn't felt in a long while … protected and safe. Silence settled around them as he simply held her, letting her tears work their healing magic. Gradually, her trembling melted away and her torrent of tears ceased until there was only the two of them, warm and comfortable and at peace.

Far away a hawk screeched. The vibrating, scratchy sound floated on the afternoon breeze and then disappeared.

"Brianna?"

She stiffened, suddenly afraid to look at him. No one had ever seen her this vulnerable before. What should she say?

She shifted her gaze to his, at the non-condemning look in his dark eyes; something unfurled in her soul. "I never thought I'd say this, but thank you for making me leave Teba. If you hadn't I wouldn't be here with you now. We wouldn't be sharing this moment." Her throat tightened. "And thank you for understanding my tears." She could say nothing more against the knot in her throat.

"My pleasure," he said with a grin that sent warmth sliding through her. "Let's not make that a habit, though. With seven sisters, I've had plenty of tears in my life."

Unexpected laughter crept up Brianna's throat and burst into a bright, musical sound in the afternoon air. She smiled. "I'm quite done."

Simon's laughter joined hers, mingled, merged, and floated high overhead. Brianna stared at the man before her. A breeze ruffled his hair and the afternoon sun cast him in a pale gold light. Her breath caught. The laughter inside her faded and was replaced with a quiet sense of wonder. She realized in that moment just how handsome Simon was. His eyes weren't just dark. They were midnight blue, the color of the sea. And just like the sea he was storm and calm, always changing, never the same.

The moment seemed to lengthen as Simon's laughter died, and a thick, charged silence followed. Brianna reached up and touched his face. She brushed a lock of hair back from his eyes. Her fingers strayed to the strong, straight line of his cheekbone and followed it in a single brushing stroke.

Words, dozen of them, pushed through her mind, but none of them came to her mouth. What could she say to this man who had rescued her not once, not twice, but three times — from Teba, de la Roche, and now from her father? He'd given her back her laughter and made her smile when all she'd wanted to do was run. She owed him so much.

Silence stretch between them until it was broken by the call of a hawk high overhead. "We should be going if we are to meet Kaden and the men as planned," Simon said.

She nodded. "It's time." It was time for so many things — time to confront de la Roche and time to step into their future, whatever that might be.

Simon started to get up, but Brianna pulled him back to her. She pressed a kiss to his lips, lingering there for only a heartbeat before she pulled away. "I love you," she whispered against his cheek. "I expect no words in return, for I know you are not fully free to say them to me. But I wanted you to know before we go into this battle what is in my heart. What has always been in my heart."

He pulled her tightly against his chest. "There will be plenty of time to speak of such things when we are through." He released her. "Until then." His dark eyes filled with promise.

Brianna swallowed back the sudden lump that came to her throat. Aye, there would be plenty of time if her vision did not come true. She closed her eyes and said a sudden prayer that for once in her life she'd be wrong about the images that had come to her.

Please let me be wrong!

Any peace or serenity that had settled over Brianna was broken by the sound of hoofbeats approaching from the castle. She looked up from her position in Simon's arms to see something she'd never expected.

Her father.

"Brianna Sinclair. Don't you run away from me," he called as he brought his horse to a stop a short distance from the tree near where they sat. He dismounted and hurried toward them.

Brianna scrambled to her feet. A wave of fear moved through her at the almost desperate eagerness in his expression.

Simon came to his feet and reached for his sword. Brianna stalled his movements, laying her hand over his.

"I'll not let him hurt you again," Simon said.

"Ready the horses. This won't take long." She stepped away from Simon, moving to her father's side. From the corner of her eye, she could see that Simon did not move away. He stood nearby, his hand firmly on the hilt of his sword.

He would protect her even now.

She would have smiled had she been less afraid. Her hands were shaking. She took a deep breath, steadied herself, and looked her father straight in the eyes. "Father," she acknowledged, as he stopped ten paces from her.

The eagerness in his expression died. His face paled as his gaze lit upon her sword. "I've taken everything from you. I've called you names. I've aligned you with the Devil himself." He released a shuddering sigh. "I've given you every reason to hate me, and to use that weapon on me. And yet, you do not. Why?"

"Because you are my father. Regardless of how you feel about me, I would never do anything to hurt you."

He shook his head. "It makes no sense. Your brothers would have sought retribution had I treated them the same way."

Brianna's fear ebbed. She straightened. "As you have more than once pointed out, I am not my brothers."

"Nay," he agreed, worrying his hands in front of him. "That you are not."

Silence fell between them until Brianna asked, "Was that what you wanted to say to me? If you are through, Simon and I are needed elsewhere." She fixed him with a pointed stare.

The man shivered beneath her gaze. His throat worked, but he said nothing, as though words suddenly failed him.

That had never happened before.

Brianna frowned. "Was there something more?"

A flicker of sadness passed over his lined face. "I came out here— I had to say—" He broke off and looked away. "I should never have forced you to go to the abbey."

The muscles of her stomach tightened at his admission. It was the first time he had ever admitted any wrongdoing on his part, and yet he did not reach out to her as a father would. He couldn't even meet her eyes. "How would my not going to the abbey have changed anything?"

"It was all my fault. I should never have sent you away."

Brianna's frown increased at her father's words. Simon took a protective step closer. With a shake of her head, she stilled Simon's advance.

Her father looked up at the afternoon sky. "I am beginning to see that if I had not sent you away, none of this would have happened ... the Templars ... your brothers' deaths ... you wearing a sword."

At his words, any hope inside her died. He wasn't here to make amends or admit to any wrongdoing. He had come to her for a salve to his own guilt. And yet this time she felt no pain, only an easing, as if a burden had been lifted from her. Her father would never understand what was in her heart, or how the dreams of prophecy were a vital part of who she was. She was a warrior and a seerer. And those things did not make her evil. They made her special.

Brianna straightened at the realization.

Simon saw her gifts as special. The other Templars did as well. And she would use those gifts now to help save others. If her father wanted nothing of that, then so be it.

She moved to her father's side and placed a hand upon his arm. His gaze shot to hers. "I forgive you, Father, for never understanding me. I was brought into this world for a purpose. I know what that purpose is now."

She pulled her hand away. "If you'll excuse us, we must leave." Signaling to Simon, Brianna hastened to her horse, leaving a startled Henry Sinclair standing alone by the tree.

"Come, Simon. We have a battle to win."

Chapter Twenty-one

The day took on an unreal quality for Simon. It was as if he had entered a space without time as he and Brianna rode across the terrain.

De la Roche was close.

He could feel the man's presence on the back of his neck. Yet they had no idea where the Frenchman was. The bastard could pounce on them in an hour, at sundown, or even on the morrow. Simon stiffened. What was he doing? He was thinking like a sheep staked out for a lion. God's Blood, he might as well bare his chest for de la Roche's sword. Nay, he had to stop thinking the way de la Roche expected.

And, he wasn't in this battle alone. With Brianna by his side, they would be a mighty force. They had experience, and together they could outsmart the villain if only all the forces they had gathered arrived in time.

"What do you think de la Roche expects us to do next?" Simon asked the woman at his side as they rode toward Pennyghael Abbey.

"He'll expect us to come charging into battle, with tempers high and swords drawn," she replied.

He'd been thinking the same thing. "Then we should do the opposite."

"Methodical planning instead of full-force confrontation?" she asked with a hint of a smile.

He nodded. "We'll have to be one step ahead of de la Roche if we are to succeed."

Her smile slipped as they arrived at the abbey. They dismounted. "Now that we have arrived, how will we signal the others?"

"Do you remember how to signal in Templar code using abbey bells?"

"Bells?" she asked, then her eyes went wide and the smile returned to her face. "Aye. The abbey's bells will be heard by half the countryside."

Satisfaction rode through Simon at their new plan. "It is time for us to turn the tables and become the hunters instead of the prey."

Brianna took a step toward the abbey below. When he didn't follow she turned back to him. "Are you coming with me?"

"Nay. You go down there and send the message while I prepare things here."

She came back to stand before him. Determination lit her eyes. "We go together or not at all." She offered him her hand.

Together. He knew she was afraid to leave him alone now that they were so close to the conflict. Perhaps he should be more afraid of being alone... He slipped his fingers between hers. "We'll go together."

At Brianna and Simon's knock, an older, gray-haired monk opened the heavy wooden door of the abbey and looked upon them with suspicion despite Simon's monk's robe. "What brings you to our doorway, Brother?"

"Are you the abbot here?"

"Aye. I am known as Brother Emmanuel."

"Brother Emmanuel," Simon pulled to the hood back from his face, revealing himself fully. "I know this is most unusual, and I apologize, but we must beg use of your bell tower to alert others of our whereabouts."

The abbot's eyes went wide as he shook his head. "We want no trouble here. It is all we can do to hide ourselves away from that scoundrel who terrorizes this land."

"That is why we are here," Simon said loosening his robe further to reveal the Templar tunic he wore beneath the heavy robe.

The door opened wider as two other monks stepped forward from the darkened corners of the entry. "A Templar?"

"The Scottish Templars are assembling for a final stand against the Frenchman, de la Roche." Simon's gaze fixed on the abbot. "It is most urgent that we ring the bells. I promise to explain all as soon as we alert our Brothers of our location."

The abbot stepped back, as did the others, and waved Simon and Brianna toward the hallway. "Down and to the right, you'll find the staircase leading to the belfry there."

"Many thanks, my Brother," Simon said a moment before he and Brianna shot forward. Their footsteps echoed through the abbey as they made their way down the stone hallway, then up the stairs to the belfry tower.

From the height of the tower, Simon looked out over the land. They had reached their destination. It was time to alert the others. With a hand on the ropes, he paused. "Dear God," he whispered at the sight of de la Roche's army spreading like a blight across the gently sloping land. They were heading toward the abbey. One light spot that could only be de la Roche's white stallion led the mass forward.

The end was near.

"Help me ring the bells, Brianna. We must ring them now."

The staccato ringing filled the air. One ring, a pause, two rings, a longer pause. One ring, then three. The Templar warning to all who could hear to gather together and head toward the sound. Together, he and Brianna repeated the warning two more times before the bells fell silent. They'd done what they could do here.

Silently, they left the tower and strode once more toward the abbey door where several monks lined either side of the hallway, waiting.

"Simon?" Brianna asked as they neared.

"I see them. They will not stop us." He tightened his grip on Brianna's hand, needing the support her nearness offered.

"Blessed Jesu, we heard your call," a tall, slender monk stepped forward. "I am Brother Andrew." He bowed. "Some of us answered the Templar call years ago, then when the Order disbanded, we gathered here to continue our lives in peace and prayer. How can we help?"

"You were Templars?" Simon stared at the monks as the impact of Brother Andrew's words slid over him. Peace and prayer. How could he ask these men, even for a day, to become once again what they'd turned away from? Or if they kept their peaceful minds, would de la Roche's army tear their lives into shambles and horror?

"An army of considerable size approaches. If I were you, I would gather the monks and flee for safety."

Two of the monks stepped back into the shadows. "We must hurry if we are to escape."

"Hold." The abbot's voice echoed off the arched stone of the hallway. "Our calling might be of another nature in this time of great need."

The abbot and several other monks gathered behind Brother Andrew. "What if we chose to stay and fight?"

"You would do that?"

"The role of warrior is not one we take lightly, but we would rather accept the yoke of future penance than see our countrymen fall."

The two monks who had hidden in the shadows stepped forward. Anxiety turned their faces ashen, but they stood behind the other monks. "If the others fight, we will stand beside them."

Simon nodded in approval. "Then prepare yourselves and meet us in front of the abbey when you are ready."

Brother Andrew bowed then turned to face the other monks. "Brother Michael, Brother Thomas, Brother Peter, to me," the monk-turned-sergeant said in a booming voice that the walls of Pennyghael Abbey had never before heard. "Brother Harold, Brother Silas, Brother Paul, you will go with the abbot. Alert the other monks that we are needed to fight once more. We have much to do and little time to do it in." The monks vanished through the open abbey doors as they set upon their tasks.

"I didn't expect that outcome," Brianna breathed beside Simon.

"Nor I." Simon paused at the doorway. Usually before a battle he felt very much alone. It was always him against death. One outcome or the other. He'd eluded death so far. Yet today, he did not feel the same aloneness as before other battles, even when he had battled with his fellow Templars. Today, Brianna's hand warmed his own, and the monks of this abbey had put aside their peace to spare others pain.

His body warmed as he reached for his sword. His hand closed around the hilt, feeling the familiar grooves of the intricate carvings as they fit themselves into the calluses of his palm. He knew with a surety the path his own life must take when this battle was over. He was not meant to be a monk. He needed peace, but not the kind he'd had in the past. He needed the peace and security of love. His gaze connected with Brianna's.

There were things in this world worth fighting for, worth killing for, worth dying for. All a man could do was to pick his causes with care and walk the path his heart told him to follow. He did not know if death awaited him this day as Brianna's dream had predicted, but he finally understood what was in his heart. "Brianna, I—"

"Simon!" Kaden shouted as he, Alaric, and Kendall rushed for them. "We were approaching the abbey when we heard the bells."

The words Simon longed to say stilled on his tongue. He would speak his heart to her when this battle was through.

With one last longing glance at Brianna, he turned toward his men. "How is Roinald?"

"He is stable, but too weak to travel with us," Kaden said. "We left him at the priory with Brother Kenneth. The rest of the monks there are heading this way along with Hector's men."

"That is good news. Come, we must ready ourselves." Simon moved to his horse, opened the saddle bag, and withdrew a white garment that he handed to Brianna. "This is yours. I saved it for you after it was taken away. I want you to have it now. Wear it in this battle if it will give you the courage and strength you'll need."

Brianna accepted the garment and stood staring at the bold red cross atop the white. "My Templar tunic." She looked up to meet his gaze. No tears shone in her eyes, but there was joy along with determination. "Thank you, Simon." With a smile, she donned the garment and fastened her belt and scabbard over the top; she tucked the Grail beneath her belt, obscuring it from view within the folds of her tunic.

Simon watched her dress. Memory flashed through his mind of a similarly dressed 'lad,' hair shorn and breasts bound. He released a soft sigh. That illusion no longer existed. There was only Brianna. Her feminine curves added shape and dimension to the otherwise shapeless tunic. Her wild hair spilled about her shoulders. And she looked every bit the warrior she had always hoped to be.

She was a warrior. She was a knight, in every sense of the word but one. And he had the power to change all that.

He drew his sword. "Kneel before me, Brianna."

Surprise wreathed her face as she dropped to one knee. "Simon?"

"As a knight, I may knight men, and women," he clarified, "on the battlefield when they show great bravery. You have already proven to me that you are brave and strong and worthy of the title." He drew his sword and brought the flat of the blade against her left shoulder. "Brianna Sinclair, do you promise to speak only the truth, to never avoid a dangerous path out of fear, to defend the weak, and protect those who have need?"

"I do," she said, her voice raw with emotion.

He brought the sword to her other shoulder and with a smile said, "Arise, Lady Brianna Sinclair, a knight of the Templars once more."

She stood and was instantly flooded with cheers and handshakes from Kaden and Alaric.

"We are honored to fight beside you, my lady," Kendall said.

She looked up at Simon then. Gratitude brightened her eyes, bathed him in its unfamiliar light, and something in his chest tightened. He felt special. Extraordinary, even. And there was something else in her eyes, something that filled him with longing, something he wanted so badly it made his stomach clench.

Images of their time together tumbled through his brain. He saw her bathed in sunlight as they travelled through the forest, wreathed in moonlight as they battled with quarterstaffs. He saw her lying against a bed of ferns with desire in her eyes, waiting for him to pull her into his arms, wrap her in warmth, and reveal the mysteries of life to her. He saw her battered and beaten after de la Roche had captured her, and he saw the strength in her eyes as she struggled to come back from the pain, learning to fight with her left hand.

An emotion both intense and primal surged inside him, erupting in a billow of breath. It was an emotion he had left behind him months ago on that battlefield in Teba. An emotion he had never expected to feel again. He let it form, let it swirl inside him, warm him in places that had long since dulled to anything but rote survival. It burst from him on a breath and seemed to fill the glorious space around him.

Hope.

For the first time in a long while, he felt a glimmer of hope even in this desperate situation.

All because of Brianna.

"Simon?"

He heard her voice through the pounding of his heart. He shook off the fog of memory, but clung to the feeling of hope. "Come," he said, reaching for her hand. "We have a battle to win."

Simon drew a fortifying breath as he appraised the battlefield. He, Brianna, Kaden, Alaric, and Kendall were all dressed in mail that lay beneath their Templar tunics. They would make their final stand against de la Roche here. In preparation, they'd set fires at intervals along the open field, with cauldrons set in the heart of the coals. The fires would help illuminate the battlefield as the day turned to night, and the tar within could be flung in hot, sputtering agony at the enemy as they advanced.

Next to the cauldrons were several bows and cloth-wound arrows that could be ignited by the flames and sent into the enemy's ranks as they thundered down the hill.

Brianna stood with the men with two swords at her back, one strapped to her side, and a dagger hidden in her boot. At her feet rested a stack of sharpened spears. The other men were similarly armed. They were few, but they were mighty. De la Roche should take heed.

"Where are the MacDougalls? Where are the monks? The five of us cannot hold de la Roche's masses back for long," Kaden said.

"They will be here. Give them time," Simon said with confidence.

"We have no more time if the tremors of the ground are any indication. De la Roche will appear over the ridge in only a matter of moments."

Simon, too had felt the tramping feet of a marching army, the heavy thud of horses and men come to attack. "Then we'd best take our places." Simon motioned toward the others, and he and Kaden took their positions. Kaden on the right flank, Simon beside Brianna. They lined themselves across the terrain. The five of them against an army of hundreds.

Simon swallowed roughly. The five of them could never hold the masses off until help arrived. He looked at each of the warriors beside him. He loved them all, and would proudly die beside them. "Until the end," he said, thrusting his sword into the air.

"To the end," they each shouted in reply, thrusting their swords high.

Simon held his sword at the ready. This was it.

The storm was not long in coming.

De la Roche appeared first, dressed in full armor. He and his men spilled over the rise and down the hillside. Simon had to admit, de la Roche was an impressive sight, riding forward, his hand curled around the hilt of Joyeuse. The late evening sun glinted off the blade, sending rays of orange and gold out before him.

De la Roche came to a halt two hundred paces from the five of them, forcing his army to stop behind him.

"Can we make this battle between the two of us?" Simon called across the divide.

Brianna drew a sharp breath beside him, but remained silent.

"Only if you sacrifice yourself to my sword. Perhaps then I might let the others live."

"He lies," Kaden growled. "Once you are dead he will continue his attack. Don't let him fool you."

Simon straightened. "I am aware of what de la Roche is capable." He had to stall for time.

Behind him, he heard the shuffle of footsteps as the monks of Pennyghael Abbey took their position behind the Templars. Twenty men stood with them, armed with swords and pitch forks and clubs. They wore no armor except for the crucifixes around their necks. Their faces wore looks of determination.

Before he could turn back to de la Roche, a loud cry of "Attack!" echoed around him.

He could delay no longer as de la Roche's army charged, thundering forward like a dark wave against the dirt.

Simon dove for the bow and arrows near him and let them fly into the massive army that approached. Before their arrows were spent, a roar of the ages erupted out of the chaos — the cath-ghairm — the call of the Highlanders. The MacDougalls had arrived. A hundred men on horseback swept across the field from behind where the Templars had taken their stand, surging with wrathful power toward de la Roche's men.

Everywhere, battle erupted. Tar was thrown, spears were tossed, and around them the clangor of steel against steel sounded above the shouts and cries of men and horses.

Simon fought alongside Brianna, the two of them making their way toward the Frenchman who now hovered at the rear of the fighting. A volley of arrows took down de la Roche's horse. The Frenchman jerked away before the beast could crush his legs. De la Roche rolled then gained his feet. His eerie gaze connected with Simon's over the fighting. Simon knew this was it. The final confrontation. Simon strode forward and raised his sword in salute.

De la Roche offered him a sneer of a smile and did the same.

They both dropped into position.

"You can leave this land in peace. Go back to where you came from and never darken the shores of Scotland again," Simon said as they began to circle each other slowly, each taking measure of the other.

De la Roche laughed. "I'll not walk away from my destiny to conquer and rule over all. Are you afraid of death, Lockhart? For that is your destiny this day."

"There is no destiny," Simon answered. "Nothing is written," or dreamed, he added in his mind, "that cannot be changed."

De la Roche lunged. As he moved he dropped his shoulder, focusing his action. The man was older than Simon and though he still walked with a limp, there was nothing but youthful strength in his motions.

If only he could knock the sword from de la Roche's hands...

Simon parried and spun to the right. De la Roche brought his sword around in a sideways sweep, but Simon was ready. His blade arced up and back, stopping Joyeuse's slice. As the swords collided, Simon kicked, catching de la Roche in the stomach and sending him staggering backward.

The Frenchman kept his feet. He grinned at Simon. "Good," he said. "Very good. A worthy opponent at last."

Simon didn't answer. He kept his body low as he watched de la Roche's body for the next attack.

Brianna clutched her sword in her left hand and faced her opponent. She could not keep her gaze on Simon for long; the Frenchman she'd come to know as Philippe leaped forward. Her breath hitched. This was it — the battle she had longed for and dreaded with equal fervor.

Gathering her strength, she blocked the man's blade and spun away. Her grip was firm, her strike confident. She could battle with her left hand just as effectively as her right.

"A girl," he said in a thick French accent. "This should be nothing more than child's play."

Brianna attacked, her steps quick and sure. The Frenchman parried, but he threw his weight off balance with his strike and Brianna slashed. Her opponent fell away, only to be replaced by another, and another.

She fought her way through the wave of men, keeping Simon in her peripheral vision at all times. She had to protect herself, but she also had to be ready to help if de la Roche gained the advantage.

Simon would not die.

Anguish filled her momentarily at the idea of him falling in this battle. She forced the thought away, giving no life to negative thoughts. She had to stay positive, think positively, in order to see this battle through.

The men who charged her fell like leaves against the wind. One after another, they came and fell. She looked out at the fighting. The monks were holding their own, as were Kaden, Alaric, and Kendall. Brianna's eyes slid across the fighting, to a familiar figure in the distance. Her heart seemed to freeze at the sight of her father. He fought against de la Roche's men.

Why? Why was he here? He'd come to the MacDougalls to gather his own protection. Why would he follow them into war? Without fully seeing them, Brianna slashed at the men who lunged at her as she fought her way to his side.

Crimson blood spilled from a wound on his chest down the front of his tunic. Icy fingers gripped Brianna's spine. Her father might not love her, but she still cared for him, still remembered happier times, times when he had cared for her. She took two steps forward then froze.

She couldn't leave Simon's side.

Her gaze shifted between the man she loved and the man who'd sired her. Simon appeared in control of the situation while her father's opponent raised his sword, turned it, and brought it down.

Brianna cried out. Her father's opponent hesitated at the sound, but for only a heartbeat. She surged forward. Threw herself onto the enemy, knocking him to the ground. Was she too late? She hadn't seen the strike, but her father lay on the ground beside her, horribly still.

Her eyes blinded by pain, her right hand shot forward, connected with the enemy's face. She felt bones cracking and the man went limp. She tossed him aside and crawled quickly to her father's side.

He lay with one hand covering the wound on his chest. Blood stained his fingers. Brianna's breath hitched once more as she felt the pain in her own body. She brushed the hair away from his face and his eyes fluttered open. His eyes were not filled with the disappointment she had grown used to seeing there. Instead, she saw pride.

"Brianna," he whispered. "I was so wrong."

"Father, don't waste your strength with talk," she said urgently. "I'll get you somewhere safe. I'll take care of you—"

"Brianna." He reached up and touched her face with cool, trembling fingers. "You are a warrior. Better than your brothers. I'm sorry."

"Hush," she said, feeling her throat tighten.

"Nay, 'tis time I told you what you need to hear, what I should have said after you returned from Teba." His voice was growing weaker. "I saw the pain I put into your eyes at Aros Castle and later by the tree. I followed the MacDougalls here to tell you I was wrong. I'd never considered that your birth had a different meaning than the one I always tried to force upon you. You saw that. I did not — until it was too late." His eyes glittered with tears. "Can you forgive an old fool?"

A single sob filled her, rose, caught in her throat. "I forgive you."

A smile came to his lips as his hand caressed her cheek. His eyelids fluttered closed and his hand fell away. His breath came in labored gasps.

"Nay!" Brianna's heart clenched. He couldn't die. Not when they had just—

Behind her she felt a presence. A slash fell against her left arm. Pain radiated. Instinct moved through her as she switched her sword to her right hand. Pain flared, then stilled as she whipped around, still crouched, and brought her sword up. The enemy fell.

She stood and sheathed her weapon. Ignoring the pain in her arm, she grasped her father's arms and dragged him back toward the open abbey doors. With her heart in her throat, she looked over at Simon to see he and de la Roche still fought. Her heart thundered in her chest as she pulled her father into the abbey.

At the doorway, she reached for the Grail she had tied to her belt and ran to the chapel entrance. She scooped holy water from the stoup near the door, then returned to her father's side. Kneeling beside him, she forced the blessed water past his lips. "Drink, father!" she pleaded. "The Grail can help you."

He swallowed roughly, taking the liquid inside himself.

"More!" she pleaded.

He took another swallow, then another, and his breathing became easier.

"I must leave you here," she whispered near his ear and placed a single kiss on his cheek. She took the final swallow of liquid in the cup to ease the pain in her injured arm then tucked the Grail back into her belt. Removing a dagger from her boot, she slid it into her father's hand. "Just in case," she said a moment before she raced for the door. She had to get back to the battle, and to Simon.

Simon. She prayed she wasn't too late.

Simon's battle went on. He lunged and parried, cut high, low, silently grateful to the Templars, and all his brothers, for all they had taught him. He would have to bring all his training to bear if he were to prevail against de la Roche and that sword.

The Frenchman's blade arced toward Simon in a disemboweling sweep, the blood grooves on the blade whistling their deadly melody as he dropped back, and let the blade swing through the empty space where his body had just been.

De la Roche was mighty, but Simon was quick. And most of all, de la Roche was arrogant, and too confident. Wielding a mighty sword was not all a warrior needed in battle. Wit and skill could never be taken away. Arrogance, however, could be exploited.

Simon gave a calculated stumble, testing his theory. He watched the arrogance, the certainty of success, flash across de la Roche's face. With it came the opening Simon had been waiting to find. De la Roche's sword swung wide. Simon jumped inside and drove his elbow into the Frenchman's face. With a half turn, the razor edge of his sword laid open de la Roche's arm and slid into his side.

De la Roche was not stopped. His sword flashed again, and slashed Simon's thigh. Simon fell to the ground on both knees.

Joyeuse flashed. The weapon arced upward, as de la Roche prepared to sever his head from his neck.

Simon tried to force all his strength into his good leg, tried to force himself up, but before he could, Brianna appeared beside him. She kicked out with her foot. The bones of de la Roche's knee shattered beneath her heel. The leg bent backward, and the Frenchman screamed with agony as his leg went out from under him. He dropped Joyeuse to the ground. The sword thumped against the earth and rolled an arm's length away.

De la Roche's face was cold — hard as iron. His eyes were burning coals of rage straight from the deepest pits of hell as Brianna took two steps forward and drove her sword deep into his body. He cried out and clutched at the sword, but his hands had no strength left. "No!" de la Roche growled. "This land is mine!"

Simon rolled and came up, ignoring the pain in his thigh. "You will leave Scotland in peace." He gripped his sword, prepared to strike again if the Frenchman so much as moved.

Brianna pulled her sword free and bent to retrieve Joyeuse from the ground. As she bent, the Grail glinted in the orange-red sunset that had fallen over the land.

"The Grail!" de la Roche panted in pain as he fell to the ground. "You must give it to me!"

"The Grail is to be used for good, not evil purposes." Brianna straightened and backed away. "If I gave you the 'water of life,' would you leave this country and stop your revenge against the Templars?"

His eyes narrowed. "If I live, this land will be mine."

"Then you leave us no choice," Simon said, bringing his sword down, severing the man's head from his shoulders. His head rolled two paces from Simon and landed face-down in the dirt.

De la Roche's body slumped, remained still.

Simon released a ragged breath and looked around him. At the sight of their fallen leader, the other Frenchmen turned and fled.

"Follow them back to their boats," Simon called out to Hector MacDougall and his men.

"Consider it done," Hector replied with a bow of his head. The Scotsman kicked his horse into motion and along with several of his men, cleared the battlefield.

Simon ripped a length of fabric from the bottom of his own tunic and tied the cloth tightly about his wounded thigh. De la Roche had knocked him to the ground, but the wound he'd inflicted would not destroy him. He would heal and go on.

The monks had sheathed their swords and were already searching for survivors. Brianna signaled to Brother Michael to come to her. When he did, she released the Grail from her belt and handed the sacred vessel to him. "Use this to heal the injured."

The monk's eyes widened. "Is this what I think it is? The Holy Grail? The cup of Christ?" He gripped the vessel, the most precious gift he'd ever received.

"Aye," Brianna replied. "Use it well."

He nodded and hurried away, heading for the abbey.

Simon stared down at the body of de la Roche near his feet. In death, the man looked as any other. "I feel sorry for him, almost, and the greed that took over his soul."

Simon clenched his fists, fighting his first instinct to make the sign of the cross over the fallen man. The image of all the Templars the villain had slain and burned played across Simon's mind before he forced the memory away. It was time to move forward in all things. Reluctantly, he reached out and blessed the listless body. "May God be with you, and may He show you the mercy you never showed anyone else upon this earth."

"Does he deserve mercy?" Brianna asked beside him, her voice ragged.

Simon turned to face her. "All men, and women," he added, "deserve mercy. If we didn't think so, then we'd be no better than him."

Admiration shone in Brianna's eyes. "You're a good man, Simon Lockhart."

"And I'm a lucky man to have you fighting by my side. You saved me with your skilled swordsmanship." He reached for her hand and brought it to his lips, placing a kiss against her palm. She had saved his life, given him purpose, and renewed his faith that good could triumph over evil. "How are your fingers?"

"In the heat of the battle, I felt no pain in them. Perhaps I am fully healed." He pressed another kiss to her palm then looked up to see the other men looking at the two of them, smiling. And yet, they also looked to Simon for leadership.

"We still have much to do."

She nodded and pulled her hand from his. "The dead will need burial, and there are the injured to attend to." Her face sobered. "I used the Grail during the battle to save my father."

"Your father is here?"

She drew a tremulous breath. "He came to ask my forgiveness."

"Did you give it to him?" Simon asked, his voice threaded with hope.

She nodded. "He was badly injured. I dragged him into the abbey and forced him to drink from the Grail."

He frowned. "Does he still live?"

Fear etched her face. "I don't know. I'm almost afraid to check on him. He is just comeback into my life…"

He took her hand. "You've faced your fears before, Brianna. But this time you'll face them with me at your side. Let's go find out."

Chapter Twenty-two

A gust of wind swirled through the abbey as Brianna and Simon strode inside the entrance. Torches lit the hallway, sending golden light spilling across the stone walls. A monk stood guard at the doorway.

"The man who was in the entry, is he still alive?"

"Aye, he lives."

"Where is he?" Brianna asked.

The monk silently led them down another long hallway and pointed to the third cell on the right. A chill went through Brianna as she stepped inside the chamber and moved to the pallet beneath the small shuttered window. A simple crucifix hung on the wall over the bed. Other than a small table near the bedside that held a single candle, the room was devoid of anything else.

Brianna knelt by the bedside. The flickering candle light revealed that her father's eyes were closed. His face was ashen. She carefully drew back the cover to look at his wound. Someone had bandaged him. "Was his wound cleaned?" she asked the monk who stood in the doorway.

"Aye," the monk replied. "I cleaned it myself, and as I did, it seemed that the wound was beginning to heal right before my eyes."

The Holy Grail.

Brianna frowned down at the seemingly lifeless man. "Then why doesn't he wake?" she said more to herself than anyone else.

"Sometimes," the monk replied softly, "a man needs more than healing to pull him through adversity. Without a reason to live, it is easy to slip away."

Simon knelt beside her. "Perhaps if you talk to him."

He needed a reason to live. She understood that sentiment only too well. "Father?" she whispered and stroked his bearded cheek.

His eyes fluttered and opened. He gazed about him for a moment until his eyes connected with hers. "You're alive," he whispered in a broken voice.

"You're awake." Brianna smiled down at him. "How are you feeling?"

"Better to know you are here." His lips tightened. "The battle?"

"Is over. De la Roche is gone as are his men. We are safe for now." Brianna stroked back the hair from her father's face.

He caught her hand, squeezed it. "I was not certain I would have the chance to say this again to you ... the battle ... oh, Brianna, I'm so sorry. It was never my wish to—"

"I know." Brianna returned the squeeze and placed his hand on his chest. "We have time in the future to say all that needs said."

He shook his head. "I wasted so much of it with my anger, my grief." A note of bitterness threaded his voice. "No more. I want to help." His gaze shifted to Simon. "My steward told me of your earlier visits. He informed me that you'd come for Brianna the first time and to ask about the catacombs the next. I am sorry I refused to meet with you. It would be an honor to store the Templar treasure in the catacombs beneath Rosslyn Chapel. And if you would allow me to help, I'd like to serve as guardian of the treasure if it will allow you and Brianna the freedom to live and move about the countryside and keep our people safe. You two belong together."

"I ... we..." Brianna said in a rush as her cheeks heated. Simon had yet to declare himself or even talk of a life together. "You are mistaken."

The glimmer of a smile touched his lips. "I might have been blind to you before, my daughter, but I can now see what is clearly before me."

Brianna shifted her gaze to Simon's as fear suddenly gripped her. There was no longer de la Roche keeping them apart, or keeping them together. They were free to do as they pleased. But she no longer knew for certain what that meant for Simon and her. He had said he wanted to tell her something after the battle was through, yet he had not.

It took all her warrior's will and patience to keep her gaze locked with Simon's. Her heartbeat sped up. She swallowed dryly, waiting. Suddenly she felt as though she were standing on a precipice. All he had to do was hold out his hands to her and she would jump if it meant making a life with him. She had been changed by their adventure and she couldn't go back to her old life of being alone and lonely.

She kept her gaze on him and waited.

Simon couldn't move, couldn't speak. He needed a moment — just a moment — to savor the look of her right now. Her hair was wild around her face and smudges of blood were on her cheek, her neck, and down her arm. Yet, despite the signs of war, she had never looked more beautiful.

He didn't know what he had done in this life to deserve her love … and in this moment, he didn't care. All he knew was that God had given him the gift of Brianna and he was going to take it. He brought his hand up in a tentative, hopeful gesture and touched her cheek.

"Brianna, marry me." Gazing down into her luminous green eyes he felt none of the sorrow that had lingered inside him since Teba. Instead, he felt powerful, larger than life, able to do any task set before him. Something deep in his soul expanded, and an aching, loving tenderness filled his heart. "I want to spend the rest of my days loving you, if only you will have me."

She stared at him, feeling dazed. His words were like a bright ray of sunlight, offering her the warmth and security she'd sought her whole life and never expected to find. But there were still things between them, things that needed said. "We will probably always battle each other. Can you live with that?"

His gaze softened. "I look forward to each and every one."

Her heart sped up. "And our daughters, if they want to be warriors, will you allow it?"

"I encourage it!" He reached for her hands, held them tightly in his own. "I want many strong daughters and sons. Is that a problem?"

"Nay," she whispered.

"Then you'll marry me?"

"I shall." The minute the words left her mouth, she felt an almost unbelievable sense of joy blossom inside her chest.

Their gazes locked. His was unblinking and filled with determination, as if he'd glimpsed what it was he wanted from this life and would do anything on earth to see it was never taken away.

Her eyes glittered with tears as the most profound sense of love warmed her to the core of her being.

"That's my girl!" her father's voice cut in, bringing them both back to the reality that they still knelt before his sick bed.

The monk at the doorway cleared his throat and if Brianna was not mistaken, tears misted his eyes. "Are you not forgetting one small thing?"

Brianna and Simon shared a puzzled look.

"Are you not still a monk yourself, Brother Simon?"

Simon's hands dropped to his side. "Aye. There is that one small obstacle that only Archbishop Lamberton can rectify."

Brianna straightened. "Then we had best get my father packed up for travel. We'll deliver him to Rosslyn Castle on our way to Edinburgh to see that archbishop."

All eyes in the room filled with surprise.

"What are you all looking at?" Brianna frowned. "We have work to do. Nothing and no one will stand in the way of my marrying this man. Do you hear?"

Simon chuckled as he rose to his feet and helped Brianna up beside him. "You heard the lady. We have work to do. Let's get to it, shall we?"

It took another day to bury the dead at Pennyghael Abbey, and three days more to travel across the countryside to Rosslyn Castle where Simon and Brianna said goodbye to her father. They promised to return with the treasure soon. But before they could do anything more, they had to see Archbishop Lamberton. Simon felt his Templar vows like a weight upon his shoulders. He longed to be free of the Brotherhood so that he could accept his true calling as Brianna's husband.

It was half a day more of hard riding before he and Brianna finally arrived at the gates of Saint Giles's Church in Edinburgh. As he dismounted, his body cried out for rest. There would be no rest for either of them until they knew the archbishop's decision.

He helped Brianna down from her horse, and tethered the animals. They proceeded into the church and up the altar, where he knew Archbishop Lamberton would be waiting.

Pale afternoon sunlight filtered in through the stained glass windows on either side of the aisle, illuminating the man at the front of the church. The cleric was not kneeling at the altar as Simon had expected; instead, he stood contemplating the crucifix hanging from the wall.

"Simon Lockhart." Archbishop Lamberton turned his gentle gaze upon the Templar tunics folded neatly in Simon's hands. The holy man's gaze shifted to Brianna with no hint of surprise. "I've been expecting you both. Lady Brianna." He bowed his head in greeting before returning his gaze to the crucifix. "It is done then?"

"Aye, Your Grace. De la Roche is no longer a threat." He would give no further explanations, no excuses. The man was dead by his and Brianna's hands. The holy man might not understand their need to kill the monster, but they had done the only thing their warrior blood had allowed. "If it is our confession you seek—"

"God has already forgiven you for that sin and all those that might have brought you here to me today." The archbishop fell silent, but Simon saw the slight clenching of his hands behind his back. The holy man continued to stare at the crucifix.

Simon turned to look at it, too, suddenly uncertain of what the holy man expected him to say. "My heart is no longer that of a Templar, Your Grace."

"Is that why you have come here today?" Archbishop Lamberton asked after a long silence. The holy man watched Simon now, and the feeling came over him that the man looked not at his person, but somehow into his soul.

Simon held out the tunics, both his and Brianna's. "I must return these to you, and to ask that you release me from my vows." Simon turned to look at Brianna who stood slightly behind him at the altar. "I wish to marry this woman and spend the rest of my days in her arms."

Again the Archbishop grew silent. After a long pause he nodded. "It has been a difficult life you have lived, Simon. Darkness and light have touched you in many ways."

"Darkness and sorrow and despair," Simon replied. "These are the forces that have shaped me. No man is immune to such things. I respect all that has come before, but I look forward to light and joy and hope with Brianna in the days ahead."

The middle-aged man's face filled with compassion. "And you think leaving the Templars will bring you this … peace?"

Simon did not answer right away. There were no easy words for such a question. "I ask to leave the service of the

Templars, but my life will never be filled with peace, not while men and kings still quest for power and wealth. That is why I must focus my attention on relocating the Templar treasure. De la Roche exposed it."

"Heaven help us all." The archbishop paled.

Simon turned to Brianna and accepted the sword Joyeuse and the Holy Grail from her hands. "He brought these two treasures back into the world, and because he did many lives were both lost and saved."

The holy man nodded very slowly as his gaze travelled over the sword and the Grail. He accepted the artifacts, then set them on the altar. "Life and death should be a decision only God can make."

"We agree, which is why Brianna and I would like to devote the remainder of our lives to protecting our people from others like de la Roche. Lord Sinclair has agreed to assume the role of protector of the treasure with Your Grace's approval."

"The task is too great for one man alone," the archbishop said.

Simon smiled. "He will have plenty of help from Brothers Kaden, Thomas, Benton, and Cameron. They are at Rosslyn Castle by now, preparing the new site for the treasure."

The dark eyes that met Simon's twinkled gently. "So you and Brianna will leave the peace and solitude to others while the two of you guard the gates?"

Simon shrugged. "We are both warriors. Someone must guard the gates in order to ensure peace for those behind them."

"That is very selfless of you both." The archbishop nodded his approval. "I grant you your wish, Simon Lockhart. I accept these tunics and relinquish you from your vows, but only if you take up another vow here and now."

Archbishop Lamberton's words sent a warmth through Simon. "Marriage vows?"

"Indeed."

Simon turned to Brianna. "Are you ready to marry me here, this very moment?" He held out his hand.

She slipped her fingers into his without hesitation.

"You're trembling." Simon tightened his fingers around Brianna's as he drew her beside him. "There's no reason to be frightened. After you've faced de la Roche, marriage to me cannot be that bad."

"It's not fear," she said softly, her gaze on her feet.

With a finger beneath her chin, he brought her gaze to his. "Then what is it?"

She blinked back tears. "I love you, Simon, with all my heart, but I have yet to hear those words from you."

He brushed his lips across her brow and stroked her hair back from her cheeks. "I might not have said the words, but tell me you felt them in my touch, and read them in my eyes, and heard them in my voice?"

"All the time," she admitted with a lopsided smile.

"Then I will say the words often as well. I love you, Brianna. Always and forever. You are my life now. Is that enough for you, my beautiful warrior?"

As he said the words she needed to hear, the world responded. Strong beams of sunlight streaked through the stained glass windows, casting a rainbow of colors across the altar, bathing the two of them, the archbishop, and Joyeuse and the Holy Grail in shades of blue and green and yellow and gold.

"Aye, it's enough." She blinked rapidly to keep back the tears. She suddenly threw herself into his arms, hugging him with all her strength. "But you certainly took your time telling me so."

He kissed her until she was breathless. "I won't make that mistake twice. I love you."

"The Templars have their treasure, but I have mine."

Simon smiled down at his soon-to-be-bride. "You find me a treasure?"

She nodded. "The true treasures of life are not silver and gold and gemstones as de la Roche believed. But in the shared moments of pain and joy."

"We have both seen enough pain in our lives. Let us hope for much more pleasure in the future. Now, let's get back to this wedding. Declarations of love are all well and good." His eyes were twinkling as he slipped his arm about her waist and turned to face the archbishop. "But we are both better with action. Wouldn't you agree?"

Her laughter rang out, rising to the arched ceiling and beyond, sending the doves in the belfry into flight.

And all who saw the birds knew that those who married inside would have lives filled with years of peace, tranquility and most of all ... love.

Epilogue

With only the light of a torch to guide them, Brianna and Simon made their way through the underground cavern that Simon claimed had once been buried. As they walked, Simon explained that many of the men who had helped in the battle had aided in digging away the collapsed cavern. With so many hands, they had managed to do a year's work in a matter of a few weeks. Simon had told her that the recovery efforts would take many more years, but he had said he could not wait that long to show her what they'd been fighting to protect. He guided her through the semi-darkness until they stood at an entrance to a chamber.

"Are you ready to be amazed?" Simon asked.

Brianna smiled. "Every day with you holds something amazing."

"Wait here." Simon disappeared into the chamber. Suddenly, bright light spilled from the entrance as Simon lit several urns. He returned to her side and grasped her hand. "Come."

Brianna entered and gasped at the sight of the Templar treasure that had been recovered so far. It was grander that anything she had ever expected or imagined.

Riches spilled over every surface. Within arm's reach were two enormous wooden cases inset with jewels from an early period in Egypt's history, and seven more of European descent — all were filled to overflowing with diamond, rubies, sapphires, emeralds, and pearls. Brianna reached down and plucked a pearl the size of her thumb from the heap. As it glowed with silver iridescence it warmed beneath her touch.

"Simon," she breathed beside him. "It's extraordinary." Her gaze wandered over statues in alabaster, silver, and gold, as well as plates and vases bejeweled with precious and semiprecious stones. In the corner was a painted dragon ship of Viking origin. A gilded chariot from Roman times. Along the far wall were other statues made from marble, obsidian, limestone, and granite from every culture — Babylonian, Egyptian, Greek, Viking, Roman, and more.

Excitement made her heart flutter as she looked past the wealth and riches to the historical importance of such a cache. De la Roche had taken the Holy Grail and Joyeuse, but there were also Herod's crown, Merlin's staff, the throne of Constantine, the Athenian Sword of Pericles, Ramses's golden chair, Octavian's goblet — treasures from every culture since the beginning of time. Brianna felt her legs go weak as she staggered to a gold chest overflowing with lustrous black pearls, diamonds, rubies, and she suddenly had to sit down. "Why are all these treasures here instead of with the cultures they belong to?"

Simon came to stand beside her. "The artifacts are here to protect them from men like de la Roche. Many of the treasures like the Holy Grail and Joyeuse can be used for good or evil purposes." He sat on the chest beside her and took her once damaged hand in his. Gently, he stroked the delicate scar along her finger. "Men like him will do anything to take what they want from this life."

"It seems a shame to keep the treasures hidden where no one can appreciate their beauty and their significance."

He nodded. "I believe it was always the Templars' intent to merely store and protect the treasures until mankind was ready for their reemergence into the world."

"Thank you for bringing me here, for sharing this secret with me." She gazed at him, loving him with all her being.

He inclined his head. "My pleasure, Lady Lockhart."

Silence settled around them. The only sounds in the world seemed to be the whisper of their mingled breathing and the pulse of their heartbeats. Then there was the rustling of gems a moment before Simon slipped a necklace over her head. "It's beautiful."

Simon arranged the chain of diamonds interspersed with emeralds so that they dipped into the hollow between her breasts. "This is the first time I've ever given a lady jewels fit for a queen." The diamonds caught the firelight and sprayed a dazzling array of brilliant hues across the chamber. "The emeralds match your eyes."

"Are these from the Templar treasure?" she asked hesitantly, allowing the gems to slide through her fingers. "I'm not certain—"

Simon smiled. "They are from the Lockhart family treasure. I removed them from the family vault when we stopped there. My mother would have approved, and truth be told, I had a feeling I might need them to coerce you into marrying me."

"You are the only jewel I shall ever need, Simon." A tiny smile came to her lips. "They are very beautiful."

"You could thank me for my gift," he teased.

Her smile broadened. "I do thank you, husband, for so many things." She lifted his hand and brought it to rest over the necklace so that he could feel the erratic pounding of her heart. Then she moved his hand downward, to rest against her abdomen. "You have given me many gifts in the past few weeks."

"Gifts? I gave you but one."

She shook her head. "You trusted me. You believed in my visions. You knighted me. You gave me a child."

He drew a sharp breath and his eyes twinkled down at her. "A child? Are you certain?"

"We are pregnant with a daughter."

"How do you know?"

Heat tingled through her as she remembered last night's joining beneath the stars. "I had a dream."

He pulled her back against his chest and slid his arms around her, his hands gently caressing her belly. "We won't know for certain for several more months."

"It will be a daughter." She smiled up at him over her shoulder. "Will you be disappointed that it's a girl?"

He chuckled. "Never. I would love her as much as I do her mother. I look forward to teaching her swordplay and archery and—"

"When she's old enough. And if it is her choice."

He laughed. "Aye, my dearest warrior. If it is her choice."

With a sigh of contentment, Brianna leaned back against Simon's chest and gazed dreamily out at the treasure that surrounded them, feeling the stirring of new life within her.

"Packing the treasure for transport to Rosslyn will take months if we are to keep the location a secret."

"There is no need, especially now. We need to get the treasure moved and you back to Lee Castle before you become heavy with child." He turned her in his arms to face him. "You want to have the child at Lee, do you not?"

Hope for their future filled her heart to bursting. She reached up and brushed a lock of his hair away from his face, relishing the rich, silky feel and the knowledge that she had the rest of her life to touch him. "You are the true treasure of my life, Simon Lockhart, and the only home I need is in your arms."

𝔄fterword

The hero of A Knight to Desire, Sir Simon Lockhart, was a true historical figure who won fame for himself and his family in the wars against the English when he fought alongside King Robert the Bruce. He was knighted for his loyal service along with nine other men who eventually made up the Bruce's inner circle. These knights were given the greatest of tasks: to go on Crusade for their king and take his heart with them for burial in the Holy Land.

Their crusade to the Holy Land was symbolic of the journey the Bruce had longed to take during his lifetime, but was never able to manage. The knights, along with twenty-six squires and a retinue of men, set off on a crusade from Scotland for Jerusalem, fighting the infidels along the way.

James Douglas wore the heart of the king in a specially designed cylindrical vessel about his neck, using it as a talisman as he and his men made their way through enemy territory.

On the morning of August 25th, 1330, their journey came to a devastating end when a false battle cry sent them into battle against the Moors of Spain before they had adequate reinforcements. They were outnumbered a hundred to one. The knights were crushed, their mission a failure.

Five of the ten knights died, along with hundreds of foot soldiers. Sir Simon Locard of Lee carried the key to the casket in which the heart was carried. He rescued the heart and returned with it to Scotland, after which the Locard family changed their name to Lockhart to reflect the service they had done for their king.

There is no documented evidence that proves the knights who traveled with the Bruce's heart on Crusade were

Templar knights. However, enough evidence exists to suggest Sir William Sinclair and his brother, John Sinclair of Rosslyn, were associated with the Templars. Both men were killed in the battle at Teba. And mixing a little fact with fiction, I created a sister for them, Brianna Sinclair, whose single-minded goal in life was to be a knight just like her brothers.

Rosslyn Chapel as we know it today was not built until the fifteenth century on a small hill above Roslin Glen. Rosslyn Chapel was the third Sinclair place of worship built for that family. The first was the chapel at Roslin Castle. The second, whose crumbling buttresses can still be seen today, was located in what is now Roslin Cemetery.

The chapel, built 150 years after the dissolution of the Knights Templar, supposedly has many Templar symbols which has led many to speculate through the ages about links between the Sinclairs and the Knights Templar. There is also speculation about links between the Sinclairs and Freemasonry because many carvings in the chapel reflect Masonic imagery.

William Sinclair, the third Earl of Orkney, Baron of Roslin and 1st Earl of Caithness, claimed by novelists to be a hereditary Grand Master of the Scottish stone masons, built Rosslyn Chapel. A later William Sinclair of Rosslyn became the first Grand Master of the Grand Lodge of Scotland and, subsequently, several other members of the Sinclair family have held this position.

These connections, whether real or imagined, to both the Templars and the Freemasons, mean Rosslyn Chapel features prominently in romantic conjectures that the Freemasons are direct descendants of the Knights Templar.

I chose in the pages of A Knight to Desire to once again play upon the connections of the Sinclair family to the Knights Templar. I also built upon the conjecture of where the Templar treasure might be concealed, by placing the treasure in catacombs deep below the earth's surface beneath the second Rosslyn Chapel.

As for what kinds of artifacts that treasure contains, no one knows for certain. I created a treasure trove of religious artifacts as well as pieces from history that would have been worthy of protecting from damage or abuse.

The Holy Grail and Charlemagne's sword, Joyeuse, were two of these artifacts.

The Holy Grail is known as a sacred object figuring in literature and certain Christian traditions, most often identified as a dish, plate, cup, or goblet used by Jesus Christ at the Last Supper, and said to possess miraculous powers, especially those of healing.

The connection between the Grail legend and Joseph of Arimathea dates back to the twelfth century poet, Robert de Boron's work, Joseph d'Amathie, in which Joseph receives the Grail from an apparition of Jesus Christ and sends the holy vessel with his followers to Great Britain.

Building upon this theme, later writers recounted how Joseph of Arimathea used the Grail to catch Christ's blood while on the cross. In order to preserve such a sacred vessel, Joseph was said to found a line of guardians in Britain to keep the Grail safe.

The quest for the Holy Grail is another facet of historical legend that has since become associated with Arthurian legend. The Grail quest first appears in works by author Chretien de Troyes, who combined Christian lore with a Celtic myth of a cauldron endowed with magical powers.

I used all these things in the pages of A Knight to Desire to give the Holy Grail its supposed powers of healing.

As for the magical sword in the pages of this book, I used one of the world's most famous swords — the sword of the great Emperor Charlemagne. Joyeuse is the traditional coronation sword of France. The name of the sword translates to "joyful." Legend claims that the sword was forged to contain the Lance of Longinus within its pommel, others state it was supposedly smithed from the same materials as Roland's Durendal and Ogier's Curtana, other legendary swords.

The sword was alleged to have been interred with Charlemagne's body, or contrarily to be held in the Saint Denis Basilica, where it was later retired into the Louvre after being carried at the front of coronation processionals for French kings. Another supposed Joyeuse is held at the Imperial Treasury in Vienna.

Whatever the truth is about the Holy Grail, Joyeuse, Rosslyn Chapel, or the Sinclair family, I hope you've enjoyed the facts that I mixed with a lot of fantasy in the pages of A Knight to Desire.

GERRI RUSSELL

Gerri Russell has done it all when it comes to writing; she's worked as a broadcast journalist, newspaper reporter, magazine columnist, technical writer and editor, instructional designer, which all finally led her to follow her heart's desire of being a romance novelist. Gerri is best known for her adventurous and emotionally intense novels set in 13th and 14th Century Scottish Highlands. Her most notable series to date is that of the Brotherhood of the Scottish Templars. In her spare time, Gerri is a living history re-enactor with the Shrewsbury Renaissance Faire. A two-time recipient of the Romance Writers of America's Golden Heart award and winner of the American Title II competition sponsored by Dorchester Publishing and *RT BOOKreviews Magazine*, she lives in Bellevue, Washington with her husband and children.

Connect with me online:

Facebook: http://www.facebook.com/gerrirussell

Twitter: @GerriRussell

Website: http://www.gerrirussell.net

CPSIA information can be obtained at www.ICGtesting.com
Printed in the USA
LVOW011716291112

309398LV00022B/999/P